Apex

Out of the Box, Book 18

Robert J. Crane

Apex
Out of the Box #18
Robert J. Crane
Copyright © 2018 Ostiagard Press
All Rights Reserved.

1st Edition

Prologue

She was going to be called "Big E" like her predecessors, though Eric Simmons didn't know that. All he knew was what he could see, what he could hear, and what he could taste ... and that was mostly fear.

He could almost feel it oozing out of every pore, hard-spiked adrenaline on his tongue as he walked toward the big graving dock where they were building the ship. He was sweating even though it wasn't particularly hot, his armpits soaked in the cool Virginia air.

"I have to do this," he whispered to himself. And he did. There were no other choices for him.

The dock was immense, and he wasn't even that close. He didn't have to be, not for his purposes. He wanted to be a nice distance away, especially given that President Gondry himself was coming here for this dog and pony show. There were signs everywhere, telling Simmons that the ship being commissioned today was the USS *Enterprise*, ninth of her illustrious name in the US Navy. He didn't care, though, because of ...

Man, the fear. It was just eating at him. Simmons tried to keep his eyes from darting left to right, but it was tough. There was security everywhere. The smell of the crowd was heavy, all the activity making people perspire. Who were these people? Navy families, probably, right? His gaze flicked

1

over the crowd. Yeah. Men in uniform; some women, too; lots of wives; a few little kids.

Simmons let his eyes rest on the ass of a pretty young lady, probably twenty. Maybe a Navy wife? Time was, Simmons would have been all over that. He mopped his brow with a hand, pushing the sweat off, and looked away quickly.

Not anymore. No time for that.

If he did this thing right, maybe he'd have time for that again. But now ...

Now he had work to do.

He swallowed hard and walked over to a fence, taking in the big blue sky overhead. It should have been wintery, it being right smack dab in the middle of January, but it wasn't. A freak heat wave had put the temps clear up into the low seventies, and Simmons even saw some people in shorts. He'd never spent much time in Virginia, preferring New York, Miami, Los Angeles, Aspen, Portland, Seattle—pretty much anywhere more happening than this, but at least this weather wasn't bad. It was no LA, but this he could deal with.

Simmons put his hands on the fence. To his right, a security checkpoint was forming up. They couldn't just let anybody into these parties, after all. What if someone walked their ass right onto the deck of the USS *Enterprise* and set off a bomb?

That'd be terrible, Simmons reflected with dark humor, shivering a little in spite of the heat.

But it probably wouldn't be as bad as what was about to happen.

Simmons tossed another look over the crowd, the bitter taste of adrenaline in his mouth. Working for someone else was bad enough—he'd done a team-up, he and Cassidy, with that dumbass Clary family a few years back, and that had ended in disaster and imprisonment, thanks to Sienna Nealon. Once he'd gotten himself clear of that mess, courtesy of a Supreme Court decision that opened the gates of the prison he'd been stuck in, Simmons had vowed to never be caught again.

And that resolution had lasted until some black-ops

assholes had bagged him just after his release. He hadn't even done anything to deserve it, really.

His nerves were still stinging, clanging from that day. The door to his hotel room kicked in, strong, metahuman arms dragging him out of bed as he was snoozing next to a pretty little midwestern girl, some kind of portable bugzapper on a stick shoved into the small of his back so he'd danced like he'd done the splits on a barbed wire fence.

Man, even Sienna Nealon hadn't done anything like that to him.

Simmons clutched the chain-link fence and looked through. He was detached from the crowd now, all the serious, invited guests separating into neat queues in front of the security checkpoint. Ahead, he could see the ship in question, big and grey, stretched out of the dock like a skyscraper laid flat.

Simmons had brought down buildings before. It wasn't exactly the hardest thing in the world for a man who could shake the earth—and not just for the ladies he was with, was the old joke he used.

He didn't use that joke anymore. Something about being completely consumed with terror... it really sapped the humor out of you.

A few security guards were eyeing him, but Simmons didn't care. He wasn't going to do anything fancy, just kneel down in a minute, maybe tip over after sending a shudder through the earth, give the security boys a reason to think he tripped or something before he actually keeled over.

Heh. Keeled over.

There'd be more "keeling over" soon.

A whole lot more.

Simmons felt a clutch of heat under his collar. The moment was at hand. He'd been waiting for this for a long time, waiting for his chance at freedom, at getting out from underneath everything that had come his way these last few months. The fear came down on him again like a hard weight on his back, and he stooped, breathing heavily. He was still sweating, more profusely than ever. He felt it trickle down the back of his neck, down the small of his back into his skinny jeans, and Simmons squatted on the pavement and touched the hot asphalt with one hand, making it look like he was just steadying himself.

"What are you doing over there?" a security guard asked. Military police. He was making his way over, suspicion clouding his dark features.

"Did you feel that?" Simmons asked. "I just took a break from the line and—man, do you feel that?"

He didn't actually feel a thing, but he damned sure would in just a second.

Grabbing hold of that fear that was worming around in his guts, Simmons touched the power that was waiting inside him. He pushed it down into the earth and felt the ground move subtly.

"Yeah, I felt that," the MP said, unsteady legs rocking him back and forth. "What the hell?"

"I think it's an earthquake," Simmons said, not bothering to throw in too much irony. Of course it was an earthquake. On the coast of Virginia.

Because he was causing it.

Simmons let it rip, pushing more of that stomach-churning fear into it. Months of it, pent up with no outlet for release. They hadn't let him have booze. They hadn't let him have a smoke, they hadn't even let him surf or ski or even go for a bike ride.

Months of waiting for this moment, doing nothing but fearing—fearing them, fearing *him*—and waiting for the day he'd be told how he could buy his way out of that hell with one good act of service.

This was it. Walk up to this graving dock at Newport News Shipbuilding, on this day ...

And bring the place down.

The crowd was screaming, a thousand decibels of madness in his right ear. People were running, grabbing their kids and trying to get the hell out of here, though there was nowhere to run. The earth was quaking under his feet, but Simmons felt it only in a detached way.

Everyone else was scared witless because the ground, that hard rock that they relied on every day of their lives to be steady, was suddenly not so steady. Clearly not many of these folks had ever been stationed in Southern California. This was only like a 4.1 so far.

It was time to amp things up.

Simmons poured it on, letting that fear out into the ground in waves that caused the tectonic plates deep beneath him to shudder. The earth shook, and shattered, a wide crack in the pavement forming about thirty feet to his right. The crowd was so loud he couldn't hear anything else except that MP through the fence shouting, "Holy shit!"

Concrete was splitting in the distance. Simmons was pushing the quake forward, toward the graving dock and the big ship within. That sucker was shaking, the tower stretching out of the deck rattling metal against the hull. Simmons was cranking up the power, pouring it all into the earth.

He'd sleep well tonight, one way or another. He'd either sleep the sleep of a free man, or he'd sleep the sleep of a dead man, but either way ... he'd be free.

Free from this fear.

Something buckled and burst under the ship as it rocked to the side. It crashed into the wall of the dock, upended off whatever was beneath it, and Simmons could hear concrete shattering from the force of the blow. They'd told him what to do and how to do it, how he had to pour every bit of effort he had into it, and—man, he was doing it.

He was giving the USS *Enterprise* hell. People slid off the deck sideways, dropping off the sides like crumbs skimmed off the edge of a plate. Simmons looked at the ground. Ants were welling up from one of the cracks in the pavement beneath him.

People. Ants. They all kinda looked the same to him at these respective distances.

The sound of metal tearing was like a louder, more fervent scream in his ears, worse than anything the crowd—what was left of it, anyway, that hadn't run off—was doing to his right.

The USS *Enterprise* pitched over, capsizing in its own dock. The entire side of the ship clanged again, striking against the reinforced concrete wall. It had a nasty list, forty-five degrees or worse, and it suddenly rocked back the other way, some serious sliding-water-in-a-bathtub action going on in that dock. When it rose to tilt the other way, he could see the jagged scar down the side of the ship, ripped wide, where it had been pushed violently against the sides, violently enough that the side of the ship had actually buckled.

That was all Simmons needed to see. He was only looking for a sign she was out of commission for the near future, and this damned sure looked like it.

He didn't even wait for anything else.

Simmons ran.

And behind him, he could hear the MP—damn, he should have sunk that guy into his own personal hole—radioing for help:

"—We have a possible metahuman incident! Repeat, we have a possible metahuman cause for this incident, I have white male fleeing on foot, long blond hair and, wearing a vest and a beanie hat—"

Simmons didn't wait around to hear the rest. He ran for his getaway car, thinking that—yeah, they'd come for him, probably, but this? Having the US government chasing him? He'd done that before. He feared it, but not irrationally, especially not now that Sienna Nealon was gone from their service.

And having all of them—even her, maybe—after him?

He still didn't fear it nearly as much as what would have happened if he hadn't just delayed the launch of the USS *Enterprise* by years.

He didn't fear it at all like he feared the man in Revelen …

… The one who'd made him do this.

2.

Sienna
Panama City Beach, Florida

Waking up to bad news sucks, doubly so when it's around noon that it happens.

I opened my eyes when I heard forced whispers through the walls. You know the kind; hushed but loud, lots of emotion behind them. The speaker can't quite keep it bottled up so it bursts out, like an acrophobic skydiver shoved from the back of a plane.

That was what I heard when I woke in my bed in the vacation condo. White walls, white ceilings, beach décor. There was an olden wooden oar with the words "Mike's Beach Place" painted on it in white letters. Seashells dominated the decorating scheme, printed on a strip of wallpaper border, embroidered on the towels, and glued into a box that hung on the wall.

Which made sense. I was only a block from the beach, after all.

I was staying outside Panama City, on the Florida panhandle, that little stretch less than a hundred miles from Alabama. If the rest of the state was a dangling peninsula bordered by the Atlantic Ocean on one side and the Gulf of Mexico on the other, the panhandle was the piece that kept it from breaking away and floating off to party in the Caribbean, a haven for retirees, visitors from the midwest, and vacationers from the

7

southern US. I was staying along a strip known as 30A, a colorful locale filled with lots of screaming kids and sunburned parents.

Or it usually was. It was January now, so there wasn't a lot of sunburning going on, and it was beach weather for no one, except maybe this Minnesotan.

I sat up in bed, a hangover announcing its presence now that I was up. Light streamed in through white blinds and the curtains that bordered them. I'd gone through a bottle of scotch last night—again—and it was plainly going to punish me this morning.

I was getting pretty used to this feeling by now.

I listened, trying to figure out what was going on with all the whispering. I couldn't hear it all that well, because it seemed to have stopped, but I listened anyway. I thought I could hear some intrepid soul using the pool in the off-season—crazy; it was probably fifty or sixty degrees outside—but there was no sound from the main room.

Squinting my eyes to try and block out some of the pain streaming in with the light, I put my feet over the edge of the bed and stood, tentatively. The world didn't sway around me; I guessed that meant I was sober now.

"Ugh." I made my way to the bathroom on unsteady legs, did my business, and then headed for the door. There was no problem that anyone could have been dealing with this morning that couldn't wait until I was done peeing. Otherwise they wouldn't have been whispering.

I slid open the pocket door and light blazed down the hallway. Turning left, I shuffled my way toward the condo's living room to find Reed, Eilish, Augustus, and Taneshia all sitting on the couches and wicker recliners that made up the sitting area. Beyond them was a sliding glass door to the balcony, which overlooked the pool. And yep, there were a couple crazies in there this morning, splashing it up. I could almost see the blue lips from here.

"What's going on?" I asked in the middle of a hell of a yawn. It probably came out more like, "Waaaaaaas goooooooin onnnn?" Didn't even cover my mouth. Ladylike, I know.

Reed gave me this look he'd been sporting a lot lately. I

called it the "mom combo"; it had guilt, a little worry, and a faint whiff of judgment. He didn't say anything, though, just nodded at the TV, which hung over the mantel above the fireplace.

Yes, our condo in Florida had a fireplace. And we'd been using it, too.

Taneshia and Augustus were so cuddled up, it took me a second to steer my eyes away from their overwhelming cuteness, but eventually steer them away I did, and sure enough, on screen ...

"Wow," I said.

It wasn't the wreck of the *Hesperus*, because only a few people died in that. This was the capsizing of the brand new USS *Enterprise* in its dry dock, and the chyrons at the bottom of the news screen told the tale: *Hundreds feared dead after metahuman incident at ship christening ceremony. President Gondry scheduled to attend, missed attack by minutes.*

"So Gondry's okay?" I asked, feeling a little surge of patriotic worry, even though I didn't know Gondry and he hadn't gotten my vote. Honestly, who even really knows who the VP is? I'd voted against the guy at the top of his ticket. Gondry had been an afterthought until President Harmon died. Now he was the big cheese.

Still, I didn't want him dead. And the accusatory "metahuman" tag in that chyron was a bit worrisome.

"When do you think they'll call us in?" Augustus asked. He was already twitching, and Taneshia had a look on her face that told me she wished he'd settle down.

"I don't know," Reed said, still watching me with mom eyes. "But when they do, it's going to be the three of us and Scott, I think. Just for ease of getting there."

"Scott's in Minnesota," I said, trying to suppress a yawn and failing. "Along with the rest of your team. Which means if you can pull him, you can pull anybody you want."

"Not so," Reed said, dropping the mom eyes for just a moment. "I had to send Veronika, Kat, Angel, and Chase to Seattle last night. They had some sort of meta throwdown at Pike Place Market yesterday. Nothing major, but a lot of people got scared. And Friday, Tracy, and Jamal are in

Oklahoma this morning, dealing with a runaway spiraling meta."

I knew all of those people save for Tracy and Angel. Angel had been hired by the lady I'd trusted to start up this new agency, some meta who was in her family and apparently looking for work.

Tracy, though ... Tracy was, by Reed's own somewhat strained account, a real asshole who, by some sort of miraculous transmogrification that I'd never gotten the full story on—because Reed was being incredibly dodgy about telling it—had become a very helpful sort of guy, one who practically fell over himself kissing Reed's ass on every occasion they were in close proximity. It might have been alarming if it hadn't made my brother so comically uncomfortable.

He might have been able to do mom eyes with the best of them, but I could smell his guilt when Tracy was around. He'd done something he was ashamed of in relation to that guy. I was just too busy wallowing in my own shitty feelings to dig into it.

Yet.

"I might pull in Olivia Brackett for this, too," Reed said, thinking out loud. He'd become quite the commanding commander, building up this agency I'd handed him. It was even making money now, which was a relief, because I was tapped out or cut off, most of my money taken away by Rose months ago. Hundreds of millions of dollars impounded by my Scottish nemesis, now well outside my grasp because I couldn't get to the countries where they were quartered and take possession of them.

Alas. Being a federal fugitive is such a pain in the ass. Being a flightless federal fugitive? Even worse.

I stared at the TV. "What do you suppose did that?" I asked, pointing at the wreck of the *Enterprise*. The side of the ship was completely torn open. It looked like it had been gouged on the side of the quay, a tear in the metal hundreds of feet long revealing the compartments within. "Metal-controlling type? Poseidon playing splash games in the dock?"

"I don't know," Reed said, staring at it with full concentration again. The wheels were turning, which meant he had no time to mom-guilt his baby sister. Wheee.

"And here I thought hanging about with you lot would be boring," Eilish said, her light Irish accent such a contrast with all our rugged American gutter mouths. "But it's never boring in America, is it?"

"It used to be," I said, suppressing another yawn. "Back when metas were an endangered species instead of sprouting up everywhere like genetically altered weeds."

"Yeah, I thought we pulled that plant out by the roots," Augustus said. He leaned forward, unintentionally displacing Taneshia and earning himself a glare he remained blissfully unaware of. "Didn't we get Revelen's entire distribution network in the US?"

"That we knew of, sure," Reed said, still frowning. "But it's a mighty big country, and there are a lot of wrongdoers out there looking to cause chaos."

We'd talked about Revelen enough in recent days that I didn't feel the need to go there again. When a European country takes a special interest in creating superpowered people who then go criminal and cause havoc in your country, there's not much to discuss beyond a) stopping them here, and b) stopping them there. We were still working on the former, and thinking about the latter, because I'd had too many strong people warning me away from whatever demons lurked in the country of Revelen to go charging into that den of beasts unthinkingly.

Especially now.

"I think—" Reed started to say something but stopped, pulling up his phone and then answering it. "This is Treston, go."

"Hi, this is your sister, Sienna," I said, sotto voce, earning a completely horrified look from Reed. "I'm standing ten feet in front of you right now ..."

"Dude," Augustus said, almost on his feet. "He's on with the FBI!"

"Yeah, and I doubt they can hear me, so ..." I shrugged. "I thought it was funny."

Augustus's jaw tightened. "They have their own metahuman task force now. Complete with actual metahumans."

"Oh," I said. "Oops." I hoped they didn't hear me, because that'd turn my joke into a not-so-funny incident of them kicking down our door.

"Yeah, I'm watching," Reed said, all his ire toward me forgotten as he focused on the conversation. "I'm in Florida right now, but I've got a private jet standing by about twenty minutes away. I can be there in a few hours with a team." He listened, then nodded. "All right, make the arrangements. We'll see you then." And he hung up and turned to Augustus and Taneshia. "We're up. Get packed, wheels up in half an hour. We'll meet Scotty there, and I'll send for Olivia." His jaw tightened. "Maybe Greg, too, since he's offered to be on our reserve payroll in case of emergency."

I recognized that as a sign of nothing good. "What?" I asked, and he didn't answer, just stared straight ahead. "Reed … what is it?"

He drew a long breath, then let it out, slowly. "They have a suspect, and … he's known to us."

"Oh, man," I said, putting a hand to my face. My list of rogues was pretty short these days, and one popped immediately to mind, someone who could move—well, mountains, or the earth, and definitely shake up an aircraft carrier within its berth if he were of a mind to. But I didn't say this. Instead, I said, "Who?"

"They've placed Eric Simmons at the scene," Reed said tightly, getting to his feet. "When confronted by the military police, he fled. They've got a helicopter over him right now, and they're following him back to wherever he's going." His jaw tightened, my brother suddenly serious, no more trace of the mom combo. "They're waiting for us to make their move."

3.

Simmons

Eric Simmons was getting away with it, and he could barely believe it. He'd crossed the bridge down into Norfolk with ease, before they'd even known what hit them, and now he was crossing the Chesapeake Bay Bridge, heading north into Maryland, where he'd disappear on the back rounds and vanish, heading north to Delaware. By tomorrow morning, he'd be safely tucked away in New York City. Maybe he'd catch a flight to Asia, wake up in Kuala Lumpur or spend some time surfing on Australia's Gold Coast. It was summer there now, after all ...

Simmons steered the SUV through traffic. It wasn't his preferred car; he would have liked something smaller, maybe a little more eco-friendly than a gas guzzling SUV, but beggars couldn't be choosers, and the fact that it rode a lot higher than one of those cars made him feel like he was king of the road, looking down over the lesser drivers in their itty bitty cars like he was the mack daddy.

Oh, yeah. Simmons was making it.

The Chesapeake Bay Bridge dove down into the second tunnel ahead. He was about halfway through the four-mile length, just marking the minutes, planning to ditch this vehicle when he reached the other side, pull off and use a second getaway car that had been provided for him.

It was all going according to plan thus far, the tunnel

darkness shrouding him, his beams and the lights on the dark wall letting him see just a little further ahead. It was kind of like this plan, really—all he needed to see was the next move, and the next. Sure, he'd had it all laid out, with help from his captors in Revelen, but he only focused on one thing at a time. Wrecking the carrier. Then running back to the car. Driving off. And now, getting to the change-out vehicle.

After that … getting the hell out of the hinterlands and back into civilization.

The light ahead was blinding, shining down as the tunnel rose back to rejoin the bridge. The tunnels served their purpose, though; Simmons figured there was a ship passing over his head even now, which was pretty cool. He was no fan of what those ships did to the environment, but he respected their power, their ability to move supplies from point A to point B around the earth. And the fact that a multi-ton cargo ship could be above his head, literally, right now?

It gave him chills. Cool, man.

Simmons ran a hand through his long hair, and up he went with the slope of the tunnel, rising out of the water to rejoin the bridge. *Halfway home,* he thought, feeling like he'd already kind of won this race. After all, he was going to be rid of this car pretty, soon, before they'd get a chance to catch him and—

Orange glowed just above him, and Simmons squinted. There was a glowing spot. Something was at the entrance to the tunnel, looking down at him …

Something … human?

There was a figure on fire hovering just a few feet above the bridge surface as he emerged into the daylight, noticeable against the blinding sunlight only because of the subtly different shade they were projecting. It was not a daylight color, it was the color of a bonfire, of flames, of—

Sienna Nealon?

That was one of her tricks, covering herself in fire and coming at you, flying. Simmons squinted at the figure who just hovered there, about ten feet off the bridge deck, looking down at the traffic passing harmlessly below. A semi truck honked its horn, and the figure drifted into the other lane, letting the semi pass, albeit slowly because the driver applied the brakes, probably worried something bad would happen.

But nothing bad happened as the truck passed …

Nothing bad happened until the figure looked right at Simmons.

And then lit him up with a ball of fire.

Simmons threw himself from the getaway car by reflex alone, tearing at the door handle and hurling himself from the vehicle. Searing heat passed along his back as he hit pavement and rolled, slamming into the curb and then up, back slamming against the bridge rail. Simmons cringed. That hurt.

He pushed his eyes open and looked up; the flaming figure was still hovering there, and Simmons's getaway car was burning, traffic slowing to a stop behind him, the honking already beginning. Everyone was keeping their distance, and now there was an ever-widening pocket empty of all traffic in front of his car, no one daring to pass that flaming wreck and come closer to the fiery person who'd brought his escape to a halt.

"Dude. Well," Simmons said, cringing, looking up at the flaming person—no, it was a man, he realized on further inspection. The height, the way the flames hugged the body—he was a dude all the way, and that at least ruled out Sienna Nealon, thank goodness. "I guess you got me."

Simmons wasn't ready to throw in the towel just yet, but he was limited in what he could do against a flyer. Earthquake powers didn't tend to affect anyone who wasn't on the ground, after all.

"Get up," the flaming figure said, his voice heavy with some kind of Russian or Eastern European accent.

"You got it, boss," Simmons said, putting his hands up as he stood, wobbly, using the bridge rail against his back to support himself. "Hands behind my head?" He'd figured out the score now—this was law enforcement, probably that new FBI meta squad.

"No," the man said and drew closer. "Your powers …"

earthquake?"

"Yep," Simmons said. He didn't see any reason to say no. It wasn't like it was a serious question he could lie his way through.

The man came down to the ground slowly, feet landing on the pavement and searing the asphalt as he did so, smoke rushing off them and filling the air with the stink of burning tar. "Put your hands down."

Simmons just stared at him, then looked behind him, as though seeking advice from the nobody that was there. Well, there were people in the cars, the traffic that was piling up behind them, but ... nobody was out of their vehicles. No cops, no civilians ... everybody just sitting there.

"What?" Simmons asked, trying to make sure he'd heard the fire-man right. "You want me to put my hands ... down?"

"Yes." The answer was immediate, the voice chock full of confidence.

"You got it," Simmons said and put his hands down. He tried to think his way through this. He couldn't exactly do a ton on the bridge with his powers, after all. If he tried, it'd collapse beneath him. "Nice play," he said to the man on fire.

The fire-man strode toward him calmly and stopped about ten feet away. "And now ... we fight."

He was so matter-of-fact about it that it took Simmons a moment to decode what he'd said. "... Whut?" His head bowed slightly, he looked at the fire-man, and his mouth fell slightly open. "You wanna do what?"

The fire-man lifted a hand, palm-up, and beckoned Simmons forward with all four of his fingers, waggling them toward him. "We fight."

"Uhmm ..." Simmons's mind was racing. This did not compute. "Dude. You've got me dead to rights. I can't throw flame. I don't even know if I have the speed to dodge it. You've got me, man. I'll come with you, no questions asked. I'll do my time."

"No." The fire-man shook his head. "We fight."

"How am I supposed to figh—" Simmons started to say—

—And was interrupted by the fire-man crossing the distance between them and searing him with a punch to the face.

It cracked Simmons's jaw, made him see stars. The searing of raw nerves across his cheek came screaming into Simmons's mind as he realized that bastard had hit him. With a flaming punch.

Simmons fell to his knees and watched the fiery figure take a couple steps back. "Get up. We fight."

"Owww." Simmons held his jaw. Now his knees were complaining, too, because he'd dropped after that first hit. "I don't know who you think you are, man, but I've got rights—"

"Get up or I will kill you on the ground like a beggar," the fire-man said, and Simmons looked up at him.

Cold, dead eyes stared back from behind a veil of fire. Black in the midst of an orange, crackling head. It was like looking at a demon.

"Okay, okay," Simmons said, still cradling his jaw. Man, it hurt. This dude had done a number on him, and not a good number, like four. This was a two hundred or something. He struggled to his feet on wobbly legs. He could feel the blisters already rising on his jaw.

"Now ... we fight," the fire-guy said again, and he came at Simmons, a little slower this time. Simmons put up his hands, but took a punch to the forearm and screamed, falling back as it made contact. He screamed, stumbling away, trying to flee the pain, but it followed him.

And so did the man on fire.

Fire-man hit Simmons in the gut with a flashing punch, doubling him over and giving him fresh burns on his abdomen. All the air rushed out of Simmons's lungs and was replaced by searing air as he sucked in a half-breath, unable to choke a full one down. He was gasping from the pain and from getting the wind knocked out of him, and Fire-man was just standing there, inches away, the heat so intense Simmons thought he might burst into flames from proximity.

His gut was burning, and Simmons looked down. Angry welts and charred skin showed through a hole in his shirt.

"Ohh, man ..." Simmons muttered, trying to keep the pain bottled up.

He looked up in time to see another punch coming, and this one laid him out on his back. Simmons's eyes sprang open and found fire-guy standing over him, merciless, those black eyes just staring down at him. "Get up," came the command.

"I don't ... think I can ..." Simmons moaned. So much pain. He had second and third degree burns on his wrist, his face, his belly ... what did this guy expect from him?

"Fight, or you will die," Fire-man proclaimed. "You have to the count of ten." That thick Euro accent was like a cloud that hung over his words, and it took Simmons to a two count to realize what he was doing. "... Three ... four ..."

"Okay," Simmons croaked, rolling over and grabbing the bridge rail. He used it to lever himself to his feet, back to Fire-guy. What the hell was this? Simmons hadn't been beaten like this since the time Sienna Nealon had decided to use his jaw for a punching bag.

He was on his feet a few seconds later, and right at the nine count he shoved off the bridge, trying to mimic a boxing stance. That seemed to be what this guy was going for, after all, some kind of battle to the finish. Simmons wasn't that excited about obliging him, but he didn't want to die, so he just went along for another round. He would have tapped out if he could, just laid down on the mat if it were up to him, but no, Fire-guy apparently wasn't cool with surrender.

What was this guy's problem? A little quiver of fear made its way through Simmons's legs, and he wobbled even more. There was no way to beat this guy, but ... surely he couldn't actually be serious? He wasn't actually going to kill him, a defenseless person ...

... Was he?

The punches came a little slower this time, but Simmons still couldn't ward them off. "Come on, man!" Simmons cried as one of the hits glazed his shoulder, sending up a stink of burnt shirt and scorched flesh. He kept from crying only barely, and fire-guy kicked him in the leg, burning his pants at the shin and making him double over. Simmons couldn't even stop himself; this was MMA-type stuff, which he liked to watch but God, it wasn't any fun when someone was coming after you with it.

A hard crunch to the back of the neck dropped Simmons face-first to the pavement. Blood coursed out of his lips and nose, and his head rang through the pain of fresh burns on the back of his head. How hot did this guy have to be to burn him so bad with hits that were lasting less than a second?

Hot. Really hot.

Simmons's chin was against the asphalt, and he could smell it burning where fire-guy was standing over him. "Get to your feet by ten count, or you die," that cold, inflectionless voice said again.

"O ... okay," Simmons said, drooling and dribbling blood. He tried to cradle up, to pull to all fours, but his body was just overwhelmed. Nothing wanted to move—not his legs, not his arms, and not his head, for damned sure.

Simmons was done.

He wanted to just curl up in a ball and have it be over, but he couldn't even motivate himself to do that. It was like every part of him had quit at once, and when he heard the countdown, "... six ... seven ..."

Simmons just couldn't bring himself to care enough to try anymore.

So instead he settled right there, drooling on the pavement. This was good. He didn't want to fight anymore. He hadn't wanted to fight in the first place, but—damn Revelen—gah, he hated them. It sucked that they'd done this to him. He was all ready to just live his life, free as the wind, and they'd gone and clipped his frigging wings.

Now he was here, a dead duck on the Chesapeake Bay Bridge, listening to some Euro dude count him down to death, and without even enough fight left to object. "Nine ... Ten."

The flames above him got hotter, and Simmons could feel his back start to burn. The pain surged through him, giving him new life, new panic, and triggering his fighting instinct, if only for a second.

But with him ... that was all it took.

Simmons lashed out with his powers, more out of panic than genuine planning, and a quake wave shot through the ground beneath him.

Except it wasn't ground.

It was bridge; steel and concrete, thick enough to support cars, trucks—miles of it, built to hold tons and tons of weight.

But not built to survive an earthquake directed right at one of the supports.

He could hear and feel the bridge column buckle beneath him as Fire-guy burned the layer of skin off his back and reached bone. Simmons didn't process that, just as he hadn't processed anything else since his body and will had shut down from the beating. He didn't care, couldn't fully feel anything other than screaming pain lashing its way through his back, and it only spurred him on to strike out with his powers even harder.

It came out of him like a sudden blockage being forced out of a tight tube. One minute he hadn't been using powers, the next he was giving it everything he had, like a muscle contracting from shock to his body. He hit the Chesapeake Bay Bridge with all his powers, giving it an immediate 9.5 on the Richter scale.

The concrete supports dissolved in a second, the bridge deck itself shattered a second after, and the entire thing, from the tunnel entry all the way to the next section, exploded into dust from the sheer force of Simmons's panicked release of powers.

Simmons felt it, of course, dimly, beneath the layers of agony that Fire-man had just forced on him. But more than that, he felt his body falling, falling among the dust and steel as the bridge came down around him. He left the heat behind—thank goodness for that!—and plunged, plunged into the darkness of Chesapeake Bay below, the cold water like heaven on his burns as he drifted down into the black, the world falling in with him.

4.

Sienna

"Holy hell," I said as we watched the chopper-eye view of the Chesapeake Bay Bridge explode under the assault of Eric Simmons's powers. He'd been getting his ass kicked by that guy on fire, not putting up much of a fight, and then suddenly—

Whoosh. The bridge imploded underneath him, and Simmons disappeared in a cloud of dust while fire-guy just hovered there for a few seconds, like a candle in the night. Except it was midday.

"Wow," Eilish said. It was just the two of us glued to the TV, but glued we were, unable to move. I was watching something really astounding unfold before my eyes, and it was a unique situation, because ...

Normally, in these types of events ... I would have been there in minutes.

Instead, here I sat, in Panama City Beach, Florida ...

Powerless to do a damned thing.

The dust cleared a moment later, and Fire-guy just hung there, staring down into the dark waters below. The news choppers caught him on video, just silently floating there, watching. After a few seconds, he seemed to have decided that there was nothing else to be done, because he turned skyward—

And shot off into the heavens.

"Geez," I said, taking a breath that I hadn't known I'd been holding. "I guess that settles Simmons's hash."

"That was a pretty epic fight," Eilish said, "from one side, at least."

"What happened?" Reed asked, emerging from the hallway, suitcase in his hand. His eyes found the TV before we could answer, and he dropped the suitcase. "My God."

"That guy was pretty powerful," Eilish said. "Flying and fire. That's not a normal combo, is it?"

My lips twitched. "I've seen it before." Hell, I'd *been* it before. Aleksandr Gavrikov had both those powers.

My stomach twisted, hard. Thinking about Gavrikov was like a dash of salt in a fresh wound.

"But I mean—they're two separate powers, right?" Eilish asked, though I suspected she knew the answer and just wanted to talk about what we were seeing. "Flight's one, and fire's another. This guy has both, so … it's unusual to have two powers, right?"

"Yeah," Reed said, and I deferred to him, because I didn't want to comment. "It's unusual. Not as unusual as it used to be now that these different serums are out there, but … still unusual."

"See, that's what I thought," Eilish said, with a little satisfaction.

"What's going on now?" Augustus said, emerging from his room with his own suitcase, Taneshia a few paces behind. Augustus had—I kid you not—a suitcase twice the size of his girlfriend's, plus a backpack and a shoulder bag.

"You pack like a girl," I announced, making Augustus look over his luggage.

"It takes a lot of work to look this good, all right?" Augustus said, unabashed.

"You've been spending too much time with Kat," I said.

"Mission parameter change, I'm guessing," Reed said, staying focused on what was actually important and not getting lost in the details of Augustus's girlish packing habits. He pointed at the spectacle on the TV, a helicopter shot of the fallen bridge. "Did Simmons do that?"

"Presumably," I said, still anchored to the couch, lead in

my ass keeping me from getting too excited. Or at least from showing it. Part of me wanted to get up, to go with them, but there was enough sense and enough of a feeling like I was an old dog that should stay on the porch to keep me seated. "This new guy—fire and flying powers—had him down on the bridge, and then it went kaput. Fire guy flew off, Simmons was gone, so ... my guess is that he's out of the picture, one way or another. You'll probably have to get Scott to comb the bay to be sure."

"He's already on his way to the airport in Eden Prairie," Reed said, and then answered another call. "Go for Treston. Yes, I just—yes. We're on our way, we'll be there in a couple hours." And hung up, looking at Taneshia and Augustus. "Let's go. I'll call Greg and Olivia, have them meet us en route."

"Sounds fun," Eilish said, in a tone that told me she did not think it sounded fun. If possible, she sounded less energetic than even I did. "Be safe, you lot."

"Why?" Augustus asked, giving her a sour eye. "So you can keep fleecing us at cards?"

"Yep," Eilish said with a curt nod. "That's exactly it." She was a cutthroat card player. I hadn't dared to face her, personally, but then I had other hobbies lately.

Like scotch. Scotch was a perfectly valid hobby.

"Let's move," Reed said, and nodded toward the door. Augustus and Taneshia went for it, while he stayed anchored in place, all serious now, the mom-combo gone—or at least transformed. No guilt; just pressure. "You going to be here when we get back?" he asked, looking right at me.

I looked up. "Where the hell else am I going to go?"

"Just wanted to make sure you didn't get any ideas," Reed said, a little cautiously.

"My big idea is to count down the hours until five o'clock," I said, pointing at the bottles against the wall on the counter in the kitchen, "so I can kick off this evening's festivities."

There was a flicker of disappointment in his eyes. "All right," he said, postponing that argument for another day. "Don't drink and swim."

"Pffft, too cold for swimming," I said, brushing off that

idea. The sound of some idiot proving me wrong outside came in the form of a screech of joy.

"I left you some cash, and one of the rental cars is downstairs," he said, making his way to the door. Augustus and Taneshia were just standing there, waiting. "Don't wander far. Your disguise is okay, but a sharp eye could still pick you out."

My disguise was dyed hair and being starvation thin, a little thing that had happened during my time in Scotland, and which I hadn't exactly striven to change since I'd come back to the US. Scotch helped. Scotch, and skipping a lot of meals. "Aye aye, captain," I said, and saluted.

He bit back his response, but I could see the worry in his eyes. "Just …"

"Dude, you're the one going into danger," I said, shooing him with a hand motion. "*You* be safe. And don't forget to call your girlfriend. You promised her you'd check in on the regular, and I don't want her to be madder at me than she already is for keeping you down here for months on end."

"Yeah, okay," he said, easing through the door with something that felt like lingering regret. "Just … take it easy, okay?"

"You too, bro," I said, way too casual. Seeing him walk out the door was like a gut punch, but I waved him off anyway. "Be safe. Augustus, Taneshia … watch out for my big, worrying bro-mother, will you?"

"We got this," Augustus said, and he and Taneshia were off.

"I'll see you when I get back," Reed said.

The door slammed behind him with alarming finality, and a nervous pit in my stomach that had started to subside over these last few weeks and months that we'd been here, all together …

It started to grow again—this gnawing, aching feeling within, like a black hole aiming to consume me.

5.

How was it that the minutes leading up to five o'clock could feel so impossibly long?

They were piling up, the minutes, but not accumulating nearly fast enough. I was sprawled out on the couch still, engaging in a kind of torpor to preserve my energy and ignore the hunger pangs that rattled through my body. I kept eyeing my bottle of scotch, just sitting there on the counter, calling to me with its beautiful siren song. It was right there, for the taking, minutes and miles away.

With a sigh, I turned back to the TV screen, where a clock presented itself.

4:47 Eastern Time, it read in the bottom corner of the news icon. Thirteen minutes to glory.

"I wish someone looked at me the way you look at a bottle of scotch," Eilish said, ever helpful.

"Sometimes I wish you stayed as quiet as a bottle of scotch," I said. I actually didn't. I'd had way worse voices than her in my ear for the last few years, and now that they were gone ...

Well, Eilish wasn't a replacement for them, as such, but man ... it was nice not to be totally surrounded by silence here.

"Why don't we go out tonight?" she asked, a hint of wheedling in her tone. "You're sporting the bottle-blond look, no one's going to recognize you. There's that nice Italian restaurant down at the terminus of this road—what

25

do they call it again?"

"It's called 30A," I said, watching the clock. Twelve minutes.

"Right. They make it sound so damned iconic," she said, annoyingly chipper. I'd be a lot happier myself in twelve minutes. "30A. It just sounds cool. Anyhoo … we could go to the Italian place, or that breakfast-y all-day spot down by Publix—"

"Waffle House?" I turned my head to look at her. "They have burgers and such, you know."

"I'm not really interested in the 'and such,'" she said. "Ye ask me, you order something non-waffle from a place called Waffle House, you're just asking for trouble. Besides, those waffles—they're amazing. I don't think we have anything like them in Ireland—"

"Your whiskey's not bad," I said. But it wasn't scotch.

"Uhm … I was talking breakfast-food wise," she said, a little nonplussed by my reversion to alcohol every other thought. "So … what do you say? Or we could get some of those marvelous sub sandwiches at Publix—I know you have a hankering for that Cuban from time to time—"

I rolled at my eyes at her transparent attempt to get me to engage with the world. "You can take the car and pick something up if you want. I'm just going to chill here tonight."

"Uhm, ye've chilled here every night for the last umpteen many, to borrow one of your favorite words."

I shrugged. It appeared I was running out of enablers. "I'm a fugitive, trying to lay low. Going out to Publix or Waffle House or local Italian places on the regular seems like laying high." I frowned, trying to make sense of what I'd just said. "Or … something." Laying high sounded dirty, and there'd been no laying, high or low, for me in entirely too long.

Which was fine. Because scotch was strong, and ever ready, and he would see me through.

"But—but—" Now she was into the spluttering. "But you like Publix, don't you?"

Here I didn't shrug, but only because, yes, I did like Publix. It was my favorite supermarket ever. "It is 'Where Shopping is a Pleasure,'" I conceded. "But I don't want to go out tonight, Eilish." I looked at the clock on screen. Ten minutes.

"I don't know if I can stay in again tonight," she said, making eyes toward the door and the balcony.

"So hang out outside," I said. "Chill by the pool deck. Literally, since it's like fifty degrees. That's gotta be like a balmy summer day for a fine Irish gal like you." Nine minutes. "You could probably even work on your complete lack of tan."

She made a hard scoffing noise. "You should talk."

"No, I should shut up, watch the news, and count the minutes until five o'clock." Because damn, this watched pot was steadfastly refusing to get to boiling.

The bridge mess was … well, a mess. Whoever Fire-guy meta was, he'd prompted the wrecking of a huge span of the Chesapeake Bay Bridge. The news was all in a tizzy about it, probably because catastrophes meant ratings—I tried to imagine a scenario where I somehow got bonus pay for things going to shit and realized, with the agency still under my ownership, I kinda did.

Eilish fell into a silence that was beautiful and lasted until 4:56. Four more minutes.

"It's my first time in America," she said, now crossing straight into whine-baby territory, "and I just don't want to sit around the bloody condo all the time." She hit me with pleading eyes. "We could go walk on the beach. You could even bring your drink."

I just stared at her, my patience hanging by a strand. "You want me to walk on the beach with an aged Lagavulin in my hand?"

She nodded. "I won't mind."

"If you're feeling like you need to go out," I said, letting the words filter out ever so slowly, "why don't you just go and enjoy a fine evening alone?"

"That's no fun," she said. We'd passed whining into whatever lay beyond. Whimpering, sniveling, I dunno. It wasn't just tap-dancing on my nerves; it was a herd of elephants in tap shoes Riverdancing on them. "Come with me. Show me your beloved America."

"I'm really more interested in my beloved scotch at the moment," I said, holding my shit together by a thin thread so as not to lose it all over her. I glanced at the clock. Two minutes. Thank heavens.

Like thunder from above, a knocking came at the door in an almighty fury. I froze in my chair and Eilish's eyes widened next to me. She looked like she was about to shit kittens, maybe squeeze out a brick.

I regained my calm and meta-whispered to her. "Just don't answer it. It's probably no one."

She looked at me like I was stupid. "Someone's knocking, it can't be no one. Empty air doesn't bloody knock."

I controlled the eye roll, but only barely. "I mean it's probably no one important, just a solicitor or something."

She made a confused face. "Why would a lawyer be knocking?"

"A salesperson, you UK baby," I said. "Not a lawyer."

"You Americans. Your word choices are just strange."

The knocking came again, even harder, and I looked at the clock on the TV screen.

One minute to go.

I took a steadying breath, in through the nose, out through the mouth. I got up, started to make my way over to the beverages in the corner. The knocking sounded again, loud and horrendous.

"What if it's Reed? Or one of the others?" Eilish asked.

"They have keys," I said, brushing off her tiny, irrelevant, annoying concerns.

"What if it's the police?"

"They wouldn't knock, they'd bust the door down and shoot us, holding any questions until after they'd processed us at the morgue."

"Sienna!" someone shouted through the door, and I froze about two feet shy of my scotch.

A cold, clammy, crawling sensation worked its way up my arms, turning the skin all bumpy with gooseflesh. It made its way up the back of my neck and across the top of my head, down my forearms and wrists to stop at my hands, and, for good measure, went ahead and made it feel like someone had slid an ice cube or twelve down the back of my pants at the base of my spine. An icicle-based tramp stamp.

"Sienna, open up!" the voice came again. It was female, kinda small, but clearly pissed off. The knocking came again, a rattling, and then I heard a wheezing cough from the person standing at my door.

"Oh, f—" I started to say, but it was interrupted by another round of knocking.

"I'm going to stand out here and make a scene until you open the door," she said. "Because I know you're in there, and—"

Closing my eyes for just a second, I whirled, crossed the distance to the door in a hot second, ripped it open, and dragged the person standing out there inside before she could so much as wheeze in surprise. That done, I closed it back up, locked it, and took a deep breath.

The skinny, dark-haired waif standing before me looked at me with heat-vision eyes, even though I'd grasped onto her person for about a second, tops, but she let go the succubus-to-skin contact and, instead, gave me a piece of her mind. "You owe me," she said, cutting right to it, "and I've come to collect."

I took a moment to sigh, then turned my back on her, and with a glance at the clock—it read 4:59—I broke my resolve and shuffled over to the bar, pouring myself a drink without ceremony. I filled it to nearing the top of the little glass, brought it up to my nose, let that peaty scent fill my nasal passages, and with an eye on the TV screen clock—it still read 4:59—I gave up on giving a shit and went ahead and sloshed it back, taking the whole glass down in one gulp.

"Holy hell," Eilish said. "It's not five o'clock yet."

"Go for a jump with a pogo stick up your ass, Irish, I'm an alcoholic," I said, feeling the scotch burn its way down my throat. That done, I poured another one as my invading "guest" stood in silence, just watching, her skin mottled as she clearly built on whatever internal ragey emotions had brought her to my door. I took another breath, and this time, I would savor my drink while I waited for the first to work. I

29

waited for her to say something, but she didn't, preferring the cold stare-me-down, as though waiting for my leave to speak, when I knew in reality it was no such damned thing.

Because I knew why she was here without her even having to say anything.

She said something anyway. "You owe me."

That one caused some heat in my cheeks. I kept the glass clutched between my fingers as I stared at the little figure darkening my door—well, my entry rug, now. I took a breath, and it seared like the scotch. "I don't owe you a damned thing," I said, staring right back at her, "Cassidy Ellis."

6.

Cassidy Ellis stood on my rug, this little slip of a girl trying to engage me—me, of all people!—in a staredown.

Like that was going to work.

"I helped you out of Scotland," she said, pale face splotched with red. She looked like a Coke can.

"And you got paid ten million for it," I said. I took a whiff of the scotch in my glass, sloshing it slowly around the circle of my crystalline glass.

"A serious discount to my going rates. I also lost my house, thanks to your brother."

I looked her up and down and made a show of doing so. She was in pretty good repair, you know, compared to me. "You seem fine. Living at the Four Seasons now, with all your piles of money?"

She flushed. "No. They don't have nearly the data line access I need—you know what, it doesn't matter. You owe me, Sienna."

"You keep saying that," I regarded my drink with a lot more interest than I did her. "But I paid you, which was, as far as I'm aware, the extent of my brother's bargain on my behalf."

A small, very evil smile broke across her face. "You're right. I guess I should be asking him for the favor he owes me."

I started to say, "Yeah, why don't you go do that," but then I remembered what Cassidy was here for. With my glass

31

halfway to my lips, and watching her out of the corner of my eye, I froze.

And saw the look of triumph in her eyes even without staring at her directly. Honestly, it was like looking at the sun, it was almost blinding.

"What do you want, Cassidy?" I asked, kinda wanting her to just say it, even though I knew.

She straightened. "I want you—or Reed, if you refuse—to track down that son of a whore that attacked my baby—"

"Simmons is definitely a baby," I said, "a big one."

"—I want this mutt dead," Cassidy said, flushing brighter. "I want him—"

"I get the point, Al Capone. The guy dead, his family dead, his puppy, probably dead—look, I don't do that whole murder for fun thing, okay?" I took a sip of the scotch and wished it was a whole glass. The first I'd downed was starting to work on me, though.

"You've killed plenty of people," Cassidy said, "and for less reason than you've got with this guy. He killed a lot of people on that bridge, Sienna." Convenient for her to leave out that her baby had killed a lot more people on the U.S.S. Enterprise before this mysterious vigilante had brought his interstate flight to an abrupt halt. "My estimates put it in the range of over a hundred, probably close to one-fifty."

I paused with the glass to my lips. The news had only confirmed five or so thus far.

"Jaysus," Eilish breathed.

Yeah. It had been a bad day for human/meta relations. The best thing I could say about it was that at least I hadn't been involved in any of it. For once.

"Okay, that's a point," I said. "But this event is being treated as terrorism. They've locked down the airports, no one's flying right now, and when they do open up flights again tomorrow, there's no chance in hell I'm going to be able to get on even a private plane at this point. Security is tighter than your ass right now, Cassidy." I shrugged a little expansively, but not so expansively I spilled even a drop of precious, precious scotch. "So … what do you expect me to do to pursue this guy?"

She didn't even blink. "Call your friend the incredible shrinking man and ask for a ride."

"Can't," I said. "He works for Reed, not me, and he's already been called up."

That did deflate her slightly, enough to give me a little hope that she might come to her senses. But then I saw the look on her face, and realized it was her running some sort of scenario-style thing in her head, calculating probabilities or figuring out alternate routes like a GPS after you just took a way wrong turn. "Okay," she said after a second, "we go by car."

I would have done a spit take, but the scotch, y'know. Why waste it for comic effect? Instead I picked up a water bottle, unscrewed the cap with one hand, took a sip, everyone watching me, and then sprayed it—about five seconds late, but still frigging hilarious. "This is not *The Muppet Movie*, and you must be for real tripping if you think I am road-tripping across America with either of you."

"Oof, that hurts," Eilish said. "I rather enjoyed our Scottish excursion, you know, other than the constant fear of a Scottish ginger burning my very soul out of me."

"Either you help me or I call Reed and remind him of his obligation to me," she said, unflinching. "I'm guessing he's on the case already, and sooner or later he'll catch up with this guy. Now maybe, in the course of events, he'll have to fight him anyway, and if he kills him in the process, I'll get my desired outcome." God, she really was like a computer calculating odds. "If that's the case, I'll consider our bargain fulfilled." She leaned in a little, flushing as she did so, her skin so pale that the slightest change in mood or emotional state seemed to light her up. "But what if he doesn't kill this meta? What if he manages to beat him and bring him in with the help of your team? And then he's forced to kill him to satisfy our bargain?" She arched her eyebrows at me. "I know what you're thinking."

"I kinda doubt that," I said, staring at her. I was thinking about dashing her brains out with one punch just to be rid of her blackmailing ass, because as dumb as she thought I was, I could see the box she was trying to put me in here. I could see it coming a mile off.

And it bothered me because … I had a feeling I was going to step right into it. Willingly.

"You're thinking, 'Oh, he wouldn't kill a prisoner just because he owes Cassidy,'" she said, and the hint of a satisfied smile started to creep over her thin lips. "But he's not the same Reed anymore, is he? I saw him kill that metal bender in Scotland, without a thought, without remorse. He just killed that guy, easy as pie, because he threatened you. Now, Reed owes me—but it's because of you. So when the obligation comes due—"

"I hope you die painfully, Cassidy," I said, holding my scotch glass as tight as I could without shattering it. If I threw it at her right now, I could probably—if I aimed it perfectly—kill her with one shot.

Cassidy did not seem moved by my comment. "So you'll do it, then?" She almost smiled.

She had the right of it. If she presented Reed with this same scenario, could I be sure he'd offer to satisfy her Faustian bargain—the one he'd struck to save my life?

No. No, he probably wouldn't kill a prisoner. And this guy—this meta, whoever he was—didn't even seem like the type to go willingly or gracefully, assuming they could find him.

But … at the same time … what if all the stars did align, and Reed's team beat him without killing him? And Reed was confronted with his debt to Cassidy while in full custody of this vigilante killer who'd helped wreck a bridge that probably killed some people in the process?

Reed … the old Reed … wouldn't have done anything about it. The killer would go to the Cube, and that'd be that.

But the new Reed? The more … Sienna-esque Reed, for lack of a better word?

Shit.

Who knew what he'd do? Mom eyes be damned.

I felt my breath catch in my throat, and so I washed it down with a long drink of scotch that burned all through my gullet and down to my belly. "I don't even know if we can find this guy," I said, waiting for the burning to subside. "I mean, going by car while Reed and his crew are traveling by air? We're going to be a day late and a dollar short to any encounters. They'll be two, three hours behind him, maybe five if this guy goes to the West Coast ... but we'll be days from him."

Cassidy just stared back at me, flat, uncaring, borderline evil. "I don't care. I want him dead for what he did to Eric."

I took another breath, and it stuck in my chest again. "What if I can't deliver?"

She stared at me. "If you give it your absolute best ... I'll consider us square. But if you slack off, back off—generally don't give it your all?" She sidled up into my personal space. "I'll know. And I'll still come to Reed for a favor. One that will exact a toll on him. I'll choose it carefully—it'll look innocuous enough, but it'll take from him in ways you won't care to see the end result of."

Eilish let out a small gasp, then gulped. "That sounds ... very worrisome."

I threw back the rest of my scotch, then set the empty glass down. That hitch in my breathing subsided as the alcohol hit home, and I felt my own face flush as though I were Cassidy, a burn starting within. "You have yourself a deal," I said, grabbing her by the hand before she could dodge away. "But Cassidy ... so help me—"

"You don't need to say it," she yanked her hand away. "I don't sting you, you don't sting me."

"Sting you?" I turned away from her. "Little scorpion," I smacked my lips together. I wanted nothing but more scotch, even though the second glass had barely made its way down to my stomach, but it was time to quit, "stinging is your thing. I'm Sienna Nealon, okay?" I turned back to her. "I don't sting the things that piss me off ..." I breathed in heavily, "... I scourge them from the damned earth. Now ..." And I started to step, figuring on packing my bag, but I tripped instead, my legs feeling a little woozy.

I hit the ground, sharp stinging pains ringing their way up my elbows. I bounced back to my feet a second later, head swimming from the quick double more-than-shot. "Okay. I'm okay." I looked around. "Uhm ... all right." I nodded a couple times. "So ..." I clapped my hands together. "... Who wants to drive?"

35

7.

Packing was a breeze, thankfully. I didn't have much, and what I did have was easily shoved into my suitcase. There were no clothes waiting in the laundry, because Reed had put all of mine away for me before leaving. I perhaps should have found it awkward that my brother was laundering my unmentionables and then putting them in the drawers in my room, but honestly, I had zero interest in washing my own clothes, so it was something I'd learned to overlook in the last few months.

"We'll head north," I said as I opened the door and stepped out on the landing, bag slung over my shoulder. Cassidy was just behind me, and Eilish was bringing up the rear, locking the door as we left the condo. She'd been pretty quiet since I'd made the decision to leave. For someone who'd been so keen on getting out just a little while earlier, she'd changed her tune pretty fast.

Or stopped singing, I guess. Because of the quiet.

"Oh, good," Cassidy said acidly. "Because if we headed south, we'd be in the Gulf of Mexico within minutes, and if we headed west we'd be aiming for Texas where this meta is not—as yet."

"I notice you didn't throw in a chance to make fun of her for not saying east," Eilish said, pocketing the car keys with hardly any effort. She was slick, a practiced thief, and those movements carried into her everyday life, I'd noticed.

Cassidy flushed only mildly. "If you were to head east, you

could catch Interstate 75 or Interstate 95, both major north-south feeder arteries on the east coast."

"In other words, that would make sense, so she didn't want to make fun of me for … not suggesting that?" I had lost the thread. I blame scotch. "Anyway … northward. We go north. Maybe via 90-75—whatever she said." I waved a hand at her. "I leave the navigation to you, Cassidy."

"Fine," she said, falling into a hurried step behind me. If I looked skeletal, she looked like bone fragments strung together with dental floss. "Where are we going?"

I cast a look back at her. "I dunno. Where are we going?"

Now she flushed a shade darker, and her asthma acted up, very audible in her next breath, which sounded like an unintended hiss. "Well, given that we know little to nothing about this—this *villain*," I thought that was a bit rich coming from a lady who'd once conspired to humiliate, destroy and kill me, all from afar and with the aid of my worst enemies, "I think our first step is to visit the scene, as best we can." She whitened a little as she seemed to decide the course, "to, um, canvas for clues."

"In a place where the cops and federal agents are thicker than the mosquitos on warm nights around here?" I asked, raising an eyebrow. "I think we're a lot better off getting to within a day's drive of the scene and then waiting there until this guy shows his face again."

Cassidy was frowning so deeply behind me I could hear it in her voice. "Your plan is just to wait for him until he shows up again?"

"Uh, yeah," I said. "Were you watching that thing unfold? Where he sent the bridge to the bottom of the bay?"

She caught up with me, coming alongside me and shooting a fiery look that was probably burning holes in the windows of the other condos we walked past on the way to the stairs. "Yes. Of course."

"Then you should know," I said, really wishing I'd brought a scotch for the road, "what happened on that bridge—"

"Was an attempted execution," she said fiercely. "That man—that monster—he attacked my—"

"Mass murderer boyfriend," I said, smacking Cassidy with

my words rather than my fist—for now. "Let us not forget that Eric killed more people than this guy. And if he were still alive—"

Cassidy grabbed me by the hand and spun me, almost causing me to drop my bag in shock that she'd tried to manhandle me. Mousy Cassidy. She was staring at me with a blazing fire in her eyes. "He," she said, now straining, "is not—*dead.*" The last word came out as kind of a hushed whisper.

Drink almost got the better of me, and I was on the verge of saying, "Suuuuuure he's not." But I was about to spend hours and possibly days in a confined car with Cassidy, and some little genius part of me stopped that reply at the last second. Instead, I went with the blandly neutral, "Okay." And then followed it up with, "But it wasn't an execution, there on the bridge." I looked at her, trying to stay somewhat compassionate by dialing back my desire to hit her so hard she'd fly off the balcony and into the parking lot. It wasn't as easy as you might think, with the scotch burning through my veins.

She only held off for a moment before curiosity got the better of her. "What was it, then?"

"Looked like a bloody annunciation, didn't it?" Eilish tossed in. I gave her a nod. Mad respect. She went on. "I mean, he drops of out of the sky like a fiery avenging angel, doesn't he? That's not just a vigilante coming to—what does Sienna call it? 'Lay the smack down'?"

"Pretty sure that was Dwayne Johnson, not me," I said, maybe reddening a little. From drink, surely. "I might have quoted and possibly appropriated it as my own."

"He doesn't really say much, just throws down the vengeance on your boy and then leaves," Eilish said. "Executions have announcements—I mean, I assume. We don't really have those in the UK, see. But I'm guessing when you do them here, there's some sort of reading off of the crimes the guilty party's committed, et cetera. None of that, though. Ergo, it wasn't vengeance for your ship the bloke was after, in spite of this fire man's sandbagging attempt to fight your lad."

"Exactly," I said. "Either he's a government agent that got carried away in striking down a threat, or ..." I shrugged. "This was the start of something else." We took the stairs down a few at a time to the ground floor. "And if it was the start of something else ..."

"We'll be hearing about it soon," Cassidy said, almost numbly. That was, of course, her problem—she couldn't figure out people. Eilish, though—she knew people. She had to. They were her marks.

"Now, this guy can fly," I said, "so really, he could show up anywhere."

"Then why head north?" Cassidy asked, blinking as she tried to reason along with me.

"The eastern seaboard is the mostly densely populated section of the United States in easy traversal distance," I said. "I mean, except during rush hour. You can go from Boston to DC in—what, a few hours?"

"In perfectly optimal conditions, six hours, forty-five minutes," Cassidy said, "via the Acela Express."

"So, we could go west, hope he shows up in LA," I said, shrugging as we started to cross the parking lot toward the car. "But to cover the west coast, without aid of an airplane ..."

She got it. "You'd spend days going from LA to Seattle. Less dense, more spread out."

"Bingo," I said. "So, until we know his motive, we're going to pick the geographically closest and most populated section of America—and hope that since he's already evinced interest in *a* person, that his next attempt to get whatever he wants involves another person—one located in that giant metroplex we call DC-Jersey City-New York-Boston-whatever."

"By the sheer numbers ... you're probably right," Cassidy said, blinking and thinking. "How did you—"

"Learn people, Cassidy," I said, waiting for Eilish to fiddle with the car keys and pop the rear of the SUV. "It makes everything easier when you do."

That shut her up. We stowed our baggage and got in, Eilish in the driver's seat, me in the passenger side, and Cassidy like a black hole of churning thought in the back. Eilish started the car, fiddling with the seat, with the steering wheel, what felt like endlessly.

Finally, my patience at an end, I asked her, "What the hell is wrong with you?"

She stopped fussing with things. "Well … you Americans drive on the wrong side of the road."

I chortled. "I thought the same thing about you Brits."

"I'm Irish, not a 'Brit,' okay?" She blew air impatiently out. "But the fact remains—I'm driving and I'm not familiar with the way you do things here. Also, I'm pretty sure that since I never went through customs when I arrived on that magical SR-71 with the shrunken living quarters beneath the seat, that I'm probably going to be in big trouble if I get caught for driving without a license."

I glanced back at Cassidy and she paled. "I'm—I can't really drive very well—"

"Another area of theoretical knowledge yet to become practical in your life, Cassidy?" I took a shot at her. "Well, Eilish, you're either going to have to convince Cassidy or do it yourself, because I'm really not capable of it after two rounds of scotch."

"Three," Cassidy said.

When I fired a glare at Ms. Skinnyjeans in the backseat, Eilish chimed in. "Don't think we missed that nip you took just before we left."

"Fine," I said. "Three. In any case, I'm drunk, and cannot drive." I smacked my mouth together. "So … we're left with either Cassidy, who apparently hasn't—"

"I mean, I maybe could," Cassidy mused. "I guess I haven't tried."

"Yeah, let's not learn now, on interstates filled with truckers and busy people," I said. "Or we could go with you—experienced—"

Eilish did a little flushing herself. "Well, I've been in London the last few years, so—no, I haven't exactly been driving there—"

"Oh, for f—" I started.

"Well, I ask men to drive me places if I need a ride," Eilish said, throwing up her hands. "It's not like driving's this great, fun thing!"

"Not in European shoe cars, it probably isn't," I said, thumping my head against the headrest.

"And that's another thing," Eilish said, looking around the SUV. "It's so big! I feel like I'm going to run over a small child and not even notice in this thing!"

"I imagine the screaming would give it away," Cassidy muttered.

"But it's insulated, see?" Eilish said, knocking on the door. It made a light thump, her fist against the pleather. "Anyway—I think we should ask a nice man to drive for us. I can do that."

"How do we know he's going to be any more competent than you two?" I threw a little feral savagery into the question, a little shot. A shot. God, I wanted a shot right now. I slumped, my head in my hands. "I'm casually shrugging aside the fact that you're proposing kidnapping a man in order to chauffeur us. How far I've fallen."

"Look, there's a man coming right now," Eilish said, looking at the rearview. "I'll just step out, and ask him kindly for help—"

"Bending his will to yours," I said.

"And then we're home free," she said.

"Except for the kidnapping."

"And across state lines, no less," Cassidy said. "That's extra bad, in the US. I mean kidnapping at all is bad, but statutorily and punishment-wise, involving federal authorities—"

"Ugh," I said, gurgling into my hands.

"I'm going to ask him," Eilish said and started to get out. "I mean, he's coming this way anyhow—"

"He could be a dad on vacation with his wife and kids," I said, still speaking into my hands. "And you're going to kidnap him for possibly days, and when he gets back to his wife he's going to have to explain why he disappeared in a car with three strange young women—well, two strange young women and me, a perfectly normal young woman who just has a lot of shit happen to her—"

"Oh, hell," Eilish said, "he's coming right up to the—"

There was a knock at my window and I jerked my face out of my hands before I could even stop myself. I threw open the door and the man leapt out of the way, a step ahead, and kicked the door back at me expertly.

It caught me in the hands as I was springing out to attack, driving me back into my seat before I could deploy, so fast it just bowled me over without warning.

"Didn't come for a fight!" he shouted at me, "Sienna ... it's me."

I blinked, the painful ache in my wrists slightly dulled by the alcohol. "Who is that?" I asked. His head was out of sight, blocked by the roof of the SUV. I ducked down slightly, trying to see.

"Just me," he said, and something drifted into my view, extended from between the door and the vehicle's frame. If I yanked the door closed, it'd catch whatever he'd stuck in—

Oh.

It was a bottle of scotch.

"Timeo Danaos et dona ferentes," Cassidy murmured.

"Clearly a good friend of mine," I said, yanking the proffered scotch out of his hand. He let me. I yanked the top and took a long pull, sighing once I was done.

"Well, definitely someone who knows you well, at least," Eilish muttered, still looking a little on edge.

"Obviously," I said. *Mm. Peaty.* "Who is that?" I asked, trying to peer at the man standing there. He was definitely in fine shape, definitely metahuman, definitely ... uhm ...

Kinda yummy. And that probably wasn't the alcohol talking. He was wearing a suit, no tie, and ... shapely. Greyscale suit, pressed white shirt ...

He popped down into view, his short, dark hair impeccably coiffed. He stared at me with intense eyes, and a knowing smile, as I blinked in surprise.

"Harry Graves?" I asked, my breath escaping me once more. "What the hell are you doing here?"

"I'm here to drive you," he said, with a muted smile. "And also ..." His smile evaporated, and he grew still. Graves wasn't a twitchy man, so this came with some serious sense of setting off alarm bells in my head. He breathed, and when he spoke, it came out as a low, dramatic proclamation. "I need your help."

8.

Harry Graves was just standing outside my window, handsome face framed perfectly, a boyish smile on his actually-not-that-boyish face. And he'd brought me scotch before asking for my help.

A lesser woman might have melted.

Not me, though.

"Well, join the conga line forming for those needing my help," I said as I jerked a thumb toward Cassidy, sitting in the back seat with a sour look on her face. I wondered if she wore it because she had no idea who Harry Graves was, or if she did know but was wondering what the hell he could possibly need my help for.

Gripping the bottle of scotch that Harry had gifted me in one hand, I took another quick nip before pushing the cork back in. The scotch tingled and had a good flavor. I faux-gargled with it for a second, then swallowed it down. "Oaky," I said.

"That's a lovely review of the scotch," Eilish said, looking at me with serious doubts, "but, uhm—who is this fellow?"

Harry slipped around the front of the car and over to Eilish's window where he dropped down and knocked on it. He bent so he could look in, and she was graced with a perfect view of his good looks. Very devil-may-care.

The scotch might have been affecting my judgment, because I couldn't recall finding Harry quite as attractive as I was finding him now. Not that I'd ever found him unattractive, just ...

Humm. He was, uh ...

Tasty ... now. Very tasty.

"This is Harry Graves," I said, trying to put Eilish's mind at ease. "He's cool. He helped save the entire world once, and all metahumans another time."

"I suppose I should be grateful for that, then," Eilish said, staring out the window at him.

"Plus, I offered to drive," Harry said, a little muffled by the window. "Thus sparing you the trouble, Ms. Eilish."

"And he's a mannerly one, too," Eilish said, opening the door. "Sienna, would you kindly—"

"You can sit in the back," I said, slurring a little. "I'm not moving."

"By the way, Eilish," Harry said, grinning, "I always thought of myself less like a Hugh Jackman, and more like a Kurt Russell."

Eilish flushed. "I—I didn't say that Hugh Jackman thing out loud, did I? Wasn't I just thinking it?" She put her hands on her cheeks, which were tilting a hard red, like Cassidy on a normal day. "Wait," she whirled around on me, "is he a telepath?"

"No," I said, taking a leisurely sip of scotch and enjoying the burn, which felt less harsh than it had four sips ago. "He's a Cassandra, so he can read your future. Probably picked out a probability of you saying it, like one percent or something." I met Harry's gaze, his grin wide. "He does that sometimes to show off."

"She's got the right of it," Harry said, still grinning. "In your case, it was about a 0.001% chance of you saying that, but it was enough that I knew you were thinking it." He shifted his gaze to Cassidy. "So you've never seen a Cassandra at work, Cassidy?"

Cassidy just blinked once, then, realizing he'd plucked her thought out of the probabilities, rolled with it. "I've only read anecdotes." She leaned forward to me and didn't even bother to whisper. "His power would be so useful to you. Why haven't you absorbed him?"

I was feeling pretty relaxed before she went and said that. I caught Harry's flinch of reluctance at her comment, and figured some of my possible responses to that must have been pretty epic. But instead of flying off the handle in an unmitigated display of drunken emotion (because I was soooo gone by now), instead I said, "Why didn't you drink that super powers potion that President Harmon gave you for safekeeping?"

Cassidy blinked. "Because he would have scooped the brain right out of me and left me either dead or a vegetable. He doesn't—didn't—really suffer competitors, Sienna."

"Oh." I stared at her, having trouble holding my head up straight. "I thought maybe you realized the limits of power and decency ... or something." Eilish was surrendering her seat to my left, I realized, and Harry was slipping in. A few seconds later, I heard Eilish get in behind me, then slam the door as Harry started the engine.

"We're going to—never mind," Cassidy said, probably realizing that Harry already knew where we were going.

"Heading north," Harry said, backing the car out of the space.

I glanced at our little beachfront condo. Sometimes, when I wasn't too drunk, I did take scotch out onto the beach. Stared up at the stars. Walked with Reed. Or Augustus and Taneshia. Occasionally Eilish. The sand beneath my toes. My dyed hair blowing in the wind.

Scotch, neat, flowing down the back of my throat. Good times. Or, y'know ... as good as I could expect at this point.

"How long is it going to take us to get to this Norfolk?" Eilish asked. "I say '*this* Norfolk' because you know we've got our own."

"Yes," Cassidy said, a little acidly. "I did know that."

"This is going to be so much fun," Harry said, meta-low, so low I suspected only I could hear it.

"Heh," I said, and all the levity went out of me.

I was on the road with Eilish, who followed me around like a co-dependent, with Harry Graves, who I didn't really know that well and understood even less, and Cassidy Ellis, who usually hated me but now wanted to use me for revenge.

And somewhere out there was a meta who I apparently had

to fight, and defeat … with none of the powers I'd once boasted.

"Good thing I packed the Walther," I muttered, and put my head against the window as my brain rattled in my skull at a bump in the road. I looked out the window as we turned onto 30A, a few people walking down the sidewalks around me, heading to the beach or to the pools or just enjoying the brisk "not-really-winter, go home, Florida, you're drunk," air. (I might have been projecting there.)

"Anyone know any songs for the road?" Eilish asked, just a few notes too chipper for me.

I put my head against the window and felt the slow drag of unconsciousness pull me away. I didn't want to be awake for this crap anyway.

9.

Jamie Barton
New York City

Night had fallen on the city early, winter lowering its darkness on the canyons and towers. Jamie Barton was slipping through the night, reeling herself across the harbor on a gravity channel that anchored her to Freedom Tower on one end and the Statue of Liberty's torch at the other. She slipped over the water, watching it wash beneath her, half-asleep.

Her new cowl was a little itchy; it was mostly for effect at this point, since everyone in New York knew she was the superhero known as Gravity. She'd designed it herself. That was her job—her day job, after all, designing clothing, and boy, had that business taken off since her secret identity had come out. She was a top clothing manufacturer in New York at this point, her superhero-themed outfits selling like wildfire, as her friend Clarice would say.

Yeah … Jamie had it pretty good at this point, she had to concede, the wind whipping her hair behind her. If she was fortunate, online orders would spike again tomorrow. Because tonight she'd been photographed at the scene of a particularly large bank robbery, foiling the perps just as things were getting intense. She'd just split them up like badly behaving kids at a party, yanking them apart with simple gravity channels. Easy enough.

The Staten Island Ferry's horn bellowed beneath her, and Jamie smiled, waving down. There were a couple people shadowed on the deck as she slid over them in rough approximation of flight. It wouldn't do for Staten Island's own superhero not to wave at the ferry, after all. She reached her apogee, only a few hundred feet from the Statue of Liberty's torch, and started to adjust. She'd need to throw her next gravity channel down on the island, probably somewhere near—

A bright flame lit in the night, just above the torch, as though someone had set it on fire. Jamie paused her ascent, stopping in the middle of the gravity channel, hanging in midair. She peered into the dark and realized—

There was someone just … floating there.

And they had fire coming out of their hands.

Her first thought was, "Sienna?" but she stifled it. She'd seen Sienna just a few months ago, during that rescue mission in Scotland, and … she didn't have fire powers anymore.

No, this was someone else.

She could see the hints of his profile in the dark, even at this distance. His face was grim under the flames, mouth a flat line. With a jerk, he floated toward her, not too quickly, and stopped fifty feet or so away, just hovering.

"Who are you?" she asked, a little tentative. She wrapped a couple gravity channels around his feet, snugging him to the ground very lightly, preparing to activate them full bore should he go from looming to …

Well, threatening.

"Who I am is not important," he said, voice echoing in the cold air. His accent was Eastern European, reminding her of a Polish man who sold her cloth.

"What do you want?" Jamie asked.

"It is not about 'want.'" His voice was clear, and he just hovered there, almost blocking her. She could adjust course, dip lower, or set up a channel straight to Staten Island—and might, if he proved intransigent, but …

So far he wasn't being threatening. He was just hanging there. Like he wanted to talk.

"Then why are you here?" Jamie asked. She peered at him. Hadn't she read something on her phone earlier? Something about a meta who attacked a bridge after that carrier disaster down in Virginia? A man who—

Wreathed himself in flames? Was that it? Jamie couldn't remember. She'd been rushing around New York most of the day, dealing with one police scanner call after another. You'd think criminals would get it through their heads that Gravity was on the scene and call it a day, but no ...

"I have to be here," he said, crisply. His hands still glowed, or else he'd be barely visible, a shadow in the night in this place.

This was the most frustrating conversation Jamie could recall having since ... well, probably this morning, when she'd last talked to her teenage daughter. "Oooookay," Jamie finally said, wanting to give up and shrug, just walk away like she had with Kyra. But it wasn't entirely wise to leave a man with flaming hands and flight powers at your back while you were riding a gravity channel home. "Well ... unless you have some other need of me, I'd like to call it a night—"

"There is need," he said. "You ... have power."

Jamie just hung there, waiting for more. "... Yes?"

"I have power," he said, and the flames grew brighter. "We must ... test powers, one against another." His English broke a little in the middle.

"I'm not looking for a fight," Jamie said, preparing to scoot back on the Freedom Tower channel and laying out a few more delicate ones from herself to other points that she could throw the switch on in case of emergency. Two at different spots on Liberty Island, one attached to the statue's waist, and a final one onto the Staten Island Ferry some two miles out by now.

The man just hung there, fire burning at his fingertips, and then suddenly ... it started to glow brighter. "I am."

His attack was dramatic, fire flaring at her in an orange glow, bulbs of it streaking toward her in the night. Jamie yanked herself down on one of the gravity channels, the one planted at the edge of the island below her. It pulled her back and down, and at the same time, a second later, she activated the two she'd subtly attached to his feet, and his glowing hands were yanked in the other direction.

Have to avoid the flames, Jamie thought, tempted to slap herself for thinking the obvious. Of course she had to avoid the flames. Who would want to jump through them willingly—

Oh. Right. Sienna Nealon.

But Jamie wasn't crazy like that, so she just bent and let the next gravity channel whip her around the base of the statue as the ones she'd left on the man did the work of pulling him down. She'd slide around the base of the statue as her channels worked, and she'd catch him near the ground and set up a flux around him, a field that even fire couldn't escape. Once that was done, she'd—

A roar reached her ears just before a power burst of water came ripping out of the harbor and engulfed her. The freezing wash soaked through her costume in a bracing shock. Her skin went numb, her breath left her in a single, urgent exhalation, and she halted in place.

Her mouth opened of its own accord, to let the air out in a rush, and she blasted out the other side of the sudden wash, trying to wrap her analytical mind around what had just happened.

She was still a hundred feet above the water, and it looked—well, not calm and placid, because it was the harbor, but it was relatively still. How had that water come rushing up to—

Her answer came a moment later when another blast of it shot out of the harbor like an erupting geyser and flew at her. The harbor's surface below looked like a bank of cannons firing off, pelting frigid water at her. Soaked to the skin, Jamie dodged, even though the blasts were not particularly hard. They didn't carry the power that, say, Scott Byerly's attacks did, but they certainly had enough force that she didn't want to be hit by them—

Just as she was steering her way around the Statue of Liberty, a gust of wind hit her with a fist-like impact. Jamie's immediate gravity channels released—they were a series she was guiding like spokes off the Statue's waist—and she dipped before she caught herself on one that was reversing gravity, anchored to the ground, keeping her aloft. She tumbled forward but not down, thankfully, and came around the statue's waist to find—

The man was just hanging there where she'd anchored him, hands still burning, his back to her, waging his own war against the channels she'd set up against his feet to drag him to the earth. He was moving down, slowly, their drag eventually winning against him, though he seemed to be fighting them with his flight.

Well, let's speed this up, Jamie thought. She reached out, intending to increase the drag—

The sound of something behind her made her use the statue to set up a repelling channel, and she vaulted away from the statue just as another series of water blasts peppered the surface. They chased her as she dodged them, dipping lower to the ground as she moved away from the most concentrated center of the gravity channel that was holding her aloft. She threw down another at the edge of Liberty Island to keep her from dropping as she moved out from the center of power of the one she'd used before. That was the problem with using gravity channels to keep aloft; once you got too far from them, they weakened in their ability to keep you rising. It was why she always had to use the Statue of Liberty as a guidance point for getting to and from Staten Island.

Jamie anchored to the torch and pulled herself back up in a blindingly fast ascent, riding the channel like she had a bungie cord attached to her belt. She flew up and around as the torch's surface was blasted with water behind her.

Her mind was racing, the cold seeping in, slowing her reactions. Hypothermia had to be on the way, if it hadn't settled in already. How would that affect her, as a metahuman, Jamie wondered? Surely she was more resistant to it than a normal person, but the way she felt—soaked, teeth chattering—didn't seem that terribly different from what a normal person would be experiencing.

She could also feel herself moving just a hair slower.

This man, this meta—he was using fire powers, water powers, and it felt like air powers, in addition to the power of flight. Two of those, Sienna had before ... well, Scotland. The others, Reed and Scott had possessed.

But—her mind wrangled with the thought—those powers didn't come naturally together. They were—

Another blast of wind sent Jamie tumbling sideways. She landed another anchor on the statue's torch, then started to secure another to the ground, trying to just maintain her altitude. It wouldn't do to—

Water blasted her, finding her in the air and submerging her, causing Jamie to once again exhale mightily. Darkness squeezed in at the edges of her consciousness, and freezing liquid started to seep up her nose, forcing its way into her mouth.

She gagged, but it only got worse. It forced its way into her sinuses, chilling her as she choked, mightily, the freezing water pushing down her throat and into her belly, seeping cold through her entire being.

The gravity channels she'd laid down—dozens in the last few minutes—started to release, one by one, as the water invaded her, choked her—

Drowned her.

And Jamie Barton started to fall as the light of consciousness began to fade. The man with the flaming hands was in front of her for just a moment, and his face was frozen in brief satisfaction. There for but a flicker and then gone as he was gone, flying upward—

No.

She was tumbling down.

Jamie dropped, one of the channels steering her, almost by accident, to the edge of Liberty Island. It pulled, one of only two she had left, her brain reduced to mere instinct as she warred with the water that threatened to drown her.

She burst free of the liquid entrapping her, but it was within her now, water in her mouth, in her lungs, streaming out of her nose as she plunged toward the surface of the harbor—

Jamie Barton hit the water lightly, the second-to-last gravity channel she'd set up at the edge of the island cushioning her to a drop of a mere six feet; into the frigid harbor she plunged. The gravity tether's job done, it released.

And left her with only one. Operating on the instinct, grabbing hold of it like a drowning woman—which she was—she activated it.

Darkness followed, and Jamie struggled. She broke the surface seconds later, heaving up water, heaving up liquid, heaving up …

Death.

She was choking, she couldn't breathe, it was in her and everywhere, like a weight pushing all the air out of her. There was a steady tug, dragging her through the water, waist high, but her head was out, her chest was out of the freezing water, but it was in her, drowning her, and she jerked, furiously, trying to get it out of her, out of—

Voices in the distance. Shouts in the night.

She felt a thump, her shoulders against something. City lights glared, twinkled, in the distance, but Jamie's mind was panicked, frenzied, only on one thing.

Breathe. Can't—breathe!

"Hang on, hang on!" someone said, male. Someone grabbed her shoulders, dragging her up.

"Get her out, get her out!" Someone else seized her, pulling her up, up, from where her shoulders rested hard against—

The Staten Island Ferry.

They pulled her out, onto the deck, and water streamed out of Jamie's mouth. Darkness was pressing in on all sides, panic at a fevered pitch. She was drowning, drowning on the ship's deck, but—

Water streamed from her mouth, and she took her first hacking, wheezing cough.

"She's got water in the lungs," one of the people surrounding her said. His face pushed in, in the haze. "We're going to get you to Richmond University Medical Center, Jamie. Don't you worry. We got you, okay? You just relax. You're—"

Home, Jamie thought, as the darkness swelled around her, swirling, and took her into it, there on the deck of the Staten Island Ferry.

10.

Sienna

I woke up with a hangover. The night was like black tar poured outside the window where I rested my head. No moon, no lights waited outside the glass as I blinked at my own reflection staring back at me, just ink-stained night and the refracted instrument panel of the SUV behind my shadowed face in the window.

Smacking my lips together, I pulled my aching head off the glass. A cool feeling persisted against my cheek where it had rested against the flat window, and a thumping pain radiated out from within. I was getting used to hangovers—sort of. As used to them as you can get, I guess.

"Well, good morning, sunshine," Harry Graves's voice greeted me from the driver's seat. I made a low moan as I turned toward him, and found the bottle he'd gifted me corked and resting in the cup holder. I stared at it; it was the perfect size, and I suspected he'd planned that when he'd bought the damned thing. Precognitive asshole, showing off.

As if in answer to my thought, he tossed me a bottle of ibuprofen that I caught, just barely. I opened it and dumped three into my hand. I swallowed them without liquid, and though I was sorely tempted to embrace the hair of the dog that bit me, I found the bottle empty when I gave it a look.

"You dump the rest out?" I asked.

"Not me," Harry said. "Your Irish lady did."

I turned my head to give Eilish a piece of my mind, but she was sleeping, conked out in the back, mouth open, head back. A soft, ragged snuffling was coming from her open mouth, and mercy won out. I let her sleep.

Cassidy was lit by a computer screen, tapping away without saying anything. I knew she'd noticed my awakening, so I figured she didn't have anything to add at present, and I didn't give enough of a damn to ask her what she was up to. Instead I faced forward, staring into the darkness ahead, where a single light about a quarter mile off aided our headlights in telling me we were on a two-lane road with nothing but green around us.

"Where the hell are we?" I asked.

"Last sign I saw said we were in Ashville, Alabama," Harry said, and he broke into a grin that I found … well, I should have found it infuriating. I was surprisingly neutral on it at the moment, though. "We're heading north, taking the road less traveled."

"We were supposed to be on I-75 or I-95," I said, massaging my scalp. It didn't help.

"No, we're supposed to be heading north," Harry said, "and exactly this way. Trust me."

"Why would I trust you?" I asked. "You took my instruction and promptly discarded it in favor of doing—I dunno, whatever the hell you wanted to do." I blinked at him, his rugged chin. "What the hell are you doing, Harry?"

"I'm driving," he said, still grinning. Still not infuriating. Must have been his boyish charm. "Trust me."

"Ugh," I said, pitching my head forward and giving my kinked neck muscles a chance to not annoy the hell out of me by screaming like my head. "You didn't answer why I should trust you the first time I asked."

"Because I know what I'm doing," Harry said.

"Yes, but I don't know what you're doing," I said, "and two-way communication is so important to trust and also your continued survival."

He made a production of letting out a grand sigh. "The interstate corridors back east are being fiercely watched right now. Cops, Department of Homeland Security—there'll all be on it. And while you've a neat little trick to mask your face on cameras, it's not going to help with the immense number of patrols rolling through there at the moment. I caught a probability—if we took those routes, you were going to get spotted, and all manner of hell was going to descend upon the back of our necks. Ergo ..."

"You're taking us through rural Alabama," I muttered, still rubbing at the base of my spine. "Where the roads are twisting and the cameras are less plentiful."

"Like I said, it's not the cameras you have to worry about," Harry said. "It's the watching eyes. You may be looking not quite like yourself these days, but it's hardly a foolproof disguise."

"No kidding," I said. "It certainly didn't fool you."

"I do like to think I'm no fool," Harry said, with that everlasting sense of levity he seemed to bring to everything, "but of course ... we all get caught with our pants down sometimes." He looked at me slyly out of the corner of his eye. "Or ... with nothing on, maybe."

I was still slightly drunk, coming out of that bender, and damn if he didn't get me to blush. The first time we'd crossed paths, Harry had knocked on my hotel door when I'd been wearing nothing but a towel. I'd thought he was Reed, so I'd answered, and in the course of events—I thought he was a villain at the time—I'd attacked him and my towel had gone kaput, leaving me properly naked and trying to kick his ass while he'd dodged my every attempt to lay a hand on him and watched me try with amusement.

That he was reminding me of this now was ... annoying. And only mildly embarrassing.

Maybe more than mildly.

"Don't be an ass, Harry," I said, trying to make it sound warning.

"Well, I can't help it, really," he said, that smirk—gahhh, I should have wanted to club him, but he was—I was pretty sure—modulating his delivery to keep on my good side, and damn if it wasn't working, even though I knew what he was doing. "I'm not really being an ass—I might be showing mine, a bit." Here he grinned. "Surely you can identify with that."

Not subtle. I blushed deeper. It wasn't like I hadn't endured many bouts of public nudity in my life—I mean, I burned off entire wardrobes for the years I had fire powers, in public and elsewhere, before I discovered the secret of cloaking myself in it like clothing afterward. There were photos on the net. I knew it, and had made my peace with it.

Harry was rubbing my nose in it, and I wasn't ready to kill him. Marks to the man who could read the future for—to my complete surprise—making me smile, ever so slightly. How the hell did he do that?

"Yeah, I can identify with that," I said, suddenly thankful that I was sober enough to not be slurring. I let the silence hang for a moment. "So ... what do you need my help with?"

He didn't take his eyes off the road. "It's not time for that yet," he said. "I'll tell when we're getting closer to the moment."

"Great," I said dryly, "I love surprises."

"Of course you do," he said.

"I actually don't," I said. "I hate surprises."

He gave me a sidelong look, taking his eyes off the road for way, way too long. "Don't worry," he said smoothly. "I can read the future, remember? I could steer us all the way from here to—well, where we're going—and never run off the road."

"That's still really creepy, Harry," I said, my nerves ... well, they were fine. It took me a second, and then ...

Yeah. He could see the future. Of course it wasn't a problem for him not to watch the road. If the car started to bump, he could correct because ... he'd see it coming in his future probabilities.

Nifty.

"You don't like the kind of surprises you're regularly confronted with," he said, looking me right in the eyes. "Villains popping up like a jack-in-the-box you never asked for. Enemies showing themselves at times you didn't expect to see them. Governments turning on you, the press blindsiding you out of nowhere. But a normal surprise? Reed showing up when you least expect him to?" He smiled. "You like a good surprise every once in a while, Sienna Nealon. You just need to have more people in your life who give you the pleasant ones, instead of the unpleasant kind."

"Huh," I said, contemplating what he'd said. "Okay. Maybe."

He just grinned and turned back to the road in time to bring the car back between the lines. "You wait and see."

"Still," I said, watching him out of the corner of my eye while crossing my arms and pretending to face forward, "I don't think your need for help is going to fall into the category of 'pleasant surprise,' Harry."

"Why would you think that?" he asked. He already knew the answer, the bastard.

"Because no one has ever asked me for help and it turned out to not be something horrific," I said. "It's never, 'Hey, Sienna, help this little old lady cross the street.' Or, 'Babysit this lovely, charming kid who will give you no problems at all'—"

"I don't think you've done much babysitting," Harry said.

"I've watched Greg Vansen's son Eddie on at least three occasions now," I said. Greg and Morgan had been up to visit us twice since I'd come back from Scotland. I suspected Reed of trying to draw me out of my drinking shell. It had worked, inasmuch as I'd managed to postpone my normal five o'clock drink to after Eddie went to bed at eight. Progress, probably, by my brother's standards. No need to mention that I hadn't been unsupervised with Eddie during those visits. "That kid loves me." Mostly true. I hadn't stolen his soul, and he seemed to like to involve me in his Lego projects, even though he was much better at them than I was.

"Duly noted."

"My point is, no one comes to Sienna Nealon for the easy stuff," I said.

"I like how you've gotten to the point that referring to yourself in the third person is natural."

"They come to me for crap no one else can solve, usually involving face punching."

"How's that face punching business going lately?" Harry

asked.

"Poorly. I haven't punched any faces in a while. My knuckles are getting soft."

"Well, I come with opportunity, then," Harry said.

"I didn't say I wanted to get back to it!" But ...

Of course I did. I missed punching people in the face. Only worthy people, people who had earned a good punch, of course.

"Don't worry," Harry said, prompting me to frown again. "All will be explained in time."

And before I could respond to that bit of cryptic nonsense, Cassidy piped up. "I've got another hit on this attacker."

I turned in my seat, twisting my neck and sending a shooting pain up to join the hangover headache. "Oof," I said. "Where?"

"New York City," Cassidy said, not looking up from the glow of the screen. It cast her in an even paler shade of white. She looked up, gaze flitting to me for just a second, watching my reaction. "Looks like he just beat the living hell out of an old friend of yours." And she spun the computer around so I could see the headline emblazoned across the top of the screen.

I saw it ... and my stomach dropped like we'd hit the world's largest speedbump.

GRAVITY FALLS

Attack on local hero leaves her future in doubt—authorities are not saying whether Jamie Barton is even still alive.

11.

I sat in the passenger seat of the car heading down that Alabama back road, stunned. I'd seen Jamie Barton just a few months ago. She'd helped me escape from Scotland, helped save my life at a time when I wondered if I had any friends left. She'd been one of a couple of handfuls of people who'd put their lives on the line facing off against the strongest metahuman on the damned planet to help save my life.

Now she was possibly dead, and I didn't have a damned clue what had happened.

"What the hell?" I asked, directing it to Cassidy.

She glanced up at me. "I'm looking." And she drove her gaze down again.

I looked at Harry, who sat with pursed lips staring into the distance. "What do you know about this?"

Harry shrugged. "I don't really know this Gravity gal."

"It's just Gravity now," I said. "And I don't care if you know her—do you know what happened?"

"I've been sitting here with you this whole time," Harry said, turning to favor me with a boyish grin. "How would I—no, I don't have an iota of an idea. I'd need to know this lady to be able to look into her future."

My mind raced. "What about my future?"

He paused, just waiting. I wondered why, but after he didn't speak, I lost patience. "Because I'm going to try and contact her, of course."

"Of course you are," Harry said. "How?"

"I don't know, a phone call," I said, my already exhausted patience somehow finding a further level of exhaustion to sink to. Post Marathon status, maybe. About to yell, "Nike! Nike!" before collapsing dead.

"I'm sure that'd be satisfying," Harry said, "but what are the reasons you can't do that—and what are the reasons you shouldn't?"

I squinted at him, and he smiled. "What is this, twenty questions?"

"See, this is something you learn after a little time spent gazing the future," Harry said, settling back, still paying most of his attention to me and not the road ahead. "I could have this whole conversation in advance of you by three whole sentences. I know everything you could possibly say—"

"Pine—" I started to interrupt.

"—apple," he finished.

"—Sol," I said spitefully. I totally had meant pineapple.

"So I could go ahead and skip most of our conversations," Harry said, and he nudged the empty scotch bottle with an elbow, "just head you off in a way you'd never realize you'd even been … let's call it 'handled'—"

"Wh—"

"Because 'manipulated' is an ugly word," Harry said. "That's why." He looked at me knowingly. "I could head you off at every conversational pass. I know what you're going to say before you say it. Even the crazy stuff like—"

"Bene—" Cassidy piped up from the back.

"—ficient," Harry finished for her.

"Mal—" she started to say.

"—volio," Harry said.

"Very good," Cassidy said coolly, then went back to typing.

"But if I have one side of the conversation, always," Harry said, "it's not really a conversation, is it? So, yeah, I play twenty questions with you. Fifty questions, or a hundred questions, even—and when I'm doing that, know that it's not because I'm being a giant, throbbing hemorrhoid." He cracked a grin. Charming. Damn him. "It's because I actually do want to have a conversation with you, and because I don't want to be a dick and act like I'm reading your mind when I'm really just excluding you from our talk by jumping ahead of you in time. Because doing that means I'm the only one learning anything in our conversation, and that seems unfair to you."

"I want to know where you learned charm, Harry," I said, after giving his little explanation a moment to digest. It sat well with me.

"Why?" He smirked. "You wouldn't take any advice I have to give you in that area, would you?"

I grunted. He was right about that, too. "Fine. I want to talk to Gravity."

"Why?"

"Because I want to know what happened to her," I said.

"Read a paper," he said. "Or just wait for Cassidy to find video of the incident in question. It's on the net and she's zeroing in on it as we speak."

"Interesting," Cassidy said as I tossed a look over my shoulder. She'd paused for a quarter second and now she dove back into her computer, tapping even more furiously.

"I'd still like to hear it from Jamie's own voice," I said.

"And what happens when your voice gets heard over the airwaves?" Harry asked. "Or however they work those cell phones?"

"It's—" Cassidy started

"It's a little too complex for me, Cassidy," Harry said. "Just illustrating a point." I blinked; he'd shut her down without being rude about it and simultaneously complimented her intelligence without being hammer-on-the-head obvious about it. I looked at Cassidy out of the corner of my eye and she nodded a little appreciatively.

Damn, Harry Graves was slick.

"The NSA would intercept my call from a cell phone," I said. "Voiceprint analysis. And they'd pounce on me after they traced the call."

"Let's say they didn't," Harry went on, "because Cassidy is brilliant at that sort of thing, obscuring phone calls—"

"Thank you," Cassidy said, and in her voice I heard … gratification?

Like, genuine ... pleasure?

I didn't recall ever hearing that from Cassidy before. Ever.

"—let's say you got away free and clear. And Jamie Barton gave you ... a long and florid explanation that never made the press." He settled a hand on the wheel, gently guiding it, still not looking at the damned road. "What would you be giving your enemies?"

"A recorded call," I said, and then I got it. "They'd know I was after this guy."

Harry's smile brightened. "Probably not the greatest idea to give the feds a big, blinking arrow telling them which direction you're going."

No, that wasn't a good idea. At all. "What about—" I started to ask.

"Don't assume that just because Jamie Barton fought this guy," Harry said, "that she knows what he wants. She doesn't. He's mysterious. And my sense is, he's going to remain that way until such time as he decides not to be anymore."

I sat there in the silence, and my stomach turned a good flip over, either from the scotch or the worry now afflicting it. "Do you know what he wants?"

Harry just shook his head. "Too many branching paths. The farther out I look, the less likely I get the right scenario."

"Excuse me, what?" Cassidy asked, leaning forward.

Harry took a breath. "It's like this, Cassidy—my view of the future is a series of forks in the road. I can see the probabilities associated with each path. It's 99 percent likely that Sienna is about to say, 'Porcupine scuttlebutt,' for instance," and he looked at me.

"Porcupine scuttlebutt," I said lamely, because ... yeah, I'd been about to say it. For the sake of randomness.

"That's immediate," Harry said. "That's easy. Only a one percent chance she wasn't going to say it—I mean, I'm rounding, it was more 98.5% to 1.3%, with the remainder going toward other, extremely unlikely possibilities—me pulling over the car and successfully initiating an orgy, for instance—"

I slapped him on the arm, and he didn't dodge. Probably

because I didn't put much sting in it. "Very low odds. Below zero."

"Not below zero," he said, still smirking, "but threading that needle successfully in order to buck those odds is in the incredibly thin percentages. Near enough to impossible as to make it not worth my time to try. A shift in the winds is enough to kill it, and not only kill it but to do so prejudicially, meaning you toss my ass out on the side of the road for the attempt. Right, Eilish?"

"Jaysus," Eilish said, stirring. I hadn't even known she was awake.

"The immediate future is easy," Harry said again. "But the next decision after that, the percentages are less sure. They get clearer up until the moment the decision is made, and the event happens. Even minor, unnoticeable events have an effect. You're talking to someone you like, you're plucking up your courage to ask them something—maybe to go to dinner. The wind shifts, suddenly you smell bread from a bakery down the way." His voice was smooth, soothing. "It reminds me you of when your mother used to cook cinnamon rolls when you were a kid. It pauses the conversation for a second; you lose the thought. You pick up again and go in a different direction. The moment is lost, the opportunity missed—you go on, and never come back down that road."

"I miss my mother's cinnamon rolls," Cassidy said, a little stricken, from the backseat.

"The next moment another choice comes up," Harry said, "more split odds. For every decision I leap over, the path forks. Again and again. After a while, I pass so many forks that I can't keep track of them all anymore. No one could, unless they had Cassidy's brain." She made a mollified sound from behind him. "I can look forward a little. A lot, if I really sit and concentrate for a while." His face twitched slightly. "But the probabilities that I get everything right? They fade the more decisions I leap over. Sometimes, external events insert themselves into your life no matter what you're doing here. For example—Franklin Delano Roosevelt was going to die no matter what I did on the morning of April 12, 1945.

Things were going to change in the US after December 6th, 1941 whether I called the War Department and warned them what was coming the next morning or not. My small decisions were not going to influence that—they were going to influence me. So ... I don't know about your friend Jamie Barton. I don't know about this guy that you're chasing, either. I can look ahead, but clarity escapes those moments because every choice you make in the next few days affects what happens when you come to them. Your frame of mind when you get there," he not-subtly nudged the empty scotch bottle again, "the questions you ask when you face him—if you face him—determine the outcome, determine what he says, whether you get to the bottom of what he wants. So I've got no answer for you. You'll have to find this one for yourself when the right moment arrives."

"But I do try and face him?" I asked, fighting against the hangover. A little worry was gnawing in the pit of my stomach, some small thing tearing at me, wondering ...

What the hell was I doing?

Why was I going in the direction that I was?

"Lot of decisions ahead," Harry said, and now his smile was not nearly so charming. It was more ...

Reserved. Hesitant.

Scared?

I pondered that question, and his answer, as we rolled on through the Alabama night, silence fallen over us as I stumbled on in my own uncertainty for a few miles, wondering why I was doing this thing at all.

12.

My head spun like the tires as we rolled on through the night. It was hard not to let my thoughts just roll and whirl and go on of their own accord as we passed through small towns in Alabama, one after another, a neverending parade of Americana under the moonlight.

I wondered if Jamie Barton was okay, whatever hospital she was in. I wanted to talk to her, to ask her about this flaming angry avenger guy, but Harry had convinced me not to try. I was still toxic in this country thanks to my being wanted. Or unwanted, depending on your perspective.

The car was quiet after the conversation ended. Harry seemed content to let me dwell in my own thoughts. Eilish went back to snoring gently a few minutes later, her part apparently done. Cassidy even gave up on finding more detail, I guess, because the next time I looked back she'd put away her laptop and gone to sleep, hair over her face and her cheek against the cold window.

That left me and Harry, and Harry stared at the road, giving me my privacy—or as close as I could get in a car with three other people. I looked at him out of the corner of my eye for a while, wondering what the hell was after him, or what problem he was dealing with that left him in need of my help.

My help …?

Once upon a time I'd been capable of giving quite a lot of help, if asked. I'd had superhuman powers of flight, of fire—

hell, I could even turn into a dragon if need be, though I did it very seldom.

Now? I could punch faces pretty well, drain souls through physical touch, and reach out to people in their dreams—

"Oh," I said, a little tingly.

"Night night," Harry said knowingly, a little smile perched on his lips.

"You could have reminded me earlier," I said, putting my head against the window and closing my eyes. "Ass."

"Knew you'd get to it in your own time," Harry said as I slipped into the darkness.

It took a few minutes for me go into shadow, into the darkness, but pretty soon I found myself in a quiet place where the world, and the sound of tires thrumming against pavement, had receded into silence. I looked around, and all was quiet, all was shadow.

I was dreamwalking.

"Where am I?" a voice called in the dark.

I turned, and there was Jamie Barton.

She was wearing a new iteration of her costume, stylish-bordering-on-dazzling, and looking around like she was hunting for something in the darkness. "Hey," I called out to her, and her eyes alighted on me—

Holy hell. She looked ...

Terrible.

"Jamie," I said, whisper quiet.

"Oh, Sienna," she said, shaking her head. Her hair was wet, her clothing was waterlogged. It was also cut and torn in places, and I wondered how that had happened. She squished when she walked. "It's you."

"It's me," I said, a little tightly. "How are you feeling?"

"I'm ..." she hesitated. "I'm ..." Her eyes went a little blank. "Did ...?"

I just waited, my head cocked slightly. I didn't want to interrupt her as she thought things through. Having been the tragic recipient of a few beatdowns-into-unconsciousness in my time, I wanted to give her the space to come back to it in her own time. If she was concussed—well, comatose, now—she'd probably remember the event in question soon, but maybe not. I definitely didn't want to prod her too hard.

"Do you know what happened to me?" she asked, blinking her eyes at me, brow furrowed in concentration.

I nodded once, hesitant. "Yeah," I said. "Ish."

She stared into the darkness, into the distance. "Did ... did I just ...?" Her hands found her face, and she touched herself, as though trying to absently recall if she was still here.

"What do you remember?" I asked gently, easing a little closer to her.

"Oh my goodness," she said, quiet in the dark. "He ... really kicked my backside, didn't he?"

Jamie Barton wasn't much of a swearer, so this aversion to saying *ass* was probably a good sign. Maybe it meant she hadn't totally lost herself in the incident. Memory loss? Not fun. I could sympathize.

"I didn't see," I said. "But it didn't sound good." I sidled closer to her as she stood there in the dark. "What do you remember?"

"I don't know, little bits," she said. "I was on my way home, and—" She stopped, blinking. "Wait. What are you doing here?"

"I'm dreamwalking," I said. "Helping out, you know."

She squinted at me in intense concentration. "I thought you were in hiding. The law is after you, Sienna."

It was kind of touching that even after a severe ass-whipping, Jamie was worrying about me. "I'll be safe, but ..." I shrugged. "I dunno. I'm curious. Can you tell me about the villain?"

She folded her arms in front of her, and water dripped from her sleeves, which had small tears in them. No blood seeped out from beneath, and I was left to wonder if this was her vision of herself after getting smacked around, or if her costume had genuinely had been torn. "He was hovering by the Statue of Liberty as I was heading back to Staten Island. He was all aglow with fire—I couldn't see him very well. He just sort of ... loomed there. Reminded me of you—you know," and she got subdued, looking at her feet, "before."

Recalling for myself the trauma of getting your ass handed

to you unexpectedly, I knew the best thing I could do right now was shut my mouth and just listen, ignoring her conversational misstep. She didn't need me interrupting in order to work her way through the ... incident.

"He said something ..." She shook her head. "Something about ...?" She concentrated, like she was trying to remember. "I don't know. About having to fight? It's all a blur."

"It's okay," I said.

"It's not okay," Jamie said, looking up at me. "I know what you're thinking—you're going after this guy, aren't you?"

I took a breath. "Wouldn't be my first choice, Jamie. Honestly ..."

"You're depowered, Sienna," she said. "This man—he's too much for you. He has fire powers, he used wind and water attacks—"

"Wait, wait—what?" I perked up at that.

"He did," she said. "His hands were burning as he hovered there, he shot at me with powerful water, nearly drowned me, and he used wind to bat me around—"

"Those powers don't—" I stopped myself from talking, my head was spinning so fast. "He had to have an accomplice."

"Maybe," Jamie said after a moment. "It was dark. Maybe I didn't see them."

That stuck in my head. What if this guy did use all those powers? Flight, fire, wind, water—

No. I didn't want to let things get too wild in my head. Occam's Razor. The simplest solution was the best, and like she said, it was dark. He probably just had an accomplice.

He definitely wasn't an incubus stocking powers to use against others.

I shook my head. "Is there anything else you remember?"

Jamie just stared at the ground. "Is ... is Kyra all right?" She looked up at me. "Do—do you know if—"

"I'm sure she's fine," I said.

"You don't know that, though, do you?" Jamie's eyes went wild, looking around. "You have to let me out of here. I have to wake up and—"

"Jamie," I said softly. "Even if I break the dreamwalk, it's possible you won't wake up now. Your body—you took a beating. You need time to heal."

"Sienna," she said, stepping toward me, "my daughter. What about my daughter?"

"I'm sure she's fine," I said. "This guy, whoever he is— he's the one who took down the bridge in Virginia earlier. He's ... targeting metas, I guess." That sent a little shiver down my back.

"But how do you know she's fine?" Jamie asked, just blinking and looking around. She was starting to get agitated, and I knew my exit cue had arrived. "Maybe he was after her and—and afterward he came for me—or tried me at home first—"

"It's all going to be okay," I said, "try to rest. Heal. And when you wake up, Kyra will be by your bedside, as worried about you as you are about her right now."

She locked on my eyes. "But how do you kn—"

I broke the dreamwalk and sat up in the car, staring into the darkness ahead of the windshield wildly, like Jamie Barton's accusing face was going to leap out at me, poke a finger into my eye, and ask me again, "How do you know that she's okay?"

Because, of course, I didn't.

And worse, I thought, looking around the car and finding Cassidy and Eilish still sleeping, and Harry glancing back at me, coolly, probably totally aware of what I might say ...

Worse ... even if Jamie's daughter had been kidnapped, been taking by this super powerful meta in New York City ...

I was in Alabama, at least a day's drive away.

There wasn't a damned thing I could do about it right now.

"She's fine, by the way," Harry said, and when I looked over at him. "The daughter. She's fine. She gets mentioned in a news article tomorrow, by her mother's bedside waiting for her to recover."

"Good," I said, but it sounded hollow, because ... it was. A hollow feeling, empty thoughts. Kyra was safe; that was good, but ... if she hadn't been ...

The old Sienna Nealon would have been there in hours, with either the FBI or her own agency to help spearhead a rescue attempt if needed.

Now?

Now all I could do was sit back, uneasily, in my seat as Harry Graves drove me on through the night, the thought of my near-powerlessness almost overwhelming me as I tried to quell the fear that rose inside me like the darkness outside.

13.

"I need to stop and pee," I said. The clock on the dash read 4:45, and I assumed AM, since it was still pitch black outside. There was a glow on the horizon suggesting there was a town up there, and I was still letting Harry do his thing in silence, because I didn't have much to say until now.

"I know," Harry said. "There's an all-night gas station two miles ahead, just through the town. We're getting on the freeway after that."

"Oh?" I asked, peering into the dark ahead, as though I could see this mythical town ahead around the bend. "What's the town called?"

"Ardmore," Harry said.

That meant nothing to me. I'd been all over the country, but only spent a little time in Alabama. "Wait, did you say we're getting on the freeway?" I turned to him. "I thought you said that was a no-no?"

"The I-75 and I-95 corridors are being watched pretty hard," Harry said casually, steering the car into a slight curve. Woods surrounded us on either side, and the SUV's heater chugged to give us warmth. "But this is I-65, and the Department of Homeland Security isn't God—their eyes aren't everywhere at once. Or, in this case, police patrols aren't elevated here—yet." He gave me a warning look, one that I took to mean, *So don't do anything stupid to cause them to elevate.*

I raised an eyebrow at him. "Well, your earlier fears appear

72

to be unfounded. You didn't say anything there and I felt I learned something anyway." He smirked.

A few minutes later we pulled into Ardmore and into a gas station. I didn't see any sign of the freeway, but it was probably ahead somewhere. This was a smallish town, complete with various storefronts and some restaurants. I saw a Mexican one that looked intriguing, but unfortunately it wasn't open at 5 AM.

I popped out of the car while Harry quietly woke Cassidy and Eilish with an announcement that we were stopping for a bathroom break. While he was doing that, I swiped the credit card Reed had given me for gas and other contingencies and then started the tank to filling. That done, I followed Cassidy and Eilish in staggering toward the store. Well, Cassidy staggered. Eilish composed herself a little better.

Cassidy stumbled through the front door and didn't even wait to hold it for me. I caught it nonetheless, not overdoing it on the metahuman power display, but having to hustle a little to keep it from shutting right in my face. Cassidy had paused just inside the door, her thin frame blocking the entry as she scanned the store. Finally her head turned and eyes alighted on the "Restroom" sign and off she went again, looking like she was the one who'd downed half a bottle of scotch, not me.

I followed behind her, walking past the beer cooler. The light within was off, shading all the Budweisers and Millers and all else in darkness that wasn't exactly complete. I smacked my lips together as I went by, almost running into Cassidy again just outside the women's room, which was in a little corridor off the store.

She was rattling the door handle, staring at it stupidly as though it would open if she just pulled a little more. "What the hell?" she mumbled, like she had a mouth full of cotton.

"Eilish is in there," I explained, then had to tug her skinny arm away before she busted it with her meta strength. Cassidy may have looked like a stick figure, but I'd tangled with her, and while she was on the low end of meta physical abilities, she could still level a three-hundred-pound human linebacker with minimal effort.

"Oh." Cassidy looked up at me, and I realized her comprehension must have been running at incredibly low levels. She had dark circles under her eyes, making her look a little like a drug addict when coupled with her natural paleness. I tried to recall the time and remembered it was nearing five in the morning. Cassidy turned back to staring at the bathroom door dully, waiting for Eilish to exit. Finally, apparently in frustration, she turned to the men's room and tried that handle. It opened immediately, and in she went, locking it behind her with a heavy click, still seeming like a zombie.

The lady's room door opened a few seconds later and Eilish came out, looking a little better than Cassidy in terms of how put together she was. She yawned right in my face as she held the door for me, and I went in as she said, "Might want to not sit down." I looked at her blankly, and she elaborated: "Trust me."

When I got inside, I found she wasn't wrong. Someone did not care to do janitorial work in this particular bathroom, so I held my nose and got finished quickly, never daring to touch the seat. When I finished, I washed my hands and avoided looking in the mirror, continuing a habit I'd been embracing since Scotland. I caught a flash of my dyed-blond hair and sunken cheeks, and that was all I needed to see. Onward.

I popped out into the store to find Eilish with her arms full of junk food. "And you," she said, grabbing a bag of Cheetos off the shelf to add to the pile she was already carrying like a chipmunk readying herself for winter. Even though winter was getting close to done, at least in this part of the country. She passed the candy display. "Ooh," she said, snatching up a Snickers bar. "And you ..."

I wandered over to the beer cooler and away from her junk food mission. I didn't need any of that. I paused next to a display advertising a forty-ounce malt liquor that sounded intriguing, even though I had to kind of squint to see it with the cooler lights off. I doubted it had the flavor of a good scotch, but it was just before 5 AM, and I wasn't feeling picky, so I grabbed a six pack and headed toward the counter.

There was an older, heavyset woman standing back there with her arms folded, just watching us. She shifted her attention to me as I came up and put the malt liquor on the counter.

"Oh, honey," she said, coming up to the counter. Her nametag said she was "Joan." "I can't sell you this."

I was feeling pretty good until that happened, when suddenly I got a little cross. "Why the hell not?"

She blinked a little at my reaction. "It's Sunday, doll."

My eye twitched when she called me "doll." "What the hell does that have to do with anything?"

Joan took a step back. "Now ... you just settle on down now. It's Sunday. You can't buy alcoholic beverages here on Sunday. At least not until after noon."

I blinked. I paused. I took a breath. "Why the f—" I took another breath.

"It's against the law," she said, looking at me over half-moon specs.

The door bell jangled, and someone cleared their throat behind me. I turned and looked.

It was Harry, and he was looking not so subtly at me.

I sighed. Apparently I'd been about to cause the sort of scene he'd explicitly warned me against in the car.

I pressed my lips together, my mouth all dry, and said, "Fair enough," grabbed the malt liquor, and headed back toward the cooler. I put it inside gently, trying to keep from tossing it so hard it sprang a leak, and then beelined for the door. Eilish was at the counter, a mountain of junk food in front of her, as Joan stared down at all the crap she was about to buy with a jaded eye, like she'd seen a hell of a lot worse than this gluttonous rampage. "And ... maybe some of these," Eilish said, ransacking a plastic case filled with beef sticks on the counter.

"Nice recovery," Harry said once we were outside, under the fluorescent glow of the overhead lights.

"This is bullshit," I said, stalking back toward the car. "I bet I could buy cigarettes today, no problem. Or lotto tickets.

Damn you, Sunday."

"Well, you should probably moderate your vices," Harry said amiably. "You want some lotto tickets? Or some cigs? I mean, they're hell on humans, but all they'll do to you is make you stink like flaming dog crap."

I turned and gave him a withering glare. "No, I do not want to smell like flaming dog crap, thank you very much." He wasn't wrong; the smell of cigarettes held an extra aroma of stink to the finely tuned meta senses. I couldn't stand to be around a smoker for very long without wanting to kill them and toss their body off the nearest bridge just to be rid of the smell.

That ... might have been the alcohol craving talking. Or maybe not.

The door to the station swung open and out came Cassidy, looking much more alert and awake. "Come on, come on," she said, gesturing to us. "We should get going."

I raised an eyebrow at her. "We're not going anywhere until Eilish gets done paying for her stuff." I nodded at Eilish, who I could see through the window talking to Joan, who was watching her with one eye cocked curiously while ringing up the plethora of junk foods. She picked up a pack of Twinkies and rang them, nodding at something Eilish was saying.

"Does she have any money?" Harry asked.

"Uh ..." I tried to think about it. It wasn't like Eilish worked, and I didn't know if Reed had given her any money before leaving. "Uhm ..."

"Rhetorical question, Sienna," Harry said. "You might want to go take care of that before she causes a scene by shoplifting. Because she will get caught. That Joan is no spring daffodil. She's seen some shit in her time."

"Yeah, yeah," I said, grumbling and heading back into the store.

"Have fun," Cassidy said, a little too singsongy for my taste. I gave her a look as I went inside.

"That'll be ... two hundred eighty five dollars and ninety three cents," Joan said as I let the door swing closed behind me.

Eilish's mouth dropped open, but I'd known her long enough to know that it was all an act. She was faking outrage, and I got a bad feeling as to why. "That's outrageous! I won't p—"

"I'll pay," I said, brandishing my credit card.

Eilish started to say something to me, then shrugged. "She'll pay," she said to Joan, a little smile of self-satisfaction spreading across her face.

I stepped up to the counter and slipped my card into the card reader. "You were just about to cause a scene," I muttered, meta-low.

"What? No," Eilish said. "I was going to grab a little something for the road and leave this bird scratching her head and restocking shelves for a bit, that's all."

"Harry says there was about to be trouble," I said, still talking uber low. Joan was looking around, the bag in her hand half-filled with Eilish's absurd number of junk food purchases. "You were going to get caught.

"Y'all hear that buzzing sound?" Joan stared at the ceiling. "I think one of these fluorescent lights is about to go bad."

"Better call maintenance," I said, grabbing the receipt as it printed before Joan could. I signed it, completely illegibly, and handed it back.

Joan gave me a half-assed scowl, more disappointed than bemused. "I *am* maintenance, doll. Night shift, you do anything you have to."

"Maybe it'll fix itself," I said, trying to be cool as I grabbed the first bag of junk food. It was not light. "Could just be a power surge."

"Maybe," she said, a crease forming between her eyebrows as she finished bagging the fifth(!) bag of Eilish's junk food. I couldn't tell whether she was politely choosing not to argue with me or she just knew I was full of crap and she'd been hearing the faint hiss of us talking meta low. "I guess it stopped."

"Hmm," I said, stringing the damned junk food bags along my arms while Eilish loaded up her own. How the hell had she managed to get all this to the counter without bags? "Welp … have a good night."

"Damned near morning now," Joan said as I went for the door. "Oh, you want a copy of your receipt?"

"No," I said, "I think all this crap is plenty enough reminder for me about what I spent." And I turned and walked out, Eilish a few steps behind me.

"I was not about to cause a scene," Eilish hissed once the door had slammed shut behind us. Joan was still looking around at the ceiling within, as though she could locate that mysterious sound just by staring long enough.

"Harry says you were," I said. "How would he know about it if he didn't see it come through in a prediction?"

"He's probably making stuff up," Eilish said. The hatchback of the SUV popped open, and I realized Harry was opening it for us.

I dumped my bags of junk food into the back of the SUV while Eilish discarded all but one of hers, after making some strategic switches into the one she kept. Part of me wanted to look, the other part of me didn't want to know, but I grabbed a Snickers anyway and peeled the wrapping off and started to eat it.

"Hey, that's mine," Eilish said.

"Technically, this is all mine," I said, waving a hand to encompass the enormous trick-or-treat result that filled the SUV's hatchback, "but I'll let you steal some, don't worry."

Eilish made a frown, and then made her way to the door again, following behind me. "Can I at least sit up front this time?"

"No."

She grunted and got in the back seat as I got in the front, and Harry started the engine. "There's a Waffle House a few miles ahead," he said. "I'm stopping for breakfast."

Eilish was halfway into an Oatmeal Creme pie. "We're stopping for breakfast? That would have been good to know before I bought all this!"

I rolled my eyes. "Why are you upset? You're not even down a dollar."

"Well, I went through the trouble of hauling all that to the counter, did you see? It was like ten trips."

I looked back at her, and caught a glimpse of Cassidy

bobbing, little wireless earbuds in her ears as she tapped away at a computer screen. I turned all the way around so I could look right at Eilish. She had a piece of brown Oatmeal Creme pie on her lip. "No thieving, you hear me?" I made my voice emphatic. "The last thing we need is to get in trouble with the law because you wanted a stick of peppermint gum, okay? If you want something, I'll buy it."

"With your brother's credit card," Eilish said softly.

"Well, I'm kind of the one who financed his venture, so ... it's sort of my money, too," I said. I hadn't been able to access my own money yet, really, save for a quick bank transfer to Cassidy once I'd gotten back to the States. I'd lost eighty percent of my fortune thanks to that damned Scot bitch. I still had a sizable fortune under my control in the Cayman Islands, but I didn't know if the feds had found that money yet, and I didn't want to transfer or make any withdrawals that might lead to me.

So, I used Reed's money. And that was totally cool and only slightly driving me nuts.

"Next stop, Waffle House," Harry said, pulling the car out of the parking lot as I turned around and sat back down. My stomach gave a low rumble. He looked sidelong at me. "Way to turn around your own intemperate response, by the way."

"Thanks," I said, the only buffer between me and a rather extreme headache being the ibuprofen he'd given me earlier. I kept from snapping at him, though. "No alcohol on Sundays? What kind of bullshit is that, Harry?"

"Uh, that'd be the law in many states," he said. "Including your own, until recently."

"What?" I frowned. After a moment's reflection, I realized ... yeah, that could have been true. It wasn't like I had ever really gone out to buy booze on Sundays when I lived in Minnesota. "Maybe," I finally conceded.

As the car pulled back out onto the highway, rolling through Ardmore, it made me think of how things had been back then, when I'd lived a normal life, unencumbered by countless law enforcement agencies hunting me, and I'd had all the power in the world.

It was almost like another life, one I could only look back

on now through a dark prism I called Scotland. If everything in my world could be divided into "Before" and "After," there was a giant black smudge in the middle marking the space between, and staining everything that had come after.

Though, really … I wasn't sure quite where to demarcate the end of "Before." Maybe it wasn't in Scotland. Maybe it when I'd exploded in Eden Prairie, Minnesota, killing a whole heap ton of meta prisoners that had meant to kill me (and scared a ton of reporters out of their damned skins, turning them against me) that I'd lost my freedom. When I'd had to start running, like I was Dr. Richard Kimble, but with superhuman powers. And pretty. I thought I'd hit rock bottom after that.

But then … Scotland. Where I'd lost … everything I had left.

I put those thoughts out of my head, shaking them off. Before? After? None of it really mattered. My life was in the state it was in, and reflecting over the wreckage didn't seem too prudent. It was liking look back at the road behind. What the hell was the point? Other than a farewell view of Ardmore—and maybe a glimpse of Cassidy now that she was peppy or Eilish as she stuffed her face with junk food— there was nothing behind me that I could change. Nothing that would make the present better.

But as I stared out at the road ahead, I had to wonder if there was anything I could change before me, either? Before, when I'd had power, the ability to influence the outcome of a situation like this was never in doubt. But now …

Was there even any hope?

Or was it all darkness, from here to the horizon, more grim surprises that would only be revealed and do further damage to my life as I came upon them?

14.

"Did you pick that gas station knowing I couldn't buy alcohol there?" I asked once we were a little further down the road.

Harry chuckled. "Even I don't control the blue laws of the states we're passing through. It's a statewide thing."

"Yeah, but you took us through this particular state—"

"We're actually in Tennessee now. Ardmore is on the border."

"Whatever, you chose this entire path," I chucked a thumb behind me, toward the service station where I couldn't buy malt liquor at 5 AM on Sunday. "We were supposed to go through Florida and Georgia."

He grunted. "Well, if you wanted this trip to end up with a visit to the federal pen, you should have said so." He smiled thinly. "I thought you wanted me to get you to this bad guy you're chasing." He inclined his head back, indicating Cassidy. "You know—totally for her and not at all for yourself."

I didn't know how to take that. "Uh."

"Classic repartee," Cassidy said. "But I think I see where he's going with this."

"Oh, uh ... where's that?" Eilish asked. "I mean—no, I totally see it, too," when Cassidy cast her a frown.

"Where I'm going with this, Eilish, is here," and Harry looked back at me. "If Cassidy hadn't knocked at your door, you'd still be sitting in Florida, glued to the television screen, watching all this unfold on the pixels."

"Actually, I'd be sleeping at this hour," I said. Harry gave me a knowing little smile, and I felt compelled to answer. Sort of. "Yeah, I'd still be in Florida, enjoying a nice boozy vacation from—y'know, fighting villains and running from the law. Most people call that a vacation. What's wrong with that?"

"Most people don't consume entire production runs of scotch in one sitting," Eilish said, mostly under her breath. Or possibly around a Twinkie. "Gyah. This is not to my taste." And she spat whatever it was back in the plastic bag. "Do you Americans not have Jaffa Cakes?"

"Never heard of them," I said. "Listen, Harry—I get where you're going with this, but come on, man. I'm a liability to any sort of metahuman response at this point. I bring down more John Laws than—"

"Than a hooker on Saturday night," Cassidy said, and she flushed when I looked back at her. "Sorry. I'm trying out my own repartee."

"Work harder at it," I said, and turned back to a smirking Harry. "I'm not—"

"You're on vacation," Harry said like he understood, but I caught a faint trace of mocking embedded in his tone.

"Yeah," I said. "And a liability. There are teams that handle this sort of thing. Reed runs them." I flipped my hair out of the way, because wearing it down was annoying.

"Is that how you felt about it before you went to Scotland?" Harry asked, slipping that dagger between my ribs.

I let that one sink in for a second, and started to open my mouth to argue when Harry said, "Waffle House!" and started to pull off on the next exit.

"Oh, good, waffles," Eilish said, "because I'm totally famished right now."

"How?" Cassidy asked, a little pointedly.

"Because I don't know what this is," she said, throwing a partially eaten Snickers into the bag, "but it's not the Snickers I'm used to. When you lot said 'road trip,' I got all excited, because last time—when Sienna and I went through Scotland with Diana—there wasn't a chance to properly stock up on road trip food. I figured this time would be different, but then I try all your American snack food and—ugh. None of it hits the spot like Walker's Crisps. None. I'm left to wonder how you people eat the way you do."

"Try the Cheetos," I said, folding my arms as we slid up the offramp and onto the road, then into the parking lot of a Waffle House. The big yellow sign hung overhead, and I kept my sullen silence as Harry parked the car and we all got out.

The Waffle House was a brick building with glass windows that stretched all the way around. Crowned with a short, triangular roof, it had a look about it that said it had been here for a while, situated at this prime piece of real estate since maybe before it had even been a prime piece of real estate. Now it was directly off a freeway ramp, which guaranteed traffic.

As I walked up to the door, Harry opened it and held it for me. I caught a twinkle of mischief in his eye as I frowned and walked in, grabbing a seat at the counter while the others filed in around me and filled in the spaces next to me. Harry seated himself on the other side of Eilish, who took the spot to my left. Cassidy plopped down to my right, setting her laptop in front of her. I stole a glance at her screen, and it looked like she'd been watching video of Jamie Barton's fight as filmed on a cell phone from the deck of a passing ferry or something.

"Hey, what can I get for you?" A guy with a little too much pep in his step for this time of morning came sauntering up in an apron with a name tag that identified him as "Mike!" (I added the exclamation point because, honestly, it fit this guy.) "Coffee? Juice? Water?"

"Coffee," I said, before anyone else could answer.

"Orange juice," Cassidy said.

"Do you have any tea?" Eilish asked.

"Sure!" Mike! said. "And for you, sir?" he asked Harry.

"Eilish," Harry said, staring at the menu, "you're not going to like that tea. It's sweet tea."

"So it's got honey in it? Sugar?" Eilish asked, frowning at

him.

Harry looked like he was holding in a smile. "Well, it's got sugar."

"That's fine," Eilish said, completely disregarding him. "I like my tea sweet."

That twinkle was back in Harry's eye, and he looked for a moment like he wanted to say something else, but held it in. "I'll take a coffee, too," he said instead. "Black."

"I'm a flagrant racist, so I would like mine with lots of cream and sugar," I said. Mike! didn't seem to know what to make of that, so he just sort of forced a smile.

"Coming right up," he said, and turned from the counter to walk on down to where a fridge waited. Almost the entire kitchen was open for us to see, right there behind the counter in front of us, but it tapered into a slightly more private area to our right, where on our side of the counter it led to the bathrooms.

"What are you going to order?" Cassidy asked, perusing the menu.

"A waffle, of course," I said, and when she gave me a curious look: "It's Waffle House. How can I go wrong ordering that?"

"That's an interesting theory," she said, and I got the feeling she was dismissing it out of hand. "What should I get?"

I looked over her skinny, rail-like frame. "Everything on the menu, girl. The fattier, the better."

She looked up, worked through that for a second, then looked back down, frowning. "Oh, ha ha. Because I'm skinny."

"I should probably do the same," I said, "but since my tendency usually leans toward the more rubenesque framing, I'm gonna hit that waffle and call it quits."

"Well, this is all fascinating, ladies," Harry said, standing up, "but if you'll pardon me, I've got to go see a man about a horse." And off he went, toward the bathroom, disappearing down the short hallway and into the bathroom.

"You know, he's quite a handsome one," Eilish said, watching him go. Mike! brought the drinks, setting her tea in front of her, and Eilish picked it up.

"Don't waste your time, Irish," Cassidy said, still staring at the menu. "He's only got eyes for Sienna."

I felt like someone had just delivered a shock down my spine that made my head come up hard. "What the—no, he doesn't!" I looked over at Cassidy, who was still staring at her menu. "What the hell are you talking about, Cassidy?"

"I'm sitting in the back seat and I'm not blind," she said. "That's what I'm talking about."

Eilish did a spit take next to me, and for a moment I thought she was going to argue with Cassidy. Instead, she said, "This tea is terrible!" Harry strikes again.

I turned back to Cassidy, rolling my eyes at the clear absurdity of her idea about Harry. Her super-powered calculator of a brain knew nil about human emotion. "I know you're really smart when it comes to numbers, but in this, Cassidy, you don't know a damned thing. He's just—"

The bell behind me rung over the door, and I turned, catching sight of a stiff, straitlaced black man as he walked in. He was over six feet tall and wearing a coat that reached to his knees. He scanned the room quickly, target-seeking, and when his eyes alighted on me, he paused, then came right for me with slow strides.

I didn't wait more than a few steps before I stood, spinning off my stool to rise and greet him. "Howdy," I said, any quibbles with Cassidy forgotten as he made a slow beeline for me, nothing else in the place getting so much as a glance from him.

"Hello, Sienna," he said, in a low, scratchy voice, a baritone that would have been damned near perfect for creating the scariest sort of ominous voice with just a little digital synth. His face was broad and flat, and there was menace in his eyes as he stopped just outside my reach. He didn't smile, didn't blink, and I could tell just by looking at him—oh, and the fact that he'd walked right in here and called me by name—that things on this road trip were about to take a turn for the worse.

15.

"Excuse me, sir," Eilish said, "would you kindly—"

Eilish didn't even get that much out before the man lashed out with a lightning fast kick and kicked her stool from beneath her so hard that it ricocheted off the counter, Eilish still on it. She didn't stay on it for long, though, because after it cracked her, knee-first, into the counter, she came spinning back and into a waiting fist. The big guy leveled Eilish with that one punch,

and her stool flew free from beneath her, over the booth behind and out the plate-glass window to smash into the windshield of an old Cadillac in the parking lot.

Eilish landed in a heap on the floor, eyes already closed. There was a mad scramble of the few other customers, dishware clattering, as they either froze in place or went for the door.

My eyes widened as Cassidy let out a little scream and hopped back, taking her computer with her and cradling it in her arms like she was protecting her baby.

"That ... was so totally unnecessary," I said.

"Being charmed by a Siren isn't within my mission parameters," he rasped, his dark eyes watching me for any hint of aggression. He was standing off, waiting for me to make a move that he could counter. I knew the posture because I'd adopted it myself more than a few times.

Unfortunately, he had me backed against the counter, which didn't give me a lot of room to maneuver without doing a flip or something, getting over it, which was going to be slow and kinda risky given he'd just moved lightning fast. There seemed to be a kind of shadowy smoke rolling off him, something I'd never seen before. It had allowed him to kick out at Eilish so quickly that I'd barely seen the movement. It wasn't what it looked like when a speedster moved, and it wasn't like a shadow-melding meta I'd fought down in St. Thomas, either.

This ... was something new. And new tended to be scary, especially when it took down one of your team with such alacrity.

"'Mission parameters,' huh?" I cracked. "Sounds like Skynet finally got pissed off enough at me to send the Terminator."

He was slightly hunched over, in a ready stance, waiting for me to make a move that I wasn't going to be making—yet. I couldn't believe I'd been dumb enough to sit with my back to the door, first of all, but second—

Shit, how long had it been since I'd trained?

London. Months ago. That was how long. Before ...

Well, before.

As a succubus, I was fast. But this guy? He was in a class of his own. Speed wasn't going to win, even if I'd been operating at top form.

"I'm not here to terminate you," he said, finally replying to my joke. "If you come quietly, no harm will come to you, and your friends can leave."

"Tempting offer," I said. "Where would I be going?"

"That's classified," he said, completely straitlaced, the same way he'd replied to my Terminator riff. Like he didn't get the joke or he just didn't care because he was so focused on what he wanted to do—namely, bring me in.

"I've hit my bag and drag quota for the last few months, thanks," I said, taking a half step away from him. I meant it to look like I was moving my stance, readying myself for a stronger defense in case he decided to come at me. "I'm afraid I'm going to have to ask you to leave so that I can have my waffle in peace. Otherwise, things are about to get ... feisty."

"You've been warned," he said, and his shoulders swayed, that shadow-smoke rolling off them, telling me that whatever his power was, he was about to employ it in spectacular fashion. "This is your last chance to comply."

"Yeah, you're totally not the Terminator with that sense of gravitas," I muttered. I bent my knees slightly, using the opportunity to hook my rear foot on the stool I'd been sitting on moments before, back when I had a hope of a tasty waffle, laden with butter and syrup.

"You have no idea who I am," he said.

"I know who you are," I said. "You're the man with a giant crease down the middle of his face."

I shifted my weight as he paused, looking at me suspiciously. Bringing the stool forward with my own version of shocking speed, I made it skitter across the floor, rattling as it moved. His eyes went low at the distractionary noise as I hucked the stool at him—

And he punched it, sending it roaring right back at me.

I dodged it by about a quarter inch—but only because I had a feeling that Mr. Blurry-with-speed was going to do something like that. I tilted sideways to do it, and it left me slightly off balance, but I'd already thrown myself into a spin, using my left foot as traction to execute a pirouette. A lot of speed came down to stance, and in this case, I knew I couldn't match this guy for quickness.

Instead, I pushed all my chips onto "Catching him by surprise." There was little to no chance that my opening gambit of throwing the stool was going to do that, which was why I had a backup plan. Wheels within wheels, ya know.

As I spun, I tilted and came low, wobbling. I brought my right leg up as I came around, trying to sweep his feet from beneath him.

My foot made contact with the side of his leg, and I realized my error immediately. Stupid, really.

He was anchored to the ground like a tree, having seen what I was doing a mile off. It was a clumsy, desperation maneuver that he'd probably picked out the moment I went into my spin. I'd hoped it look like I was—I dunno, breakdancing or something, but he figured it out.

I kicked his leg and he didn't so much as cringe. Upon impact, my spin stopped, and all I had to show for my desperation maneuver was a mild ache across my instep where I'd caught him in the back of the knee, where—dammit—he should have been vulnerable to being knocked off balance.

Instead, I was the one off balance, and still wobbly as my kick bounced off. If it pained him at all, he didn't show it. He was perfectly poised, low enough with his center of gravity that even if I'd knocked one of his legs from beneath him, he could have recovered.

He didn't need to recover, though. He was perfectly positioned to lash out, and lash out he did, with a short punch that hit me in the ribs and launched me backward.

My left foot left the ground behind as I tumbled, hitting the counter across the back of my thighs. The sudden contact arrested my lower body's momentum and I flipped, my head and upper body continuing on without obstacle and my lower body adjusting its momentum to go in the same direction.

The result? I tumbled ass-over-teakettle behind the counter and hit the wall knee first, then thumped into the griddle—ouch, hot!—and then torpedoed into the tile floor beneath.

I made contact all across my forearms, thumping my head lightly but enough that—yeah, ouch, I felt it. As I landed in a heap, I heard heavy feet thud as someone else came down behind the counter only a few feet away.

I opened one eye and looked up to find Mr. Terminator upside down, leering down at me with that frozen, expressionless face. "You'll be coming with me, now," he said, and raised a hand to deliver the finishing blow.

And there was a not a chance in hell I was going to avoid it.

16.

Veronika Acheron
San Francisco, California

Vernonika was a night owl by nature, her brain wired so that she couldn't really get to sleep until the wee, small—hell, the wee many hours of the morning. A stolen look at the clock provided the knowledge that, yes, she was well beyond burning the midnight oil, and now safely into the territory of burning the three o'clock oil. Three-thirty, almost.

Her muscles were tense, ears pricked up, listening. The darkness was complete outside, but in here in the bedroom—

It was nothing but action and excitement, baby.

That was the Veronika everyone knew. Wild to a fault. Frenzied when crossed. Furious in battle.

And in her personal life?

Well, she had stories.

Veronika loved the stories. Loved to tell them, loved to watch the expressions on peoples' faces as they took them in, digesting the exciting, emotional, sexy content she fed them. It was always a trip, watching a choice joke land, a good reference, some ribald story hit home.

Such excite, as the kids on the internet said.

Yeah. Excitement. This was what drove Veronika.

And it was the reason that she was awake now, pushing herself to stay up later, go longer, and not sleep until she'd had all the fun she could.

Wild. Crazy.

Veronika didn't have to even try and hold her breath when she felt it coming on. The bedsheets were tangled around her, damp with sweat. Her breathing was quicker, because—hell, she was plainly excited. Even having been through this before—so many times—she couldn't help but get … enthusiastic.

Sure, it was almost three-thirty now. But she could do this until four. Until five. Six, seven, eight, who cared? She'd do this all night and the next day, she reflected with undying enthusiasm as she rolled, slightly, her hand tight from overuse, a faint smile perched on her lips from the evening's enthusiasms. She reached up to mop her brow; was it hot in here? Or was it just her?

"I just can't stop with you," she whispered, a little bead of sweat drip down her temple. "No matter how times we … do this dance." She looked ahead, impish mischief in her eyes. "We get to a certain point and … I just gotta finish, you know?"

The book in her hands did not answer her. But then, she'd read *Pride and Prejudice* hundreds, maybe thousands of times now. It never did disappoint.

Veronika brushed the cookie crumbs out of her bed and onto the floor as she shifted position. Her hand was practically cramping from holding the book open this long. What was it about Elizabeth Bennet and Mr. Darcy that kept her reading all damned night? Even though she knew the outcome, even though she could quote it by heart?

Oh, who cared. It was three-thirty in the damned morning and she was still reading a book she'd read so many times before. If she didn't feel the need to justify anything else in her life, she damned sure wasn't going to justify this.

"You are too generous to trifle with me. If your feelings are still what they were last April, tell me so at once. My affections and wishes are unchanged, but one word from you will silence me on this subject forever."

Veronika sighed, letting the book fall to her chest. Nobody talked like that anymore. Certainly no man. If they did, she might be more interested in them.

A thump came on the roof, like Santa Claus landing. Veronika paused, turning over in bed, hand frozen while reaching for another cookie. "What the hell?" she muttered.

It had sounded like ... like a damned flying meta just landed on her roof.

That got her to put down *Pride and Prejudice*, fighting loose from the bedsheets, which had tangled as she'd tossed and turned all night, plucking her way through the pages. She threw a silken robe over her t-shirt and boy shorts, went down the stairs of her townhome, and out the front door.

She hit the front steps, out into the chill evening air, wind coming in off the Bay making her shiver. She kept going, down to the sidewalk and looked up, up, trying to see on the roof. It wasn't easy; the roof was flat, and two stories straight up. Her townhome was a quintessential San Francisco-type landmark, built in a row, basement just below street level, two stories rising above that. Her mother had bought it for cheap back in the seventies, and Veronika had taken it over now that her mother was ... unwell.

"Hey!" she called up into the night, trying to project her voice up onto the roof. "Who's up there?"

A man made his way to the edge of the roof and stood there, looking down at her. He was shadowed in the dark; she could tell nothing about him. He stared down at her, she stared up at him.

"Dude, what the hell are you doing on my roof at this hour?" Veronika asked. She brought her hands to her sides, ready to light off plasma if need be. She'd be damned if she was going to toss a burst up at him now; a bad throw and her house would go up in flames.

No, her mind was in one place now—kick this guy's ass and go finish the story of Elizabeth Bennet and Mr. Darcy, dammit. Not like she didn't know how it was going to end, but still. She didn't like to be left hanging any more than anyone else. In any way.

The man stood at the edge of her roof for a moment, then floated down, his hands strangely shadowed. "You are Veronika Acheron," he said, reaching the street a few seconds later, a delicate leaf making his way to the ground, unhurried by gravity.

He didn't ask it like a question. "Yeah, and you are?" she fired back. "Other than an annoying, stalking cheesedick?"

"I seek you," he said, that Euro accent echoing down the canyon of a street. "I seek your ... strength."

"Well, you're about to get it," she said, keeping her hands at her side. "Though I don't think you're going to like it when you do get a taste."

Closer, under the streetlight, she could see him a little more clearly now. His hair was dark, skin pale, and his hands seemed to be ... writhing, catching the light, a thousand sparkles glaring out, like—

Like the Bay. The reflection of the city on the—

Shit, Veronika thought, *he's a Poseidon. A flying Poseidon. He's got water powers, his hands are wrapped in water, that's why—*

She flared her plasma to life and came at him, crossing the distance between them—only a couple feet, and meeting him as he raised a fist to her. Her hands were bright blue with the glow, and she struck at him as he struck at her, her leading plasma edge finding the globe of water wrapped around his fist—

There was a hiss and a crack, and a rush of heat that Veronika was utterly unprepared for forced her to step back or be scalded. She jerked away, the air temperature rising several hundred degrees around where they'd collided, and threw herself into a backward roll.

When she came up off the sidewalk, she found the Euro guy still standing where she'd left him, burns and blisters disfiguring his face. His mouth was a tight grimace, pain infusing his entire expression. His eyebrows had been burned off, his face red and raw as though she'd tossed boiling water at him—

But he stood there, clothes steaming, and he straightened up—

And came at her again.

Veronika blinked; seeing this guy come at her after taking a wounding like that was intimidating, though she tried not to let it get to her. He was human—well, metahuman. He could be hurt. Hell, she'd just hurt him.

Now she just needed to hurt him again.

She flared plasma, making a ball of glowing blue wide on her hand. It grew, expanded as she rose up, ready to strike at him, to burn him down to embers—

He smiled as she came, hands spread wide, no sign of that flickering light, the water on his fingers. He was just going to take it.

That made Veronika smile.

Right up until the stream of water came splashing down on her from above.

The heat roared, sizzling off the ball of plasma she'd just created. With no way for her to channel it, the raw heat ran across her skin, burning and crackling it as though she'd been dropped into a blast furnace. Control of plasma was her power, and she could diffuse a great deal of heat by swallowing it up in plasma, but this—this subtle, simple workaround—

There was nothing Veronika could do as the flash-boiled water seared her flesh, burning her skin. Her ball of plasma dispelled instantly as she dropped, nervous system overwhelmed, thudding on the sidewalk. She couldn't really feel anymore, just an overwhelming sense of every nerve firing in pain. The sky lay dark above her, a light in the distance, a street lamp, shedding the only illumination.

The dark-haired man loomed over her, staring down, curious, almost. She looked back up at him with eyes that were half-blinded, her vision blurred with tears.

Words crackled from her throat, raw and burned, wafting up to him. "Who ... are ... you ...?"

It was, after all, the only question that mattered.

He just stared down at her, dark and forbidding. She thought she saw him smile, a little.

"If you live," he said, as he started to lift off the ground, floating up, up into the darkness, "maybe someday ... I will tell you. When I find out myself."

And then he was gone, and the darkness came sweeping down on Veronika, sirens in the distance edging closer as her sense of the world faded away as surely as any thoughts of finishing her book in peace.

17.

It had been a few months since I'd gotten my ass kicked, and man, the experience had not gotten any better in the interim.

I was lying on my back behind the counter in a Waffle House just over the Tennessee state line from Alabama, my weight resting not so comfortably on my shoulder blades, my legs straight up in the air. I'd landed that way after taking a hit that would have wrecked a car, smashing into the griddle where, dammit, my waffle should have been cooking even now.

But, no, instead some yahoo with a grudge had come stalking into the place and started shit with me. Poor, innocent little old me. Depowered, just-a-vanilla-succubus me.

Now he was closing in for the kill with his super-fast-punchy powers. About to level me with a last punch, in fact, aimed right at my face. He was leaning down to do it, because he was super tall, and I was on the ground (well, head and shoulders, anyway).

Most people probably would have been unconscious by now. I would have liked to have been. Sleeping in my bed somewhere, preferably, where my entire cerebrum and spinal column would be much more in harmony and not carrying my lower body's entire weight. It was, after, generally supposed to be the opposite, but here I was, almost standing on my frigging head, about to get punched out properly by

95

some looming linebacker of a man who seemed an awful lot like the African-American version of the Terminator.

I just hoped he didn't have a metal skeleton.

He started to lean down to deliver the knockout blow, and I made use of those legs dangling over my head by lashing out and giving him a solid kick to the balls. I couldn't do much—not nearly much as I used to do—but I still had some strength, and dudes still had the ultimate weak point, and—

All the wind went out of the Terminator as he realized, too late, *Whoops! She's not out of the fight!* He didn't say that, instead going with, "WHOOOOOOOOF!" a muted version of the pained noise most guys tended to make when you hit them in the boys with super strength.

I followed up with a nice, clumsy kick to the face, taking advantage of the natural slowdown that happens right after your body takes critical damage to a crucial area. His jaw made a profound cracking noise, and his speed advantage seemed to be nullified by the fact he was in pure agony. He was doing a really good job of controlling it, though, credit to him.

"Ungh," I said, rolling over and landing a knee, painfully, on the tile floor. Terminator was on all fours, and, not being one to waste a lot of opportunities for cheap shots, I drilled him in the jaw and he slammed into the base of the griddle. "Jerk off," I grunted, getting to my feet and aiming a kick at his lower back. I hit him, he grunted, but he was tense—

He was preparing himself to be beaten on the ground. Bad sign. Take it from one who'd adopted that same posture every now and again. If someone was preparing their body in that way, a counterattack was coming.

And I just didn't have time for that. We'd been brawling for a few minutes—well, I'd been getting my ass handed to me for a few minutes before this reversal of fortune—and that meant there had been plenty of time for someone, probably Mike! my waiter, to call the cops.

This being not to my advantage and maybe to his, instead of delivering another blow, I leapt the counter and grabbed a barely-conscious Eilish by the collar, dragging her to her feet.

"Come on," I said, to her and to Cassidy, who was standing back all wide-eyed and ineffectual, waiting for somebody to tell her uber-smart-but-useless-in-a-fight skinny ass what to do. "Move!"

I ushered them both out the door in a hurry, mourning the loss of my chance for a waffle. I half walked, half dragged Eilish, who was barely conscious and moaning at the physical harm done unto her, out the door and into the parking lot as someone came skidding to a stop inches in front of us.

Harry. Driving the damned car.

I threw the back door open and tossed Eilish in as Cassidy skittered around the other side. Then, with a look back over my shoulder at the Terminator, who was rising to his feet behind the counter inside, I hopped in the passenger seat and Harry floored the accelerator. The SUV took off with a roar, and we skidded onto the street and straight onto the entry ramp to I-65 north about a half second later, causing some semi driver to lay on his horn in full-fury pissedness as he came to a stop with a hearty ROOOOOOOOOOOOAR of his engine brakes.

I looked back in time to see the Terminator come leaping out the hole in the window that he'd made with Eilish's barstool. He hit the pavement running and disappeared as we moved down the onramp far enough that the slope of the earth obscured him from my sight.

All I could do was hope that we made it out of there before he could get to his vehicle and begin an honest pursuit. But for the moment I sat there, breathing in, my aching side, back—hell, everything—crying out at me, as we rolled onto Interstate 65 and Harry accelerated up to 80.

I did not stop looking back for many miles.

18.

"Shit, what if that guy has a car?" Cassidy was the first to ask the question I'd been ignoring for the last five minutes as we boogied up the freeway at high speed, the speedometer needle buried against the right side of the instrument. Harry was keeping very careful control of the vehicle, sliding in and out of traffic brilliantly.

"Oh, he does," Harry said, breaking his silence. He lifted a hand and something dangled from within his fingers. "Where do you think I got these spark plugs?" He shot me a grin.

I just stared at him. "Wait ... you sabotaged his car?"

"Damned right I did," he said.

I thought about it for a second, then my voice went frosty as I watched Harry stiffen, subtly. "You knew he was going to bushwhack us before you stopped at that Waffle House, didn't you?"

Harry just sort of shrugged, and I hit him on the shoulder. Not too hard, but enough that he cringed, and suddenly I knew why he'd tensed a moment earlier. He'd been anticipating the hit.

"Yeah, okay, I knew," Harry said.

"How?" I asked. "Who is he?"

Harry shook his head, not looking at me. "Don't know. But he's tied up in this whole thing somehow, so this was a necessary meeting and also ..." he seemed to be deciding how best to say it, "... your best chance for survival."

I hit him again, and he grimaced. "Dammit, Nealon ...

sometimes, I swear ... associating with you definitely brings its own sort of pitfalls. Pain being one of them."

"I haven't mangled you beyond repair yet, Graves," I said, which was about the most charitable thing I could manage after he'd just copped to walking me into the worst beatdown I'd experienced ... in three months. "Count your blessings given what I just went through in that Waffle House." I seethed in silence for a moment. "What the hell are you playing at?"

"Me?" Graves kept his eyes on the road for once. "I'm just the driver."

"The driver who can see into the damned future and just walked me into an ambush. Try again."

"I told you—this guy was going to cross your path regardless. I just tried to engineer it so—"

"A warning would have been nice!" I hammered Harry's arm. "'Hey, Sienna, this stop isn't so much about waffles as it a chance for you to get your skull beaten in by some superpowered goon with the personality of a freaking android'!" I thumped him again and again on the bicep, and he just took it.

"My arm's gone completely numb," Harry said, shaking it out as soon as I delivered the last blow. "I hope you're happy."

"I was happy on the beach in Florida," I said, crossing my arms in front of me to keep from physically abusing Harry any worse than I'd already done. I could have broken bones and done so much worse, but I kept a lid on it.

"Bullshit," Harry threw back at me, a little angry, probably from the pain.

I chewed on that one, gritting my teeth. "Fine," I said at last, "I wasn't *happy* happy. But I had scotch, and I was safe, and—"

"Yeah, you were living the high life in your little dog run," Harry said, now more animated than I'd yet seen him. "Make sure you don't go any farther than your shock collar comfort zone would allow. And keep diving into that bottle, Nealon, eventually when you hit the bottom maybe you'll find an answer to how pathetic your life has become."

"I already have an answer for that, Harry," I shot back, "I'm on the run from the frigging law, and I got my ass beat and my powers stolen by some ginger with a mad-on for me. I'm entitled to sit back and tip a few—"

"Bull. Shit." Harry thumped the wheel and the car shook as he took us slightly over the bumps at the side of the road, then got us right back on the straight and narrow. He turned to me with blazing eyes. "You can sit and drink and feel sorry for yourself all you want, but don't turn around and tell me that it's because you were happy wallowing."

I wanted to hit him again, but I didn't, because I wasn't sure I could restrain myself from using lethal force. Hell, I didn't even know what lethal force was for me anymore, without Wolfe strength.

"Looks like I missed some good times," Eilish said woozily from the back seat.

"I didn't ask for you to come along and become my cryptic asshole shaman spirit guide," I said, trying to ignore the distraction.

"Well, I needed your help, so—here we are, anyway," Harry said. "All part of the service."

"Me getting my ass kicked by the Terminator is part of your service? Your service sucks. Like—Comcast bad."

Cassidy chuckled, and we all turned to look at her. "That was funny," she said, blushing. "Their service is bad-award winning. If there was a J.D. No-Power award, they would get it."

"I don't need your damned help, Harry," I said, still steaming.

"Yeah, you were doing great without me," he said. "Just keep a little something in mind—you may have just run across this guy now, in my company, but he's been hunting you for a while. So he would have found you down in Florida, eventually, and then you wouldn't have been in a position to at least outrun him when he knocked your ass sideways."

That annoying little factoid had an infuriating ring of truth to it. I'd been hunted by the best, and this Terminator guy—he was right up there. If I'd had my old powers, sure, he might not have been as much of an issue. A few fire blasts, boom, he's pre-cremated and my problems with him are over.

Now, thought? His super-speed punchy powers damned near caved my freaking head in, and my own punches were not nearly so lightning fast.

How had I fought guys like this before?

Oh, right. I cracked my back, and felt for that empty space where I used to carry a holster. Well, I had a Walther in my travel bag, a gift from one Manannán Mac Lir, and it still had a few rounds left in it. "Cassidy," I said, "be a not-pain-in-my-ass and hand me my bag, will you?"

She shrugged, put aside her laptop, and reached into the back, pulling up my bag and one of Eilish's countless candy bags with it. She tossed it to me lightly, between the gap in the seats, and the candy bag broke loose and showered the rear floorboard with Twizzlers and Almond Joys.

Eilish moaned. "My head hurts so, I don't think I could stomach any more of your American candy right now."

I reached back and grabbed an Almond Joy, furiously ripping the paper off it and then throwing the wrapper back in her face. "Fine, then! Our candy is too good for you anyway." And I took a big bite of almond coconutty goodness as I unzipped my bag and pulled out the Walther box.

"Please don't shoot me," Harry said, and I froze, contemplating it for just a second before I tucked the gun into my waistband. "It was long odds, but it was a possibility," he said when he caught me frowning at him.

"Throw me into an unexpected fight with an unstoppable ass kicker again and the odds are going to get a lot less favorable for you, bucko," I said after I practice-drew the gun and then checked to see if it had one in the chamber. Of course it did; they were pretty damned useless without one in the chamber. At least that old habit died hard.

"Oh, good," Eilish said, leaning forward so I could see that she was sporting a big bruise across her pale forehead. "The angry, drunken American is now armed. You people are crazy."

"Why?" I asked, not particularly perturbed about Eilish's characterization of me, unflattering as it was.

"Because you just tucked a gun into your waistband," Eilish said.

I stared back at her. "I got this gun in Scotland."

She started to open her mouth to protest, paused, then said, "Yeah, but, you're carrying it in America now."

I just stared, still. "And ...?"

She stared back, apparently trying to construct her argument and not having much success. "You people are gun crazy."

"Well, in this case, it's a problem solver for me," I said, shaking it off and turning back to putting away my bag. That done, I tossed it to the back of the hatchback area. "As in, if I can, I'm totally going to blow the brains out of that asshole the Terminator, and then my problems with him will be over."

"But is that really the way you want to be solving all your problems?" Eilish asked, like that was some kind of compelling argument.

"The ones that involve people wanting to harm or otherwise kill me? Hell yes," I said. "That is how I want to solve them. With bullets to the head for all who threaten my wellbeing in a serious manner." I looked sidelong at Harry, who let out the thinnest smile. "Judgment reserved on where you fall into that category, Graves."

He didn't argue back. Which was wise.

We passed a sign warning us that the next major city ahead was Nashville, somewhere in the near distance, and I quietly seethed about getting my ass handed to me—this was becoming a habit—by some rando meta in a Waffle House who apparently had beef with me. What was his deal? Kidnapper for unknown parties? He didn't seem like a government stooge, since they usually came in teams, a swarm of stinging pains in my ass.

I'd have to file him under mystery for now, which left me with two to unravel—three, counting Harry "I might be trying to low-key kill you" Graves. Why the hell was he hiding behind my skirt (metaphorical, not literal—I don't wear those)?

"Uh, Sienna?" Cassidy piped up from the back seat.

"Tell me you have a read on who that asshole was," I said, turning, my hand brushing the soft cloth seat. "And that we can go to his house and just wrecking ball it to the ground right now, so that when he comes home he finds himself in a rough approximation of my old house, burned and—"

"No," Cassidy said, shaking her head urgently. She spun the laptop around toward me so that I could see the screen, and when I did ...

My freaking guts felt like they'd fallen out of my body and dropped through the floorboard and onto the highway, left behind as the wheels spun on through the night and carried us away.

METAHUMAN MASSACRE

Cute lede, I might have thought any other time, but the subhead gave me chills in its dense simplicity, and it took my brain another second to process through the information.

Veronika Acheron had been attacked. Outside her house.

And suddenly it started to feel ... so very clear.

I knew Eric Simmons.

I knew Jamie Barton.

I knew Veronika.

This guy who flew, who had fire ... he was targeting people I knew. And the guy in the Waffle House? He'd come for me, personally.

Somebody was sending a message to me, loud and clear.

This was war.

19.

Kat

Los Angeles, California

This was the part of California weather that Kat liked best. It was winter but hell if it felt like winter. The day had been in the eighties, and now the temps had fallen with the sun to somewhere in the low seventies. Cool enough she could feel the prickle of it on her skin, but not so cold she'd need to flee the hammock in the backyard of her rented house.

She lay there, under the dark sky, the moon the only visible light, a few clouds passing overhead, and took a slow breath. Her mission was complete, successfully. Her team had done well—sure, Veronika helped keep them on course, but it was Kat's team, really. Reed had made that clear to her. She was pretty content to let Veronika think she was in charge, but Kat knew who the real star was.

She yawned, checked the time on her cell phone. The backyard wasn't exactly expansive, but it was a pretty good size. Palm trees lined it, swaying in the light wind. A few other types of trees were present, too, giving it the feel of a garden oasis. They'd survived the drought, which was nice. Lots of trees, lots of other greenery hadn't. It made Kat so super-sad to think about it.

One of her legs hung over the side of the hammock, brushing the grass beneath with her bare feet. It tickled at her toes, swaying to touch her. It was a neat thing, the way greenery bent for her, bowed to her, wanted to touch her. Like she was a queen, and every seed was one of her subjects.

So here she sat, at four in the morning, ruling over her subjects, her kingdom. Tomorrow they were going to do some filming for her TV show, *Beyond Human*, and ... and ... and ...

Kat let out a lazy sigh. Could life be any better? She did her service with the agency, was making millions with her TV show and associated merch; ratings were way up now that she was back on the job, seemed like people really responded to the metahuman policing procedural format that they'd switched to in the second season.

Yeah. Life was good, and only getting better.

The only downside, she frowned—between the glory of the weather and all the success ...

It was such a little thing, but ...

She couldn't see the stars here. The only ones she saw were the ones at Wolfgang Puck's restaurant or the Four Seasons. Alas.

That was life, though, wasn't it? Tradeoffs. It was all right, though; she had a vacation planned for Anguilla, because she still had to squeeze a little bit of the lux and glamor into her show to provide her fans with that amazing escapist feel, so she'd see the stars again soon enough. She had a private villa booked, and it'd be glory itself, staring up at the stars from the beach, no light pollution to blot them out. She could see Cassiopeia ... Orion ...

Kat blinked; there was a star, albeit ... one she didn't know. It was glowing, right there, faintly in—

Oh. It was moving. Probably just a plane.

No. It was arcing down, toward her.

A nervous tingle ran through Kat's scalp. That ... wasn't a good thing, was it?

She started to get up. The faint glow reminded her of a star—maybe even two, it was hard to say, just that distant glow, like a plane coming in for a landing.

That wasn't a plane, though. It couldn't be. They didn't look like ...

That nervous tingle became a full blown warning, something telling her to move, to seek cover, and she followed that instinct without hesitation, that gut reaction that carried her to the edge of her yard. There was a Moreton Bay fig tree here, and she knew it well, could commune easily with the roots. She sent it a simple request: "Protect me."

It swept down with its branches and scooped her up, bringing her into its enveloping canopy, shrouding with leaves and branches. She lay there in its embrace, held in the sway of the wind, and looked out through the smallest of gaps that it provided.

Something floated down into her field of view, into the back yard, seconds later. She blinked.

It was a man on fire.

He hovered inches off the ground, looking at the back of her rental house. "Katrina!" he called, toward the house ...

He hadn't seen her. Kat didn't dare breathe.

"Katrina!" he called again, at the back of the house, as though speaking to someone within. He waited, long seconds, and then cast a ball of fire at the far end of the structure, landing it on the roof above the garage. It blazed wildly, spreading within seconds to cover the entire thing.

Kat did not dare move, nor speak. She only watched as the roof blazed bright, and the man called, "Katrina!" louder and with increasing fury, adding the occasional, "Come out!" every now and again.

The house burned, sirens wailed. The roof started to collapse, and Kat remained in her hide-out. The heat of the flames wilted the leaves around her, their intensity growing by the minute.

Finally, the man could stand it no longer. He sank to the ground, just for a moment, and turned away from the blaze.

Backlit by the flames, she stared at him. He was but a silhouette against the glowing ochre; frightening, he loomed, a figure in the dark with nothing but malice for her.

Still, she said nothing. Breathed only the shallowest of breaths, wrapped tightly in the embrace of the tree.

She watched him as he turned, his profile exposed. There was no satisfaction there, as he watched the fire blaze. "You are weak," he said, almost so low she couldn't hear it, and then floated off the ground.

With one hand, he reached out to the swimming pool at the back of the house. A motion was all it took; with one hand he snuffed the flames and with the other he commanded the pool water to drown the ashes of the burning house. The hiss of heat exchange overrode the sound of sirens growing closer and closer.

His task done, the man flew into the sky, disappearing out of her view within seconds. She waited a minute, then two.

The fire trucks arrived. She could hear the fireman on the lawn, doing ... whatever it was they would do when they arrived at a house already burned and put out.

Another minute passed, and she could wait no longer. She bade the fig tree to release her, and then she was on the ground, reaching for her cell phone, dialing the number by memory.

What time was it on the east coast?

It didn't matter. He answered, a moment later.

"Reed," Kat said, not waiting for an exchange of pleasantries, and ignoring the thick sound of cottony sleep in his voice, "your guy—the one from the bridge—he just showed up at my rental house and burned it to the ground after trying to call me out. Like, Old West style."

The voice at the other end of the line snapped to instant wakefulness. "What?"

"Yeah," she said, staring at the pillar of black smoke, the glow of the blaze now gone from the LA skyline. "Reed ... I think we've got a problem ..."

20.

I was a buzz of nervous speculation after seeing the news about Veronika. It wasn't helped by the news that came blazing across the wire minutes later:

Kat Forrest rental house burned; fate of starlet remains unknown.

That was the sort of headline that added a further element of sickness to my stomach. I'd promised her damned brother I'd look after her, after all, and it wasn't until the update came in a few minutes later pronouncing her completely fine—Kat was smart enough to hide from this attacker—that I let myself breathe again.

But at this point … it was pretty damned impossible to take this particular sign for anything other than what it seemed to be.

Someone was trying to kill my people.

"Sienna …" Eilish said, breaking a lovely silence in which I was cursing myself, cursing that I was ever born, and cursing lots of other things, too.

"What?" I asked, trying not to let too much of my anxiety loose on her. She hadn't asked for it, and odds were good that, as another of my associates, she was now under threat.

"I was going to say, 'I hope you're not blaming yourself,' but I think we all know that'd be wishing for a unicorn," Eilish said, leaning forward a little tentatively. "Guilt isn't going to make you feel any better."

"Oh, who cares if I feel better?" I asked.

"Not I," Cassidy said, still browsing the web. When I gave her a frown, she shrugged. "What? I just want you to kill this guy. Whether you feel great or terrible in the process is immaterial to me. Unless feeling good helps you kill him more efficiently, in which case … would you like me to get you some sort of mood elevator from a local pharmacy?"

"I wouldn't mind one," Harry said. "Things are getting a little down around here."

"All I want is some scotch," I said, watching another sign for Nashville pass me by. "Is that too much to ask?"

"At this hour on a Sunday in Nashville? Yeah, probably," Harry said.

"Oh, I always wanted to see Music City," Eilish said, bouncing a little in her seat.

"We're working, we're not here to do touristy shit," I said, gloom and doom settling over me. "I need a drink, you know, to keep functioning, that's all. Maybe in Kentucky—" I soured and stopped talking when I caught Harry subtly shaking his head. "Well, shit."

"Pretty sure this is the actual definition of alcoholism," Eilish said, but she didn't sound too judgmental about it.

"While you're doing definitions, you should look up 'nosey,'" I said.

"As in, sticking in your nose in the business of others?" she asked.

"As in, 'You're about to get popped in the,'" I said.

"Oh." She sat back, conveniently out of my reach. "Irritability is another sign of alcoholism."

"Leave the diagnoses to the properly trained clinicians, will you?" I sat facing forward, watching the green hills roll up and down in front of me. So these were the hills of Tennessee? Not bad. Even I could see that in my somewhat aggravated state. That pissiness thing, though, it was like an itch under my skin I just couldn't wait to scratch. "I miss flying," I said, trying to make it sound innocuous so someone—Eilish—wouldn't see the rake I'd set up until she stepped on it.

"I bet," Eilish said, right on cue. "The wind in your hair,

on your cheeks—all that. I bet it was grand."

"Yeah, that was great, too," I said. "But I mostly miss not having to be stuck in a car with a bunch of yahoos who are either wittingly or unwittingly trying to get me killed."

That shut them all up, which was kind of the point. I was on a simmer, heading toward a hard boil. I didn't need this shit; my team was being attacked on the West Coast, my known associates had been attacked in New York City and—technically—Virginia, though I didn't much want to be associated with Eric Simmons or his egghead-yet-idiotic girlfriend.

All I wanted was to sit on the damned beach in Florida and drink my effing drink. Was that too much to—?

Harry swerved hard, taking us off on a sudden exit next to a rest area sign he'd almost passed. Cassidy gasped, catching her laptop before it slid off her lap, and Eilish made a kind of merping noise you might normally associate with a too-cute CGI creature in a modern sci-fi movie.

For my part, I just hung on and looked daggers at Harry. "What the hell was that?"

"I apologize, ladies," Harry said, guiding us into the rest area and pulling up in an isolated parking space toward the front of the lot. There was an old bathroom building to our rear and a sprawling scape of green space in front of us complete with picnic areas. The sun was starting to rise, and a few big semi trucks were pulling in, probably to bed down for the day. The parking lot was speckled with cars, people taking a few minutes to use the bathrooms and stretch their legs.

And here we sat, pulling in as Harry threw the car into park and then looked at me. "A word, please." Then he got out and slammed his door behind him.

"I don't think it's just going to be one word," Eilish said. "I've got to go to the loo again, though, how about you?"

"Yep," Cassidy said, opening her own door. "Enjoy your ass chewing, Sienna." And they were gone.

I was just sitting in the passenger seat, steaming. Harry Graves was going to chew my ass? After trying to feed me to the Terminator without a word of warning?

Cassidy had seriously misapprehended whose ass was going to get ripped a new one. I got out of the car and slammed my own door, causing the SUV to wobble. I took my sweet time and went around to the rear of the hatchback, opening it and fetching a Snickers bar. I opened it and took a bite, thinking to hell with Eilish and her failure to appreciate great chocolate.

I took my time, glancing between the seats and up ahead at Harry, who waited patiently on the grass in front of the SUV, like he had all day. He knew by probability when I was likely to be done making him wait, so he probably also knew his failure to react was driving me slightly nuts.

Or maybe he just knew my patience was bound to run out soon, because it did. So I slammed the hatchback and headed off down the slope at the edge of the parking lot and down the rolling green park space to where he waited.

"What the hell do you want?" I asked, figuring niceties were unnecessary. He'd seen that coming a mile away, I was sure, since my skin was crawling and I was so irritable I would have gladly battered his head around just to relieve some of my building stress.

"Peace on earth and good will toward men and women," Harry said with a lazy sigh, slight smile on his face. "But since I am unlikely to receive that gift anytime soon short of some sort of apocalypse that leaves everyone dead, I'll settle for extracting that chip from your shoulder."

"It's a mighty big chip, Harry," I said, pausing to trash my candy wrapper in a conveniently placed garbage can by one of the picnic tables. "I'm not sure you have the strength to lift it."

"Oh, it's huge," Harry said. "Why, I'd say it's the approximate weight of the world—or it used to be. Now it's just a big piece of rock with the words 'Sienna Nealon's Emotional Baggage' written all over it. Same weight, less responsibility."

I narrowed my eyes at him. "Can you read your own survival percentages? Because I calculate they're dropping with every word you speak."

"Nope," he said cheerfully. "That's the thing about being a Cassandra; I can't read my own future."

"I'm no seer, but I'm starting to guess there's going to be a lot of pain and tooth loss in it very soon."

"But I can see yours clear as the nose on your face," he said, turning his back to me. Probably figured I wouldn't hit him like that. He was probably right. Probably. "I know what's going to happen to you now, what's going to happen next—don't get me wrong, it branches, but there are some definite, external events in your future that … well, they push you back on a defined track in spite of all the uncertainty that comes between."

He looked over his shoulder at me. "And this, Sienna … is one of those events."

I scoffed at him. "Your fortune telling sucks, Harry. If you knew so much about my damned future at a distance, why didn't I see your ass in Scotland? Seems to me that whole thing must have caught you by surpr—"

I stopped when I saw the look on his face, because it was unlike anything I'd quite seen from the freewheeling Harry Graves … ever before.

It was guilt.

"You knew," I said, little chills running down the back of my neck. "You read me before, either in Chicago or when we were fighting Harmon. You … you knew what was going to happen to me in Scotland." I took a step closer to him, and he stayed still, looking out at the sky, refusing to look at me.

I saw it anyway. Guilt was a unique expression to Harry Graves; I guessed he didn't wear it often.

"Reed said he tried to get ahold of you, through Veronika," I said, blinking at him. "You knew what I was walking into in Scotland, you knew about—"

"Rose," Harry said, a little hoarsely, and it sounded like agreement. "Yes. I knew about Rose. Sort of."

"And you let me walk into—into *that*—anyway?" My voice went low, raspy, too, and I was suddenly anchored to the spot. I wanted to leap forward, to grab him by the throat—sincerely, this time—and shake him until he answered.

"Yes," he said softly.

I took a staggering, unplanned step back instead. "…

Why?" I felt weak, dazed, like Rose had just clobbered me over the head. Which was ridiculous; I'd shredded her brains with a bullet and we'd burned her body to ash. Her days of hitting me, touching me—of ripping me apart—were done.

"I don't know if I could properly explain to you the shape of the future," Harry said, blinking, "but I'll try. I saw Rose coming, yes, much like I saw Mr. Shadowpuncher—"

"I really prefer, 'Mr. Waffle-Interruptus' or 'the Terminator,' if you must."

"I don't think the 'Waffle-Interruptus' one is going to catch on," Harry said, "but yes ... I saw Rose coming like I saw him coming." He took a couple steps away from me, and I couldn't decide if he was sad-pacing or just stepping out of my punching range. "And messing with someone's future beyond a few seconds ... it gets complicated. You remember in Chicago, I told you—"

"The world of metahumans was going to end," I said.

He nodded. "That anytime I saw someone like us ... it was like a doomsday clock hanging over their head. Don't get me wrong, I see those every day, because people die every day. But in this case.." He shrugged. "Let's just say, I saw that ... for everyone ... coming from Scotland. In the not too distant future. The probability was rising before you went over there. Now ..." He shrugged. "It's gone. That doom is over."

I turned my head so as not to look at him. "My ... souls ... told me before they ... died," That was a hard word to say, "... that Rose wouldn't stop with me." I clenched my eyes shut. "I guess they were right."

"They were right," Harry said. "Let's say I tipped you off earlier? Warned you about trouble in Edinburgh?" He shook his head. "Every single instance I looked at ... you would have died if you interrupted her game before she was ready to play with you. She would have killed you and just been done with it."

"Proving once again that supervillains shouldn't play with their food," I said quietly. "The Scott Evil approach is best."

"I don't really know what that means, and I'm totally fine with you not explaining—oh, movie reference, got it," he said. "Never heard of Austin Powers before, hm." He shook his head. "This is the danger with warning about the future, with messing with time." He walked a little closer to me, and his eyes were sincere and intense and bright. Striking.

Kinda maybe a little … pretty.

"… every action has consequences," Harry said, grave as his surname might suggest but which in practice he seldom was. "I can read the probabilities, but I can't tell you the definites because the moment I do—they stop being definite because time and choice are slippery things. If I'd sent you off to Scotland with Rose's name and the danger she posed the moment I saw her in your future—saw what she was going to do to you—your survival odds went to zero. Believe that. Just the same as if I took us any other road but this one, on this trip, trying to avoid this so-called 'Terminator' you just ran across."

I pushed my hands against my forehead. "Dammit, Harry," I said, putting pressure on my scalp. "I hate this. I hate—"

"You hate the fact that my mere existence makes you feel even less in control of your life than usual, lately," Harry said, and here his smile turned … comforting. "I don't blame you for that."

"Good, because *I* get to throw the blame right now. It's my damned turn after getting my ass kicked."

"I'm just asking you to trust me," he said.

"I thought you were coming because you needed my help?" I stared him down.

"I do need your help," he said. "I have a unique problem and you are the only one that's going to be able to solve it."

I just stared at him, feeling a little ragged. "And that is …?"

"Not yet," he said, wagging a finger at me. "Besides, you have a little more steam to let out at me."

I paused; I'd been about to tear into him again for not being a little more forthcoming on at least what kind of help he expected from me, but that took me aback. "Dammit, Harry," I said, because he'd totally caught me off guard and pre-empted my assault.

He grinned. "I know. But I don't like being yelled by you any more than—well, anyone. I don't thrive on it, see, so I avoid it when possible. Your ire, I mean."

"You're doing a pretty shitty job of it so far."

"I'll work on improving my game as time goes by," Harry said, looking out over the green, sloping hills where the park led down to endless trees. "But ... about what you were going to say to me ..." He glanced sideways at me. "You know you're not yourself lately."

I rolled my eyes. "Duh."

"You know you're not going to beat the bad guys like this. In your current frame of mind."

"Oh, are you my fight coach now?" I asked, now irritable once more.

"You could do worse." He grinned again.

I threw a punch, he dodged it. Another, he dodged it. Three more, a kick, then a spin kick—wobbly, because my balance was pretty crap after months of no practice.

He turned back every attack, naturally.

"You know, I've killed a Cassandra with my bare hands before," I said, staring him down.

"You've killed a lot of people with your bare hands." He sounded distinctly amused. "I'm not going to be one of them."

"I thought you couldn't read your own future?"

I came at him again, twice as furious. I was a little faster than he was, but I played careful. The last time I'd fought a Cassandra had been on a rooftop, and he—Phillip Delsim—hadn't been particularly skilled at hand-to-hand. Harry wasn't that skilled, either, but he was more practiced, though a hair slower than I would have expected. He turned every attack aside but missed every opportunity to counter me and strike a blow of his own.

Then he spun me around and slapped me—extremely gently—on the belly, which told me he was choosing to pass up on those opportunities, not just watching them sail by unnoticed.

I redoubled my efforts and soon I was wheezing, breathing heavily from the fury of the attacks I was throwing.

He caught my last kick. "That's enough. Someone's about to look." And he let my leg go.

I doubled over, trying to catch my breath. "Gee, thanks ... sensei ..."

"You've had a little time to wallow," he said, standing upright next to me. "But that's not you. What would Sienna Nealon do?"

"Sienna Nealon is ... going to kick your ass here in a second," I wheezed, "as soon as ... whoever is looking is ... done doing so."

"Keep going like this for another thirty seconds and you'll be heaving up that candy bar," Harry said. "It's enough for now. We'll work on your cardio more later. Cassidy and Eilish are waiting at the car."

"Let them wait," I said, pushing myself back up. "You asked what Sienna Nealon would do?" I looked out over the trees, taking a few steps away from Harry to turn my back on him. I just stopped talking there.

"Yeah?" he asked.

"Sorry, figured you read my answer ahead," I said.

"I did," Harry said, easing in behind me. "But this conversation is not just about me."

"It's not?" I played coy. I liked playing coy. Unless it involved dressing up as a giant goldfish. (Yes, I know it's spelled koi, don't be a douchebag about my lame puns.)

"It's about the fact you sent your friend Dr. Zollers away without so much as a hearing," Harry said. "It's about that bottle you keep hiding in."

"You want me to talk it out?" I was still breathing heavily, my skin chilled with the perspiration beneath my clothes. "Are you my therapist now, too?"

"Well, you sent your real one away," he said. "So ... yeah. Lucky me, getting to crack open that delicate Sienna shell."

I just stood there, staring at the trees. "The Sienna shell got pretty well cracked already, Harry."

A pause. "I know."

"'What would Sienna Nealon do?'" I asked quietly into the morning. I waited for a response.

None came.

"No, really, Harry ... what would I do?" I asked, turning to look at him as he came up to my shoulder. I was being earnest. "I honestly don't—there's so much I don't remember anymore. Reed and I will be having a conversation and he'll tell me about this time, doing something—there was a mission in Colorado we went on together, and he mentioned something about it and laughed—I just ... I couldn't remember anything about it." Little cold prickles fell down my arms, down my shoulders. "Harry ... there are holes in my head, in my mind." I looked back at the woods. "So when I ask you ... 'What would Sienna Nealon do?' it's not me being funny, or playing—"

"I know," he said softly.

"I really don't know anymore," I said, my shoulders shaking. "I don't know what she took—don't even know what I'm missing—just that—there's so much gone, Harry ..." It wasn't the chill that had me shaking, but he steadied me with an arm. "I wake up in the night and—and I don't—" I let out a gentle sob, and then one that was not nearly so gentle.

"... And I don't know who I am ..." I said, as he put an arm around me, taking me into his embrace. "I swear to God, Harry ... there are days ... nights when I wake up ... when I don't even know who I am anymore ..."

"I know," he said, taking hold of me and letting me shake, letting me pour the tears out on his shoulder, hot, wet, sliding down my face. "I know. But I promise you," he said, after a few minutes like that, just holding me while I cried, "that I'm with you ... and I will show you—again—exactly who Sienna Nealon is ... by the time this is all done." I could hear the smile in his voice, and it gave me just the slightest breath of hope. "And the world ... they're going to remember, too."

21.

"I have to talk to my brother," I said, once we were a few miles down the road. "But he's not going to be sleeping right now."

The sun was rising, the horizon brightening as it rose to our right. We were heading north, almost to Nashville, Harry at the wheel. I assumed he knew what he was doing.

"Sounds like a phone call is in order," Eilish said.

"The problem with the phone is—" I started.

"The NSA will be listening to his calls," Cassidy interjected, "hoping to catch a whiff of you. That's why he assembled the team to come to Scotland almost entirely in person."

"Exactly," I said. "So I need a way to talk to him that isn't going to trip their alarms."

"Who cares if it trips their alarm, so long as it doesn't lead back to you and definitely incriminate him?" Eilish said after a minute. "After all, it's not what they know, it's what they can prove."

"Spoken like a true criminal," Cassidy said, but she wasn't sneering, she was more … calculating. "If you just want to talk to him and you don't care if they hear, you could call with a voice scrambler on. It's what I use when I need to hide my identity. I even have a program on my computer that can handle it. Couple that with a little call origin bouncing—I could set up a phone call with him that could last at least a few minutes without the NSA tracing it back to us here."

"Interesting," I said, though I was really feeling a sense of stark terror. I looked to my left and sure enough, Harry was white-knuckling the steering wheel. He caught me looking and nodded once, which I took to be an affirmation of the fear I was thinking but barely daring to say.

If I called my brother now, even with the voice scrambler, the NSA, the government—the interested investigative parties—would have enough reason to be suspicious that they'd probably start watching him a little more carefully.

Which meant he could no longer hang out on the Gulf of Mexico with me and escape notice.

Which meant ... if I made this call, I was saying goodbye to seeing Reed, in person, for the foreseeable future.

I took a deep breath. There was this kind of warring clash within me. Why was this so hard?

That clinging desire to sit on the patio at my rented condo, stare out at the blue waters while inebriating myself to the point of numbness ... I was having a hard time letting go of it.

What else did I have to look forward to?

Oh, right. Getting punched in a Waffle House, getting dragged off to jail or somewhere else, and just generally enjoying the feeling of crawling through broken glass in order to try and return to some semblance of feeling normal—whatever that was before all the scotch and memory loss.

"I've carved out a real wonderful life for myself," I muttered.

"Not exactly George Bailey, are you?" Harry said with a slight smile. "But yeah ... you've made some friends."

"They're all great," I said, "but it's my enemies that have driven me harder down this path. Still ..." I sighed.

Something in me felt like someone had grabbed my heart and squeezed tight, with meta strength, every time I thought about just giving up and going back to Florida to be alone with my scotch and maybe the occasional margarita. You know, to break the monotony of scotch.

I didn't want to leave this fiery asshole flying around, wrecking my friends. And I didn't want to leave the

Terminator rolling around out there, either, doing who knew what besides attacking innocent—well, okay, "innocent" was a strong word, but still—girls in search of waffles.

That told me a little something about myself, something I hadn't actually forgotten, but that had gotten buried under a few months of rust. "I need to make this call," I said. "Set it up, please, Cassidy."

"Wow, that's brave," Eilish said, "cutting yourself off from your brother when he's been helping you all this time. I mean, you'll probably have to stop using his company credit cards after this, too, won't you?"

I clenched my teeth. Hadn't thought of that. "Yes," I said. "I suppose I will. So I hope you've got some gas money, Cassidy, because the revenge portion of this mission is going to require you to pay the daily expenses."

Cassidy shrugged. "I can float you some basic expenses, but nothing outlandish."

"And here I was hoping to R&D a full working replica of an Iron Man suit to use to destroy my enemies now that I'm more vulnerable."

Cassidy's brow creased, folding in thought. "You don't seem the type."

"Well, desperation does crazy things," I said. "The call?"

"Give me a couple minutes," she said, and went to pecking away at her laptop.

Eilish took the opportunity afforded by the silence to pipe up, as usual. "So … this us done with the condo in Florida, then?"

My jaw tightened. "Yep." I found her presence suddenly so annoying, and I couldn't place my finger quite on why. She'd been around for months, sure, but that wasn't it. She was always snarking, and not really doing anything useful. She'd been helpful in Scotland, no doubt, but as I sensed her behind me, all I could feel was irritated.

What the hell was Eilish even doing here? Why had she followed me back from Scotland once that was all done? She could have been dropped off in London or Ireland or wherever, but …

Instead she was following me, and suddenly I was really

annoyed about all the baggage I was picking up on this trip. Like I didn't have enough going on without managing this Irish girl when I was already incredibly irritable. I wasn't exactly a world-renowned diplomat, but that wasn't a formula for anything good.

"Just as well," Eilish said. "I was a bit tired of sun and sand and—I don't know, whatever you want to call that wintery mess that you have on that coast. I mean, don't get me wrong, it was a bit like summer back home, but still … if I'm to spend time on the beach, I'd like it to be a warm one."

"Well," I said, a little tightly, trying not to let my irritation with Eilish consume me, "it's about to get hot for us, so … I guess you get half your wish."

I heard her gulp, then Cassidy said, "Okay. I'm ready." And then she tossed me something.

I caught it and only then opened my palm to see what she'd thrown. It was a small Bluetooth headset, and when I looked at her, she nodded, so I put it on. It fit in my ear and had a very tiny boom mic that extended about halfway down my cheek. It didn't fit very well, and I couldn't shake the feeling that it was going to fall out at a critical juncture during my call.

"Sound check," Cassidy said.

"Uhmmm … scotch?" I asked.

"Microphone is functioning normally. Let me know if you can't hear the ringing." Her head was back down, focused on the laptop.

"What ringing?" I asked, and then a second later I heard it. "Oh." It was a telephone ring, in my ear.

A moment later, there was a click as someone picked up. "Hello?" My brother's voice was taut.

I paused for a second as I debated the best way to approach this. Hopefully the voice scrambler would be in place already. I glanced at Cassidy and she nodded, so I said, "Hey, bro."

My voice came out sounding absolutely terrible, like a garbage disposal trying to grind up a tin can.

"Who is this?" Reed asked, sounding somewhere between suspicious and appalled at the tenor of my voice. It was pretty bad.

"It's me, bro," I said. "Come on, catch up. You can't sit around all day trying to think your way through this like Rodin's statue."

"S—what the …?" I could tell he got it. "What happened to your voice?"

"Been gargling rock salt," I said. "Does wonders for my vocal range. Listen, I only have a few minutes." Cassidy helped up two fingers. "You heard about Kat and Veronika?"

He hesitated. "Are you out of your mind, doing this? I mean—are you freaking kidding me?"

"Focus, focus," I said.

"Yes," he seethed, "of course I heard about Kat and Veronika. Kat's fine, by the way. And Veronika …" His voice trailed off.

"Yeah …?"

"We don't know yet," he said. "Just like Jamie Barton, she's been … worked over. She may make it, she may not, depending on how well her meta healing abilities kick in." He picked up a little steam now. "Why are you calling me?"

"I kinda got bushwhacked," I said, figuring it wouldn't do to lie. I also figured that if they hadn't worked it out already, the government was going to get the picture about the Waffle House incident quickly, but I felt no need to tie that to this call, mostly for evidentiary purposes. "I'm in motion, and, uh … back in the game."

"For f—no, no." I could envision him shaking his head on the other end of the phone. "You should be—safe." Conducting this conversation was like trying to fight with one had behind your back. He couldn't say the things he wanted to say, and neither could I.

"Safe's a relative term these days," I said. "Jamie Barton probably thought she was safe heading across the harbor. Veronika definitely thought she was safe at her own house. Are you noticing a pattern with these attacks yet, Reed?"

I bet his jaw was just chock full of tension. "I noticed the pattern." Which was me, of course.

"Then you know 'safe' is an illusion right now," I said.

"Besides, there's another player who's come off the bench. Not sure if they're related. I'm sure you'll get deets soon."

"Look," he said, "none of this is conclusive. We can speculate about the connection between these ... victims," he seemed loathe to say it, and almost ground the word out between his teeth like chewed cud, "but there's no definite, final piece of evidence that says, 'Hey, I'm targeting the known associates of'—well, you know."

"Hey," I heard a voice in the background say. It was Augustus. "They spotted our guy in Minneapolis. Wheels up in ten."

There was a long pause on the other end of the line. "Shit," Reed said at last.

I glanced at Cassidy; she had a single finger extended, then lowered it. She mouthed, "Thirty seconds," and I nodded. "Starting to sound like that connection is firming up," I said, ignoring that grinding metal sound of my voice being scrambled. "Who goes to Minneapolis in January if they can avoid it?"

"It's still not definite," he said, but dear God, was he a shit liar.

"Sounds pretty definite to me," I said.

"Please," Reed said, "let us handle it. I'm bringing everyone we've got left. This guy is going down. There's no reason to—to expand the scenario to include undue risk to ... other parties."

"That's the sweetest thing anyone's said to me in years," I said, pretty dryly. "But you know that's not how it works." And by 'it,' I meant ... well, me. Even with everything in a haze, I could recall that much about myself.

Bench sitter? That was not Sienna Nealon.

"I know," he said, and there was so much tension in his voice that if he'd had a wooden spoon clenched between his butt cheeks right now, the handle would have snapped. Because meta strength, of course. Yeah, we had super-powered gluts. It was all part of the meta package.

"So ... this is kinda goodbye for a while, I think." I tried not to sound too choked up because, scrambled as my voice was, it'd probably sound like a trash compactor crushing a metal garbage can. Or a Transformer making love to a steel beam. Horrible, either way.

"Sounds like it," he said, and man, did I feel the regret. "You know you can call me anytime. One way or another." Subtle reference to dreamwalking. So subtle it couldn't be used against him in court if he ever got charged with aiding and abetting me. My brother was a smart man.

"I know," I said. "Same goes—a little differently, though."

"Just ... stand back, please." He was begging. "Let us handle it."

"You'll have a little bit of time before I insert the risk into this scenario, or whatever the hell you said earlier." I felt a lump in my throat, like I'd swallowed my own fist. "Take care of yourself, Reed. And the others, too."

"Will do. Hopefully, after today ... you can go seek out some other exotic locale and just chill for a while. Job done." He sounded pretty confident. "And either way ... I hope I see you soon. Somehow."

"Me t—" I started to answer, but the line clicked dead. I looked back and saw Cassidy nod. She'd killed it at the buzzer.

I took the headset off and wordlessly handed it back to her. "Harry ..." I said.

"Minneapolis bound, I know," he said softly. "We'll take I-65 north through Kentucky, then make our through western Illinois. It's about thirteen hours from here if we drive straight through."

"Let's drive straight through, then," I said, and stared at the road ahead. The sun was rising to my right, and the city of Nashville was ahead.

And somewhere, thirteen hours beyond it, was Minneapolis and St. Paul, the Twin Cities of Minnesota.

Home.

I was going home.

And the thought that I wasn't going to make it nearly in time for Reed and his battle with this metahuman who'd been attacking my friends and associates destroyed any of the joy I might have felt at the prospect of seeing home again.

22.

"Where are we?" I asked as Harry guided the car into a rest area a couple hours later. I shouldn't have bothered asking, because as soon as I did, I saw a sign on the rest area roofline—"Welcome to Kentucky," and it had one of those information booths visible inside the glass front of the building, just like any visitors center when you crossed a state line.

I'd completely missed our entry into the Bluegrass State, and our exit from Tennessee. It might have been nice, under other circumstances, to just enjoy a road trip like this.

But when a deadly metahuman was pursuing your friends, and they were heading into a confrontation with the bastard, it was hard to pay much attention to the natural wonders of America. My mind was on kicking ass and taking names.

Well, hopefully kicking ass and taking names. Getting your ass kicked and your name taken didn't really bear dwelling on.

Harry slid the SUV into a parking space and shifted it into park. He blinked a few times, moving at a pretty slow clip for him but still incredibly fast compared to most humans. He rubbed his eyes a couple times, and I realized that it was getting toward noon, and he'd been driving all night.

He threw open the door just as Cassidy did the same behind him. Eilish opened hers behind me, and I got out as well. We all looked a little stiff, given that we hadn't stopped since the ass kicking back near the Alabama line. I looked at

Eilish; she was probably bruised beneath her clothes, unless her meta healing was stronger than I supposed. She walked a little more gingerly than the rest of us, though she moved quicker than Cassidy, who just freaking dragged.

Cassidy had been on her computer for most of our drive, not saying a word. That was common in the car, the silence, for which I was generally thankful. The loudest noise was the slightly labored breathing of Eilish over what I guessed was a cracked rib or two. My assumption was that by tomorrow she'd be a hundred percent, but again, I didn't fully know her healing capabilities.

"I wish I could sleep more," Eilish said as we entered the rest area. A couple women were behind the counter in the visitor's booth, one smiling and facing us as we came in, another talking to a guy in a flannel shirt with a baseball hat on. She seemed to be giving him the tourist spiel, and was handing him brochures about the natural wonders of Kentucky, which I listened to with one ear while dragging myself toward the restroom, my tiredness far out of proportion with my day's efforts.

"Sleeping just wastes the day," I said with a healthy serving of sarcasm. Like we could waste the day any more effectively than sitting our asses in a car.

"I'm going to need to waste some of the day here when we get back in the car," Harry said, pulling away from us to head to the men's room, which lay to our right. "Decide among yourselves who wants to drive."

I looked at Eilish; Eilish looked at me. She shrugged, and I started to look at Cassidy, but she'd already disappeared into the women's room, seriously dragging ass. "I'm injured," Eilish said, suddenly favoring her side more dramatically.

I started to argue, then just shook my head. "Fine, I'll drive," I said. Might as well; it may have been a while, but it was probably like riding a bike. Hopefully Rose hadn't sucked the memory of how to do so out of my head.

Eilish held the door for me, cringing at the movement. I ducked into the bathroom and found a row of stalls. There must have been twenty of them, and fortunately less than half were occupied, so I picked one and in I went. It certainly smelled better than that gas station.

Once done, I came out and washed my hands, looking at myself in the mirror. Everything seemed to be about where I left it. Hair? Still bad, mussy and messed, cowlicked where I'd slept on the window. The blond notes were starting to fade, allowing my darker roots to show through. I had a couple centimeters before I'd have to deal with that, though I was sure a reasonably tall guy could already see them pretty clearly.

My face still looked haggard. The dark circles hadn't grown but hadn't receded, either. My throat looked skinny, and I tried to assess myself as an enemy would. It just made me look like a prey animal, being this thin, like someone could grab me by that neck and snap it with so much greater ease than they could have before, when I was ... sturdier. The fact that my double chin had completely evaporated should have made me look so much hotter.

But instead I just looked ... dead. Even after three months of regular feeding, of sleeping in a warm bed instead of wherever I could find a sheltered spot, of being in the same place rather than being run all over the Scottish countryside, I still looked ...

Skeletal. Like I'd left a quarter of my body weight along with my memories. I looked to either side; there was no one out of the stalls. I lifted my shirt and yep, I could still see my ribs.

Needless to say, this was not something I checked very often, even in the privacy of my own bathroom. Avoidance was key to my strategy of ... well, avoiding my problems.

My wrists were like little tubes, and when I lifted my pants legs, my shins and knees were bony and exposed. I wore slightly less baggy clothes now, but I still swam inside them.

"Holy shit," I whispered to myself. I could eat a thousand waffles and I wasn't sure it'd make a dent in this ... this ...

I didn't even have a word for it.

"Whew," Cassidy said, the sound of her stall unlocking filling the air just before she popped out and hit the sink next to me, splashing cold water on her face. Eilish joined us a moment later, taking the sink on the other side of me. The

Irish woman still looked sour, but when Cassidy came up from her splashing, she looked—

Uh.

Positively chipper.

"I feel great," Cassidy announced, mopping her face with paper towels. The cadence of her speech was lightspeed compared to where it had been when we'd entered the bathroom a moment earlier. I stared at her skinny frame, which ... shit, I looked thin compared to her, which rang like an alarm bell in my head. She mopped quickly and delicately at her forehead, and then under her eyes, no makeup coming off on the towel because ... well, she didn't wear any. "It's a beautiful day," she announced, staring at herself in the mirror, and for a second I thought she might lean forward and kiss her own reflection. She seemed to think better of that, though, probably calculating the bacteria per square inch on a rest area bathroom mirror, and out she went, humming something awfully jaunty.

"Didn't she just lose the love of her life a day or so ago?" Eilish asked, watching her with brow furrowed.

"Yep," I said. "Didn't she just enter that bathroom stall looking like death itself was about to claim her?"

Eilish threw me a look, one which turned frozen quickly, and I caught the significance: *You're one to talk about looking like death,* that was what she was thinking. But she said: "Uh, yeah."

I analyzed all the available data and came to a quick conclusion. "Shit," I said.

"Yeah," Eilish said again. "What do you reckon?"

"Amphetamines," I whispered, meta-low, in case there was a random narc hanging out in one of the occupied stalls. "I reckon amphetamines in some form."

"Should we say something to her?" Eilish asked, pushing the water on and rinsing her hands. She, too, was speaking meta-low.

I laughed, and it came out short and super bitter. "I don't think I can deal with the irony of me hosting an intervention for anyone else right now," I said. "Besides, her ... whatever ... is none of my business."

"Hey, amphetamines are serious business," Eilish said. "I had a friend who died from them."

"They're truly terrible," I agreed, "for humans. Which Cassidy is not. And it's not like she smoked them, so—I dunno. This doesn't sound like my problem."

"A fine friend you are," Eilish said, looking at me in the mirror, the disappointment thick.

"In case it escaped your notice," I said, looking right back, "Cassidy is not my friend. Cassidy is someone I had pay ten million dollars to in order to help me out of a life-threatening jam when all my friends showed up for free. Now I owe her a favor, and she's dragging me out of my—I dunno, hibernation—to collect. If you think this favor I owe her includes worrying excessively about her consumption of illegal drugs that may not even adversely affect her function? You'd be wrong. That is way outside my purview." I shifted my gaze back to my skeletal self in the mirror. "Besides … I think I've got other things to worry about right now."

"Yeah, worry about yourself, I guess," Eilish snapped. "I'm starting to see you're quite good at that." And she stormed out before I could offer anything but a sputtering reply, leaving me alone with my reflection, the girl in the mirror a stark reminder that not only should I feel like I was alone in this, but that I wasn't even truly myself right now …

If I could actually remember who I really was.

23.

"You figure out who's going to drive?" Harry asked me, catching me in front of the tourist counter. He'd just been leaning there, studiously ignoring the attentive stare of the lady waiting behind it, who looked hopeful that he might ask her some question about Kentucky that she could jump in and answer.

"I guess it's me," I said, glancing at the woman behind the counter as Harry pulled out of his lean and favored her with a winning smile that she returned as I frowned. She looked to be about twice his age, but he gave her the full charm, even though he was clearly sleepy, and headed for the door as she watched, leaving me to catch up.

"Good choice," he said as we went through the door. "Because the Irish gal will eventually take us into the wrong lane, and Miss Brainy-jumpy … well …"

"Yeah, she's got a problem," I said, and he gave me a sympathetic smile. "What the hell was that about?" I inclined my head back toward the rest area door as we stepped out into the brisk day. No snow on the ground, but the grass was all brown and the sky had clouded over.

"With the lady behind the counter?" he gave me a smile now. "I got her to focus on me, because if she'd looked at you for two more seconds, she would have recognized you and dropped a dime on us."

"Oh." I didn't stop, just kept walking with Harry as he meandered slightly right, taking us across a stretch of brown, winter-dormant grass. "What about now?" I asked, wondering why we were wandering a strange circuit, currently heading away from the car.

"Oh, I just wanted to stretch my legs for a minute," he said. I kept following him as we crested a very small hill and started back toward the sidewalk that ran the length of the parking lot and would, eventually, lead us back to our SUV. "Though I can't pretend it doesn't have an added benefit."

"Which is?"

"There's a man in a car over there who'd fawn all over you—quietly—if he recognizes you. Big supporter, big fan." He nodded at a run-down station wagon with Illinois plates. I could see the guy he was talking about, dressed up in a fleece pullover and with close-cropped blond hair. "He doesn't believe the media line about you."

I stared at him, blissfully unaware that his hero—me, apparently—was watching him from less than twenty yards away. It was a weird feeling, knowing things about people that didn't have the first clue that you knew of them. "He's one of the few, I guess. Does that make him crazy?"

"Or at least a particular kind of 'woke,' maybe, in the parlance of our times," Harry said.

"Figures you'd be a fan of *The Big Lebowski*," I muttered.

"The wh—oh, it's a movie," Harry said. "Never seen it."

"That's a shame. You'd like it. The Dude abides."

Harry paused, stared off into the distance. "Hm. I will like it."

I frowned. "I thought you couldn't read your own future?"

He kept walking slowly back toward the car. "You're going to want to keep the speed at seventy or lower. Any higher and you'll catch the wrong kind of attention."

"Hey, Harry?" I asked, and he paused. "Should I, uh … do anything about Cassidy?"

He took a little breath, like even the guy who could see the future was uncertain. "Eventually," he said. "You'll know when to say something and when to do something."

"That's … super not helpful advice."

"It'll be helpful when you actually need the help, which you don't yet," Harry said, continuing his walk. "You ever hear the proverb about manna from heaven?"

"My mom wasn't big on religion," I said, falling in step next to him. "That may have come from being raised by the original Valkyrie, who actually knew gods."

"Your view on religion is immaterial, it's a good story," Harry said, as we passed the car. I raised a hand to point, since Eilish and Cassidy were lingering outside, absorbing some of the not-so-lovely weather. Eilish shot me a questioning look as we went by; Cassidy was again buried in her laptop, on the hood of the SUV, humming something very quietly. I couldn't tell for sure, but it sounded a lot like "The Girl From Ipanema." But at a very high tempo.

"Oh, yeah?" I asked, trying to focus on what Harry was telling me.

"Yeah," he said. "See, God provides food—manna—every day to the Israelites when they're in the desert. It just appears, tons of it, enough to feed them for the day. The anxious among them would gather more, but it would rot by the morning. And the next day, boom, more manna on the ground."

He stopped, and I stopped with him. "Lovely story," I said. "I'm sure you told it for a reason."

"My powers, the way I am … I'm like manna from heaven," Harry said, with a grin that was nowhere in the ballpark of humble. "I'll tell you what you need to know, when you need to know it. Let's not overcomplicate this."

I sighed. "Harry … admittedly I don't know the background of that story, being only passingly familiar with it, but here's what I see—those people were dependent on their god for food. Which is fine, if it's your loving god who has led you out of slavery or whatever and is steering you toward—was it the promised land? I really don't know. Anyway, you, I do not worship—"

"You could start any time, I won't mind." Damn, how he was grinning.

"You, I do not trust. Not to feed me—because I still haven't gotten my waffle—"

"But you're fed!"

"I can only eat so many Snickers bars before even my meta

metabolism carb crashes, Harry. Anyway, forgive me for not, y'know, bowing and trusting you to dole out the information I need. Those people were not in charge of their own destiny, they were kept, because that's what you do to dependents. You keep them in food, in clothing, in whatever they need." I stared him down. "You control the supply of information so they make the choices you want them to make. You don't give them any agency that way, and me, Harry? I make my own choices, okay? Have since—"

"Since the day you walked out the door of your own house, I know," he said. "But you've had people controlling that flow of information the whole time."

"Not by my choice," I said.

"Yeah, by your choice," he said. "By your choice to associate with them." He leaned in a little. "If you hadn't overheard where Reed was going next, do you believe for one minute he would have told you to go to Minneapolis?"

I started to reflexively say "yes" and then I bit my tongue.

Because the answer was not only "No," it was "*Hell* no." Reed would not have told me that trouble was heading to Minneapolis. He would have let me find that one out on the news whenever the clash happened.

"Even your brother controls the flow of information to you," Harry said. "This is what we do as humans, we try and take care of those closest to us."

"I'm not that close to you, Harry," I said, and then I realized I was only about a foot away. "You know what I mean."

"Yeah, I got it," he said. "And you're right. But—like I said before, I need your help, and part of the service rendered here is that you get my annoying insights whether you want them or not. And sometimes that means you get your information spoon fed, just like you would get it from any of your other friends. I'm just more honest and more informed than they are."

I felt my forehead reach boiling. "Can't you just treat me like an adult and tell me the whole truth? Just get it all out there—'Here's what you'll be facing this episode, better gird yourself, Sienna girl'?"

He chuckled. "The human mind is a funny thing. Maybe one person in a thousand could handle that kind of guidance. Probably less. You ever heard that old sod about 'When the student is ready, the teacher will appear'?"

"Tell me you're not casting yourself in the role of teacher as well as therapist, fight instructor, and—I dunno, client? What else would we call what we're doing here?"

"So you're gonna pass on that whole deity-worshipper relationship? Because I feel like that would encompass it all." The grin, again. Toothy, amused, and kinda boyishly adorable.

I stared at him and part of me wanted to kill him.

The other part, though …

What the hell else could I do, though? Tell the man who could see into the future to take a flying effing leap, that I'd muddle through this on my own? I *could* do that, of course, and maybe I'd be none the worse off for it.

On the other hand, now I had Terminator after me, and this other guy—Fire Guy—after my friends and family. Unless I could prove to myself Harry was actively working against me, his particular power set would come in awfully handy were I to keep going down this crazy road.

And me? I just kept going down the crazy roads.

"It's okay," he said, amusement bleeding out, "you don't have to convert today. The Church of Harry will be around and taking donations for—"

"Oh, shut up before I make a martyr of you." I folded my arms in front of me as he chuckled under his breath.

"You can kill me—actually, you can't, probably—but my legend will only grow stronger."

"Argh." I put my face in my right palm. "I swear to—"

"Me?"

I gave him the dagger look. "I swear to you, Harry, I just want an easy break. For the shit to stop hitting the fan. For things to stop exploding around me, for trouble to stop rolling my way—"

"You were seeking trouble for years, Sienna," he said. "It was your addiction, and … maybe just like other addictions, it's the sort of thing that doesn't just fold up the tent and leave when you think you're done with it. Consequences follow behavior, they don't come first." Now he sounded all serious. "You made a name for yourself as a hero and a villain, whether you meant to or not. Much as you might wish you could say 'Uncle—'"

"I'm not calling Friday."

"—it's not just a matter of waving the white flag and calling it quits, unless you want to give up and go to jail." He gave a light shrug.

I sighed. "Tell me this, then, because ... back when I was working a case, I knew I'd reach a conclusion of some sort, and then I'd be done, at least with that one. This running thing." I looked the wide world around me, or at least the borders I could see within the leafless trees that girded that Kentucky rest stop. "Do I ever get out of this again, Harry? Am I ever gonna ..." I let my voice trail off. My eyes went unfocused in the distance.

Even after months on the beach in Florida I was just so ...
Tired.

"I'm just so ground down, you know?" My voice was raspy again. I was feeling ... everything. The weariness. The lack of drink. Like I'd been emptied out and nothing replaced it. "Running for a year, then this. I mean ..." I tried to find a way to ask the question that was weighing on me like ...

Like the weight of the world.

"You'll find your way out again, Sienna," Harry said softly. "I can promise you that. You will find your way out of this, and you will be happy. And sad. Normal again, I guess you could say." He smiled. "You'll find a new normal, but, yes ... this, too, shall pass away. And someday ... I can't say when ... you will be happy again." He smiled, and this time, I could feel a thrill of hope at his words. "I promise."

24.

Reed

I stepped off the plane in Minneapolis to find Governor Bridget Shipley waiting for me, clutching her hands, blond hair cut in an overgrown bob that reached the top of her shoulders. Governor Shipley was a pretty stately lady, and I'd met her enough times in the past to recognize the nervous tension in her as I descended the steps from the Gulfstream, my team following behind me.

"Mr. Treston," she said, taking a few strides to greet me as I came lightly off the last step. We were standing on the tarmac at the private terminal at Minneapolis-St. Paul International Airport. A 737 roared in the distance as it came in for a landing, passing over the Mall of America toward the north-south runway. The governor extended her hand, and I shook it, carefully, trying to not break it with my still-newfound strength.

I'd lived as a meta my entire adult life, and I'd always been strong. But what President Harmon had done, giving me a power boost? It had boosted everything. Strength, speed, dexterity. I wasn't exactly exploding Coke bottles with my grip by accident, but I didn't want to lose control on the Governor of Minnesota's hand, either. The consequences would be a lot more dire than a little Cherry Coke on my new suit.

"Rolling out the red carpet for us, Governor?" I asked,

pausing to look her in the eye. I wasn't her biggest fan; when Sienna had run into trouble, Shipley had been one of the first to pull out the long knives for her, making her life harder at a time when she didn't need it.

In previous meetings with the governor, I had been in Sienna's company. They'd been congenial, filled with praise and mutual admiration.

That had evaporated as soon as my sister hit hard times. I wasn't keeping a shit list or anything, but if I had been, Governor Bridget Shipley would have been right at the top. I suspected Sienna wasn't likely to forgive her, either, if she were to ever find her way out from under the mountain of trouble she was presently buried in.

"I'm just glad you saw fit to come back to us now, when we need you most," Shipley said, smiling thinly. Sanctimonious, of course. A true politician, this one.

"Well, I might have been around more if I felt like I was welcome here." I said that with the dryness of a good sherry.

"You are more than welcome here, of course." She didn't bat an eye. Provided this incident resolved well, and with a decent helping of assistance from her party, she'd probably be a contender to Gondry in the next primaries—assuming Gondry continued to fumble around in the dark like a monkey seeking a football to hump (and I figured that was a fair assumption).

"Well, I don't like to travel anywhere alone," I said, turning to watch Augustus and Jamal coming down the stairs, Taneshia behind them. Friday had the luggage, and he was just behind them. Olivia Bracket followed a step behind, with Tracy bringing up the rear.

I frowned. Where was Scott? And Greg Vansen?

"And family is important to me," I said, offhand, trying to complete my snide insult of the governor. I wasn't sure it hit home, because she had a wicked good poker face. Or maybe just passed on the opportunity to insult me since I was here to help her.

"You've built quite the team," she said. "I remember when it was … almost just you."

I shot her a sideways look and decided to avoid the topic

ROBERT J. CRANE

of Sienna, because ... well, two could play at this politeness game. "I still have elements of a second team in position on the West Coast. Protecting one of our people who's injured."

"I heard about that," Shipley said, falling into line beside me as I stepped away to let the others disembark. "And the incident in New York, and with the bridge in Maryland—it's got people on edge." She met my eyes, still betraying nothing. If she was panicking, she was good at keeping a steel lid over it.

"Well, they have good reason to panic," I said. "Between the *Enterprise* incident and the bridge, that's a lot of dead and injured. I'm sure seeing one of the perpetrators show up here isn't helping you keep things calm."

"We've seen worse," she said, levelly. "The string of murders back in 2012, for instance, when your sister faced off with that ... animal." She shuddered lightly under her heavy coat; I knew she meant Wolfe. "The destruction of Glencoe. The battle over Minneapolis when your sister killed Sovereign."

Now she was leaving oblique references behind. "Funny that you should mention the common denominator there," I said. "Because it seems like one person solved all those problems for you."

Her expression darkened. "Really? Because it seems to most, once they know the full facts of the situation, that all those problems had one common denominator."

"Then they should remember the old maxim about correlation not equaling causation," I volleyed back, trying to be just as light as she was but probably failing.

"Mr. Treston—"

"I love it when someone calls me 'Mister,'" I said. "I can always tell they're about to say something either very respectful or very not."

"I hope we don't see your sister," Governor Shipley said, maintaining that straitlaced calm. "Because given the current climate, I'm about one step away from activating the Minnesota National Guard to help deal with this crisis. And if Sienna were to show up—"

"I like how you still call her by her first name, even though you've totally disavowed ever knowing her." My cheeks were burning. Bad sign. Usually a storm warning tended to follow.

"—she's the sort of incendiary element that would necessitate that decision," Shipley finished, leaning back slightly to straighten her back. She looked like a pillar, standing there on the tarmac, snow at the edges of the concrete where it met the grass. "I hope we can resolve this peacefully."

"We'll do our best," I said, holding inside a lot of other, nastier replies that I could have fired at her. None of them were productive or useful for the task at hand, though, so what was the point? Other than the short-term emotional satisfaction of basting the woman in vengeful rhetoric about how my sister was innocent and persecuted and—

Hell. No one was going to listen to that. I didn't bother saying it to Sienna—because she knew—but the sum total of all of her bad decisions in the past sure had come roaring back to kick her ass with a vengeance when the Eden Prairie accusations came along.

"How's the view from the ground?" Scott Byerly asked, striding over to me from where he'd just disembarked the plane. Governor Shipley was striding off, her message apparently delivered. I'd certainly gotten it loud and clear: *Deal with this— and heaven help your sister if she shows up to assist.*

"My view feels like it's currently from under a bus," I muttered, meta-low. "Or at least that's Sienna's current view." I shook my head in a thinly veiled fury. "She does all these things to help the state, to save lives, and the minute things get a little dicey—boom. She's persona non grata, no trial, no—"

"Well, she didn't exactly hang around for a trial," Scott muttered under his breath. I gave him a daggered look and he shrugged. "I mean, I probably wouldn't have, either, under the circumstances, but ... no one's told Sienna's story, at least not anywhere someone like Shipley would have heard it. All she knows is the party line—Sienna blew up that corporate park in Eden Prairie, killed a ton of newly released prisoners that she apparently had a grudge against—"

"That had shown up at our freaking offices with ill intent,

Scott. Hell, two of them damned near killed me. That's the part I don't get about everyone's reaction—do they think these people were just innocent souls out for a walk, by coincidence, by our offices, when the shit went down?"

"Well, come on," Scott said, looking around. Beyond a tall fence nearby, a road wended its way under the grey sky, light traffic passing. "You know how it was covered by the press at the time—that was when the bombs dropped about how Sienna killed M-Squad. And she already had all those other public image issues—beating the hell out of Simmons on that internet video, punching that reporter when he blindsided her—you start adding things together, maybe it doesn't make it too hard for people to get the wrong idea, especially if they're predisposed to believing that everyone Sienna put in the Cube was wrongfully imprisoned."

"That's such a load of bullshit," I steamed, even though I shivered when a subzero breeze blew through. "You saw what some of these people did. You—"

"Preaching to the choir, man," Scott said. "I was in charge of the FBI squad that hunted criminal metas for a while, remember? I know what happens out there, even if it's not exactly broadcast to the world." He shrugged. "But good luck getting people who have the seen the bad and somehow missed the good to change their minds now that they're entrenched in their current position. Because I don't know if you've noticed, but a common failing of humanity is a real failure to appreciate our own potential fallibility of judgment. You wouldn't think so, given how many people have completely effed up their own lives, but—here we are. Personally, after evaluating how my life has not turned out the way I wanted, I might look around and think, 'I don't know if I have this figured out.' But not most people." He shook his head. "There is an awful lot of absolute certainty out there from people who have made terrible, awful choices that have brought their lives to ruin."

I took that in, and then smiled tightly. "Thank you for that simple truth, Scott."

"Don't mention it," he said, returning my smile. "And don't despair. I'm sure we'll get this thing cracked before

Sienna shows up."

I stared over his shoulder. Blinked a couple times. "Yeah. We really will," I said quietly, raising my voice to the point where it was audible to all. "One way or another."

He turned. Saw what I saw. His whole body tensed, like mine.

Because the guy we were looking for? The meta who'd trashed the Chesapeake Bay Bridge, who'd attacked Jamie Barton in New York, who'd attacked Veronika and Kat in California …

He was hovering over us, looking down at us all, cloaked in flames from head to toe.

And beneath the fire, a dark line appeared where his lips would be—a shadowy smile that chilled me like the wind.

25.

"Scott, cover!" I shouted as Scott sprang into action. He was already drawing moisture out of the air and pushing it in front of him, pulling whatever water vapor hadn't frozen in the below-freezing temps and shaping it into a shield in front of him. I took position behind him, figuring if this guy was going to start tossing flame bursts, I wanted to have a little something between me and him while I started to work my magic with the wind.

"Taneshia, Jamal!" I shouted and could see them already moving. Blue electricity sparked down their hands as they lanced bolts toward the villain hovering over us.

A bitter wind ran over me, one that I wasn't controlling, and something in the air seemed to change.

"Oh, shit," I muttered. But it was too late to do anything about it.

Mr. Flaming Super Evil was grinning, a thin shield of water distorting the air in front of him. Somehow, he had Poseidon powers, too, and had done a much lesser version of what Scott had. It was thinner, covering him in a semi-spherical arc in front, but a thread extended from it across the space between us, into Scott's forming shield.

Taneshia and Jamal's lightning bolts crackled along the surface of his impromptu shield as Mr. Flaming Super Evil darted back. The electricity sparked as it made contact with the water and then ran through it, lightning crackling—

And ran down the thread connecting his shield with Scott's—

When it reached its end, the lightning jumped to the nearest target, trying to ground itself.

And found Scott's extended hand, only inches from the shield.

Scott jerked as I leapt back, unable to do anything but keep from joining him in a shocking hell. Scott jerked and spasmed, lightning running through his body like Darth Vader at the end of *Jedi*.

He stayed standing for a moment after the electricity had passed, and then the water shield he'd been forming splashed onto the tarmac, freezing as it landed. Scott toppled after it, smoking under his clothing, limp as though someone had just ripped his spine out.

"That is one," Mr. Flaming Super Evil said in an ominous Euro accent of the sort that villains in 80's movies used religiously.

"Full court press!" I shouted and blasted at him with all the wind I could summon. He formed a shield of his own, a smaller, less powerful screen of wind, and my attack rolled over him and to the side, toward the Gulfstream jet.

I looked over and saw Greg Vansen next to the plane. He started to shrink, but the diverted wind caught him as he disappeared. He struck the plane a moment later, denting it and sending it skidding a foot, like the wind had blown it. The only reason I knew he'd hit it was because there was a bullet-sized dent in the side where he'd struck it, and a moment later he returned to his normal size and collapsed on the tarmac, limp as Scott.

"I'm gonna tear you a new super hole, Euro-trash!" Guy Friday screamed, leaping over me, swole like a … I dunno. 'Swole' is not a word that comes easily to me, because I know it's new, and it just—anyway, he leapt over me like an idiot, clearly planning to attack our enemy midair.

"No!" I shouted.

But it was too late. Friday didn't even get close to target; Mr. Flames dropped a couple feet, and the wind kicked up just behind his shield, catching Friday mid-air and sending him sideways.

Friday slammed into the Gulfstream, completely wrecking

the wing and spilling jet fuel everywhere on the tarmac. I looked over to see Olivia and Tracy getting into position near the plane, along with Jamal. They were planning something and I might have been eager to see what it was if not for ...

Our enemy grinned, and launched a tiny little spark of flame.

I shouted again, in anger, deaf because of the winds roaring furiously around me as I assaulted him.

But it was pointless. Too late.

The flame hit the spilled jet fuel, and it exploded with a thundering fury that blew me sideways. I went end over end like some angry Hercules had hurled me, landing in a melted puddle of slush that ran down my shirt, down my back, frigid water awakening me more effectively than any alarm clock I'd ever owned.

I rose, trying to look at the damage. The plane was on fire, burning furiously.

And my team ...

My team was down.

The only good news seemed to be that the explosion's force had flung my team away from the burning plane. I did a quick count over the ringing in my ears—Friday, Taneshia, Jamal, Scott, Greg, Tracy, Olivia ... all down.

Where was—

"Looks like it's just you and me," Augustus said, staggering up to me, ears slick with blood. His shoulders were covered, too; the force of the explosion had destroyed his ear drum on the side closest to the plane. He was also bleeding from some wounds on his side and arm, and a few incidental scrapes on his forehead. He looked like he'd been in a whole entire action movie, one like *Die Hard* where the hero ends up half dead by the end, not like he'd been in a ten-second confrontation with some supervillain on the tarmac of MSP airport.

"We are getting our asses kicked," I said, trying to speak over the ringing in my ears. It was angry, persistent, the sound of bells, klaxons, something. "This guy has way too many powers."

"You think he's like Rose?" Augustus held a hand up to his ear, staggering a couple steps. I guessed his inner ear had been affected by the big boom that had knocked our asses over.

"Don't know," I said, trying to find Mr. Super Evil. My head was swimming, like someone had gonged it with a little extra fervor.

Oh.

There he was.

Hovering over us.

"Shit," I said as Augustus got wiped out by a blast of water. His head cracked against the tarmac and he slid, coming to rest in a pile of snow, blood seeping off of him and turning the muddy slush red.

"Strength," our villain said as I roared toward him, launching off the ground with the wind at my back. He dodged out of the way swiftly, his flight powers engaging as I used my slower, more unwieldy winds to chase after him.

He was rising into the air now, and I hurled wind after him, furious, unstoppable winds. He dodged out of the way of every gust, rising further and further.

Which fit perfectly into my plan.

I chased him up, up into the sky. His laugh found its way back to me on the wind, and he soared higher and higher, willing me to chase him.

I did.

I wouldn't let him get away now.

Not until I stopped his ass.

The air grew colder the further I rose, chasing him like a bull after a red scarf. His laughter was a taunt, a goad that just burned me further, my blood heating up like I'd opened a vein over the burning plane.

"This—this is the way," he called back to me, disappearing behind a cloud bank.

"Hiding isn't going to do you any good," I shouted and blew his cloud away. It disappeared in a puff like it had never even been there, and for good measure I cleared the skies around us, giving us a cold battlefield of empty air in which to settle this.

The sun shone down and Mr. Super Evil stopped, looking back at me. The bastard was still smiling, that black and hollow smile beneath his flame shield. "You are strong," he finally said, seeming super pleased about that.

"You're not going to be nearly so happy about it once I cram enough air pressure up your nose to explode your lungs," I said, readying myself to do exactly that.

"I will be happy regardless," he said, pausing in place.

And somehow ... in spite of the conditions, in spite of the war we'd just been through on the ground ...

I knew he was telling the truth.

This ... freak ... was happy just to be here. Fighting me.

"What the hell are you?" I whispered, preparing my last attack. I reached down, lifting a fragment of the Gulfstream's burning wing and raising it into the air even as I assailed him with unceasing winds, buffeting him around, trying to trap him in place for my coup de grâce. It wasn't going to be pretty, slamming tons of metal into him over and over in a controlled windstorm. I figured it'd be like an improvised blender, and I expected him to come out the other side like he'd been through a real one.

And I was fine with that. Grinding up my opponent like chum, only in this case, I was the shark.

"Why are you doing this?" I asked, shouting in the maelstrom of wind I had created. The plane's burning wing was rising to us now, zipping toward its rendezvous point with his back as I trapped him in place. His command of wind was like mine before I'd been enhanced by Harmon's serum. No match for me now.

He met my gaze across the distance, flames blowing in the wind. "Do you not feel it?" he asked, electric look in his eyes, as though Jamal and Taneshia's blast had run through him.

"Feel what?" I asked. Just a few more seconds. Let him connect emotionally with me until my sneak attack connected with him and made a smear of him.

"The call," he said, staring right at me, almost through me, his eyes were so alive. "Do you not feel it? The need to ...?" He let off there, waiting.

"What the hell are you talking about?" I threw that question into the tornado of furious wind between us. "Do I feel what?"

"*It*," he said, as though that explained it all. He stared into my eyes, and—

A flash of a raven in my sight caused me to lose concentration—just for a moment, as my senses were scrambled. I'd been hit by this before, this feeling. Sienna had possessed it until Scotland, the power of an Odin-type, and she called it the Warmind.

She'd hit me with it dozens of times, maybe hundreds, but this time …

Something about it was … different. Stronger.

It caught me like a visceral slap to the face, a slap to the consciousness, and my muscles locked as the raven cawed like a scream, louder than my mind could process. It was a hideous noise, one that seeped into my arms and legs and paralyzed them, locking me into place in the middle of my tornado.

A thousand unnamed fears crashed in on me in that raven's caw, like needles of death stabbing into me. I felt paralysis, a heart attack, screaming panic infusing my every muscle group as I shuddered in the air.

The wind stopped around me, and I was becalmed, my footing disappearing like melting ice beneath my feet.

I dropped, the ground roaring up to greet me, clear now that all the clouds were blown away. I saw it rushing up, the tarmac screaming toward me, my heart thundering faster than it had ever run before. I couldn't breathe, couldn't think, and it was coming so fast—

Something stopped me a second before impact, a harsh grab at my ankle that kept me from splattering on the concrete below. The whiplash sent all the blood to my head, though, and all I was left with was fear as I snapped into the darkness.

26.

Sienna

We passed through Kentucky quickly, and on into southern Illinois about an hour later. I was at the wheel and not hating it, surprisingly. I'd never been a huge fan of driving, preferring to let others just chauffeur me around like I was a big shot. It wasn't as though I weren't capable of driving. I was reasonably smart, possessed the dexterity of a superpowered person, and had reflexes that would have rivaled an AI-guided machine.

But there was just something about driving I didn't care for. Maybe, as a total control freak, it was one of the few opportunities I got to just yield control and trust the person next to me to not get me killed. Which was a big ask in some cases. Admittedly, it was pretty funny that I, being such a deeply in-control person, would want to surrender control in such a way, but—

I blinked as I thought about that. Had I known that about myself before Rose had ripped out those memories? Maybe. I couldn't recall actively thinking about my control freakery before. And certainly not as it pertained to driving. It was a strange thing, trusting people so little in other ways and yet immediately trusting them to take control in the instance of basically the number one cause of unnatural death in the country.

"Hm," I muttered to myself, enjoying the quiet for once.

Eilish was staring out the window, a look of barely veiled awe on her face as we drove through endless, flat fields. Cassidy was still tapping away at the keyboard, having not said anything for a long while, and Harry ...

Harry was in the passenger seat. He shifted, trying to put his head against the window in a way that was comfortable (I assumed, having gone through the same thing only hours earlier) and failing.

"Trouble sleeping?" I asked as he shifted again and made another sound of displeasure.

"Now that you mention it ... yes," he said, arms folded tightly in front of him.

"Guilty conscience?" I asked with a little bit of a prickly, taunting air.

"My conscience is perfectly fine, thanks for asking," he said. "I think it has more to do with this uncomfortable car."

"Yeah, I guess windows weren't made to be great pillows," I said. "I just figured you had something on your mind that you'd yet to hit me with. Some super insight from the future or about my past that you were just waiting to—y'know, knock the pegs out from under me with in a little while. Keep me off balance."

"I think you're plenty unbalanced as it is." He was smirking again. The bastard.

"Haha," I said, with no actual humor. "You have to admit, if you were being honest, that you don't exactly seem like you're making a great effort not to knock me flat in this whole business."

"Lots of people make a lot more effort than I do to actually knock you over," he said. "And whether you want to believe it or not, Sienna ... I'm on your side in this. And I am trying to help you."

I burned a little within. "Fine. Okay." I let it go, because ... well, annoyingly, I actually did sort of believe he was trying to help me. Frustrating as I found him.

"The future is in flux right now," Harry said, trying to stretch his neck. "The near future, I mean. And, actually, the far future, too. Consequences are coming, with the chance to ripple through ... well ... with a chance for a long rippling effect." He rubbed his forehead. "The problem is, there's so much going on it's like sensory overload. So many things are happening. It's overwhelming."

"Does that happen often?" I asked.

"Not really, no," Harry said, rubbing his face, shading his eyes from the sun—and from me. "Not when I'm just walking around living life."

"What are you doing now, if not walking around and living life?" I asked. "Trying to sleep and occasionally eat and—whatever else you do. Drink and gamble, I guess?"

"I do like to drink and gamble some," he said with a nod. "But I'm not living life right this minute, Sienna." He still didn't look at me. "I'm trying to keep an eye on the future."

I frowned, turning the wheel to move us back into the right lane in order to let a BMW doing about 90 zoom past. "But you can't see your own future."

He paused, hand still over his eyes. "No."

"So ..." I pursed my lips. "Whose future are you looking into?" He didn't stir. "Mine?"

"Yeah," Harry said, and it was a slow exhalation of air that followed his words.

"Is there sex in my future?" I asked, white-knuckling the wheel. "Because it feels like there should be sex in my future. It's kinda been a while."

Harry let out a little chuckle. "Yes, Sienna, there is sex in your future."

I stared straight ahead and reddened a little. Whew. Hopefully it'd pair well with that happiness he'd promised me earlier. "Good."

"What about mine?" Eilish asked, leaning forward in the back seat. "Is there sex in my future?"

Harry seemed to think about it for a moment. "Not anytime soon." He tiled his head to look back at her, faint smile perking the corner of his lips. "Guess you're probably sorry you passed up on that orgy opportunity now, huh?"

"You're just a second-rate fortune teller," Eilish said, slumping back in the seat and doing a little blushing of her own. "I could get my rocks off if I wanted to. You don't know."

"And that's the point of my powers," Harry said. "Probabilities change. I can see a certain spectrum of them, but it doesn't mean some wild-ass, out-of-left-field shit doesn't show up at the last minute and change everything. I've been blindsided by wacky, unbelievable things I didn't see coming more than a few times."

"But I thought you could at least see those wild probabilities?" I asked.

"I can—sorta," Harry said. "It's like ..." He blinked, apparently trying to find the right analogy. "I don't know ... the big ones dominate the scene—it's like a landscape. I might not see that tiny shrub in the background until I get closer, you know? Because the lake view is commanding my attention, and past it, that forest edging up on the foreground. So I miss the bush in the background."

"Way to come through with the Bob Ross explanation of your powers," I said. "You don't have to tell anyone about that shrub; it can be your little secret."

"I have no idea who Bob Ross is," Eilish said.

"Anyway ..." Harry said. "That's how it works."

"I would have figured you'd see it all," I said, like someone had let a little of the air out of my balloon. "Like ... seeing the future would give you some sense of warm certainty." I glanced at him, head now back against the window again. "I figured you'd sleep like a baby."

"I think sleeplessness is worse for a Cassandra," Harry said.

"But ... you know how it's most likely to turn out," I said. "So ... shouldn't that eliminate the fear? Knowing that—in the end—it'll all be all right?"

"There's always fear, Sienna," he said, "because I don't know how it's all going to turn out, exactly. I just know the clearest probabilities, and they get narrower and narrower until there's only one left. And yes, I can sometimes see beyond to the big events, the ones that shake the world—or redefine it, but ... that's not the end, usually." His smile was quicksilver, it appeared so quickly and then lost all its joy just as fast. "We don't end until we die, after all."

"That's ... so very glum," Eilish said.

"But ... that's why there's always fear," Harry said. "Because there's always another trouble coming until the end." His eyes glinted, then widened. "Sienna—"

"Whoa," Cassidy said, and somehow I knew that whatever Harry had been about to say had been related to Cassidy's sudden outburst.

"What is it?" I asked, watching Harry's jaw lock out of the corner of my eye. Uh oh.

"Looks like our enemy just showed up in Minneapolis," Cassidy said as we crested a small hill that looked out over what appeared to be hundreds of miles of Illinois. She thrust her laptop forward, and I was treated to a view of a picture that looked like airport tarmac, with a burning plane in the background, orange flames and white snow, brown grass exposed where the heat had melted the snow away.

"Jeez," I muttered. "Is Reed on scene yet?"

There was silence, just for a second, and I realized Cassidy had stopped talking.

Before I could turn and see what the problem was, I felt Harry's hand on the wheel, guiding it, and I stared at him blankly for just a second before it hit me.

Reed.

He was …

"No," I whispered, and I took my hands off the wheel. "Not …" I looked at the laptop screen, and there were … bodies … arranged around the tarmac like— "No," I said again. "They can't be—"

But with damning certainty, I stared at it as Harry guided the wheel toward the side of the road, and we drifted to a stop, my foot off the pedal, my ability to do anything but stare at the picture of my fallen friends, shadows on the tarmac, as we coasted to a stop on the side of the freeway.

27.

"I don't think anyone is dead," Cassidy said, "but I can't be sure. I'm getting the MSP airport police radio transcripts in real time, and—they haven't called for a coroner or anything. Of course, that could be coming …"

Normally, I might have wanted to kill Cassidy for delivering this kind of news in a such a chipper tone of voice, but now I was hanging onto her words like a lifeline, trying to catch anything she threw my way, any factoid, any tiny data point—whatever I could get I would take, like a hungry puppy begging for table scraps.

"Here," Harry said, and he shifted the SUV into park. I hadn't even realized we'd come to a complete stop, my foot on the brake pedal.

Cars whizzed by us at 70 and higher. The SUV shook in their wake every time one passed.

"Do you know for sure that no one is dead?" I asked, even though I knew she'd just answered it. My brain felt like molasses, like it was moving in slow motion, trying to come to grips with this meteor strike of information and emotion. My hands were shaking on the wheel, wrists fluttering back and forth like a rope bridge on a gusty day.

"No, and I wouldn't even know this much if not for the fact that the entire emergency response for Minneapolis, St. Paul, Bloomington and the surrounding areas just exploded into action," Cassidy said, face lit by the screen's glow. "Apparently the governor was there when it happened, and now everyone's freaked out that this was an assassination attempt or something."

"It was," I whispered. But it wasn't targeted at the governor, and we didn't know if it had succeeded yet.

"Sienna ..." Harry said.

I turned on him, slowly. "Did you see this coming?"

He shook his head. He was pale like the snows that lay draped, unevenly, over the snowy Illinois plains. "No."

I looked him in the eye. "I believe you."

He didn't exactly let out a breath of relief, but I could see a slight loosening of his features. "Good."

"Emergency services are going to be working for a while," Cassidy said. "They're calling in more ambulances." She was still in tight concentration.

"That's ... that's a good thing, right?" Eilish asked. "They don't call in ambulances for dead people, after all."

"Yeah," I said, opening my door as frosty air rushed in. "What wonderful news." I slammed it behind me and stalked around the hood of the car, heading for the limited treeline to my right. It consisted of five pines all in a row, the tallest of which was only about ten feet, and it sat just in front of a three-wire cattle fence.

I didn't even have a proper woods to stalk off into to gather my thoughts. Illinois. The southern and western part was like Iowa lite.

I half-expected to hear a door open behind me, but I didn't, and when I reached the fence I just jumped it. Nothing too fancy, a simple meta leap about five feet over a four-foot fence. I landed in the patchy snow on the other side and almost turned my ankle.

Color me unworried. Even if I turned my ankle, a minor injury like that would heal in about two hours, even in my vanilla condition.

"Dammit," I let out a breath, and it frosted in front of me. I couldn't tell if the worry I was feeling bubbling inside was driving the anger, or the anger was driving the worry harder. It didn't really matter either way, because they were both present in sufficient quantities to choke me, and all I was doing was keeping my cool until I felt like I was far enough away from the SUV to lose it without having to worry about being watched.

But the ground was flat all the way around me, so there wasn't much hope I wouldn't be seen. No, there was nowhere to hide now; I was in plain sight of the road anywhere I went.

The despair and uncertainty felt like it was choking me, a little extra discomfort to compete with the chilling air that seeped in around my long sleeves and jeans. I should have dressed more warmly, knowing I was heading north, but here I was in the middle of snowy field, wearing no coat and watching my breath mist in front of me.

And lucky me, I got to wonder if my brother and my friends were dead on some cold, snowy runway in Minneapolis.

They'd come to save me in Scotland, and now I had to wonder if I'd missed my chance to repay the favor. They'd gone through all that hell, come to pull my fat out of the fire only for me to be too pathetic and drunk and unconcerned with everything to worry when they went into the fire themselves.

"I don't think they're dead," Cassidy said from behind me. I turned to find her picking her way across the gaps where no snow lay, patches of black earth that were fallow for winter, hard and unyielding against her little tennis shoes. She had wrapped her arms around herself and was shivering, her tiny frame covered by a heavy coat, one more appropriate for Minneapolis weather. I wondered, idly, if she'd set up shop there again, or if she'd picked some other place to park herself after Reed destroyed her house in Richfield.

"It'd be a lot more helpful to me if I knew—and if I knew how badly they were injured," I said, turning back to her. I paused, and said, "Wait ... Harry sent you to talk to me? *You?*"

"I don't know why, either," Cassidy said, shivering. "It's so cold out here, and it feels like I could be doing more at the computer, but ..." she shrugged her small shoulders. "Yes, he sent me. Said I needed to come talk to you." She almost missed a step but caught herself at the last second. She was not the most graceful meta I'd seen; in fact, she wasn't that far off from being human in her dexterity. "Said I was the only one who could come talk to you."

"I wonder why that is," I said, turning back to look at the horizon, at where the grey sky joined the flat earth.

"Hell if I know," she said, shivering as she slipped up next to me. "I think we both know my people skills are still …"

"As weak as your deadlift," I said. "Weaker, probably, since you still have meta strength."

"I never understood the point of physical strength until I ran across you," she said, cocking her head, breath still misting the air. "Eric and I, we could … I mean, he used some variant of physical strength, obviously, but … it wasn't like he had to get violent with people. We cracked bank vaults with his powers, and always when they were unoccupied. It was easy, it was lucrative, and we could just … live in the times between. Live on what we'd taken. Physical strength was about threats, about violence, about compulsion through force. I liked … to outthink my opponents instead." A trace of a smile appeared on her lips. "To present them with a circumstance so ingenious that violence was an afterthought. Persuasion by manipulation of circumstance, call it. They never even needed to know my hand had been involved in … whatever it was. I could get what I needed without being so coarse.

"Then you came along," she said, "and suddenly … all the thought in the world, all the avoidance—none of it mattered. You wouldn't stop coming. You caught Eric, and I needed actual physical strength to overcome you. So I thought it through. I brought in people skilled at that sort of thing, people who had lived by violence. I removed most of your ability to do violence through the use of the suppressant—"

"Oh, yeah?" I remembered what she was talking about, her jailbreak at the old Agency, back when I'd worked for the government and been the warden for their prison, the Cube, which was housed under our headquarters. She'd done it, too, orchestrated a hostage situation to cover up Eric Simmons's escape, used metahuman Russian ex-Special Forces operators to lay siege to us during a big event and depowered my brother. Then she'd had her little team hound me throughout the facility while I Die-Harded my way through them in order to keep the jailbreak contained.

And it mostly was. Only Simmons and Anselmo Serafini had escaped, and Anselmo had had to be carried out, scarred beyond recognition, thanks to me.

"—and you still wrecked everything and saved the day—mostly." She made a face. "Violence. You were a master of it. You killed almost every one of those Russian mercs with less power than you have now."

"I had some help," I said quietly. "Reed. J.J. Scott ... eventually."

"I don't get it, though," Cassidy said. "I mean, I know Scotland was tough on you and all, but ... you're not dead. And like I said, you're more powerful now than you were when you fought through those Russians—"

"I knew who I was then," I said, the truth crashing in on me—several at once, actually.

My brother could die.

I'd lost my way, because not only had I lost my power and my memory, but ...

This thing I'd been doing the last few years? Helping people? Fighting the bad guys?

I'd done it under the auspices of being a fugitive for the last year, which hobbled me.

But I'd also done it with incredible, near-limitless amounts of money available to me, and the power of flight to guarantee I could escape just about any situation that got too dicey. I'd turned tail and run a few times, and when I wanted to stand and fight, I had lots of power to do that as well.

Now?

I was standing in the middle of a field with the ability to punch, with a Walther PPK in my waistband, and the power to suck souls if someone held contact with my skin long enough.

It was hardly nothing, but it also wasn't the power to fly, to throw fire in any direction, to cast webs of light that could net people up like a holy Spider-man, to throw fear and paralysis into their minds, or, failing that, heal from just about any wound they could inflict or turn into a four-story dragon and rip them apart with my teeth.

I let out a long sigh.

"Why the hell did Harry send me out here to talk to you?" Cassidy asked. "I lack the soft skills for this. I mean, can you imagine a person less interested in feelings than me?"

"You're less interested in the feelings of others, Cassidy," I said, "I'm pretty sure you have your own, since I've been on the receiving end of your ire before."

"That's a reasonable point," she said, all computer-like again. "But I don't know why Harry thinks I can help you with this—this baggage of yours."

"Who am I to you, Cassidy?" I asked, turning around to her.

Cassidy stared at me with shrewd eyes. "You're an occasional obstacle to be overcome and an occasionally useful person when our objectives align. You did save me from Harmon, after all."

"Cold. Analytical. About what I'd expect of a thinking machine."

"Thank you," she said, completely sincere.

"That wasn't a ... never mind." I shook my head. Why the hell did Harry send her after me? "You're not going to have a real news update on anyone's condition for hours, are you?"

"If they die, I'll probably have one sooner," she said, and then seemed to realize what she'd just said. "Which ... would be bad, I guess ...?"

"Yes, that'd be bad," I said, and realized that her last, drawn-out sentence had been one of the longest ones I'd ever heard Cassidy try and construct, almost like she was struggling, even with her big, fast-moving brain, to put together an answer in an expedient fashion. She was taking more time to be as sympathetic as she could.

Unfortunately, she was still Cassidy, but ... points for effort.

And that drove home an old truth I'd learned a long time ago—that there was nothing you could do if you just stood around waiting for things to happen. I could stand out here in this snowy field all damned day, but there'd be no news that'd reach me here that wouldn't catch me in the car, no action I could take here that would help my brother or my friends ...

"Let's go, Cassidy," I said, starting the short walk back to the car, snow crunching beneath my feet as I put one foot in front of another and started away from the fields, away from the cold, away from nature ... and back to action.

Back to Minneapolis and St. Paul.

Home.

28.

Eilish drove. Harry gave her a long pep talk, warning her about the dangers of switching lanes, but frankly, we were on the freeway, and there was a massive divider between the left and right lanes, so he must have gotten the reading that she'd be fine, because shortly after he turned her loose to drive, he conked out and slept through almost all of Illinois.

Night was falling when he woke up to find us quiet. Cassidy had been silent; no news was good news, even though I pressed her for an update every few minutes at first, until finally I just let it go and silence reigned.

An hour past the Wisconsin state line she said, "Reed is in serious but stable condition," and I let out a breath I felt like I'd been holding for thousands of miles, for years of my life.

Little updates came trickling in on the others, too, and somewhere before we got to Madison, I fell asleep.

I woke in the dark and blinked as I saw a sign that said HUDSON NEXT FOUR EXITS.

"Where are we?" I asked, already knowing the answer.

Hudson, Wisconsin. Gateway to the state of Minnesota and entry point to the twin cities of Minneapolis and St. Paul.

Harry was at the wheel now, and he smiled over at me. "Almost home."

"Yeah," I said and sat up. I'd missed a long stretch of hilly roads and country from Madison to Eau Claire, and now we were almost to the state line, which coincided (but was not really a coincidence) with the St. Croix river.

We passed Exit 4, a truck stop exit with an outdoors store right off the ramp and a greasy spoon diner to take care of any burgeoning desire you had for oiling up your internal organs before you headed into the city.

Then we passed Exit 3—three miles to the river—the road that led south to the college town of River Falls.

Exit 2 was where all the action was—banks, big box stores, little strip malls, Hudson had most of the stuff the suburban set needed to get by on a daily basis.

Then we crested the short hill as Interstate 94 rose slightly ahead of us, and the St. Croix river spread before me as we headed down toward the long bridge below.

Exit 1 loomed right on the bank of the river; it led to historic downtown Hudson, a neat little strip of riverfront shops and restaurants and stores, a piece of refurbished Americana that thrived in the summers when the boat traffic on the St. Croix was thick from here north to Stillwater, Minnesota, and south to Prescott, Wisconsin. On the Fourth of July you could practically walk from one bank of the St. Croix to the other, and the fireworks displays ...

A little memory tweaked at me. I'd had a boyfriend, Jeremy Hampton, and we'd come down here and watched the fireworks by the shore on the Wisconsin side. They always started late, because the sun didn't set until 9 PM in the summer, the days so long they practically crawled past. It wasn't quite Alaska with its midnight sun, but it was about as close as you could get in the continental US.

I realized belatedly I was squeezing my hand as we rolled down the hill at 70 miles per hour and reached the St. Croix River bridge. There was hardly any traffic now, rush hour long over, and the clock told me it was a little after 2 AM. Some semi-trailers rolled along with us, a few cars for variety.

And when we crossed the state line into Minnesota, I realized my cheeks were warm and wet. I ignored them, and so did everybody else, but I wiped them with my sleeve nonetheless.

"How far away are we now?" Eilish asked, a little sleepily, from the back seat. I wondered how long she'd driven.

"It's about four or five miles to Woodbury, which is

basically directly east of the city of St. Paul," I said. "It's a massive suburb, tons of shopping and whatnot."

"And where are we going?" Eilish asked.

I thought about it for a moment. "I don't know. We should probably find a hotel to check into, start our search first thing in the morning." I yawned. I might have been able to do something sooner, but taking the temperature of the room around me, most of my crew seemed to be sleepy. I looked back at Cassidy; she still seemed bright and attentive by the light of her screen, but if she'd popped a little something to keep her awake, that was hardly a surprise, was it?

The miles before Woodbury, I-94 was shrouded on either side by thick woods, broken by the occasional pasture or stretch of farmland. I couldn't see the bare land in the dark, but I could see the outlines of the trees by the side of the highway as we passed, and there was something comforting about it.

"Brake lights ahead," Harry murmured from beside me. I looked; he was right. People were tapping their brakes ahead, just as we were coming up on the first Woodbury exit.

The big semi truck next to us slowed as we did. Pretty soon we were both crawling along, right under the overpass for Woodbury Drive. Radio Drive, the big Woodbury exit, was still a mile ahead.

In the darkness, the glow of headlights, brake lights and street lamps hanging over the freeway combined to give Harry a soft glow while we were under one of the overheads, and then a shadow cast by the roof of our SUV would pass over him when we moved under one. We were crawling along now at less than twenty miles per hour, inching up to the Radio Drive exit, where I could see the lights for the Woodbury Lakes shopping plaza glowing past all the brake lights on the freeway.

"What the hell is all this?" I asked, leaning forward, like moving my head twelve inches in that direction would make any kind of difference in my visual acuity. "A traffic jam at two in the morning?"

Harry's face was all screwed up in concentration and suddenly we came to an abrupt stop.

"What are you doing?" I asked as he shifted into park, blinking a few times as he did so.

He turned and looked at me, and I saw his confidence again, though he lacked the boyish smile. "We need to bail out of the car. Now."

"What?" Eilish piped up from the back seat.

"We need to go now," Harry said, turning back to the ladies in the back seat.

Cassidy didn't need to be told twice; she clapped shut her laptop, tossed it in her bag without ceremony, and was ready to move in a second.

Eilish seemed to need a little more time, fishing around in the floorboard around her ankles, gathering up her plastic bags of junk food. "So ... is this going to be a fight, then? Should I carb up to prepare myself?"

"Only if you want to crash hard in the middle of it," I said, frowning. I'd been in those kind of fights before, the ones where I wished I'd had something more than a donut when my blood sugar dove off a cliff in the midst of a battle. Adrenaline tended to keep the damage from that to a minimum, but adrenaline couldn't cover up everything when it came to crappy eating habits.

"Well, I need these," she said, shoving bags onto her arms, like she was some homeless lady from the park.

"Come on," Harry said, throwing open his door. "We need to move." He reached across the center console and grabbed me by the wrist for a second as I was about to get out. My eyes met his in the dark car, and I felt electric to the touch for a second. "We will find you," he said, and then he let go, was out the door.

"What does that mean?" I got out and watched Harry grab Cassidy by the arm and point her toward the median. She took off at a run, heading for the center of the freeway.

"Eilish, this way," Harry said, as the Irishwoman scooted across the seat and emerged on his side of the car. He helped her out and then nodded at the median. "Go."

I started toward him, but he looked at me and shook his head. "This isn't your path, Sienna."

"What the hell, are you my spirit guide now?" I asked.

He just smiled, a little tightly. "For best results ... just be yourself." And then he took off at a run after them.

I stood there, now three lanes of traffic between us, and watched them go. "What the hell is that supposed to mean?" I asked. If he was heading that way, and said it wasn't my path ...

Then, logically, whatever we were dealing with here would be ...

In the other direction.

I whirled, eyes scanning, and sure enough, in the channel between lanes directly in front of me was a figure. Tall, broadly built, his ebony skin dark in the night, he came striding toward me, full of the swagger and confidence of a man who'd already squarely kicked my ass in a Waffle House once today.

The Terminator.

29.

"Be myself," I muttered, under my breath, as the Terminator strode toward me, sheltered on either side by two big semi trucks. "That's great advice, Harry. A wonderful mantra for someone who's had entire sections of her mind wiped clean like a dry erase board. Super helpful."

The Terminator didn't bother to speak, or issue an ultimatum, or even say something cool like, "Hasta la vista, Sienna." He just came at me, picking up speed, that shadowy effect melting behind him as he ran, smoking off him like he was carrying a pound of evil dry ice in his clothing.

"Be myself," I muttered again. "Here's a question, then— who the hell am I?"

The Terminator came at me in a blur, and I reacted—a little slowly—by throwing up a blocking hand. It was old instinct, something ingrained in me by my mother over years of sparring sessions and reinforced in my adulthood by countless ones I'd forced myself to partake in to keep fresh. Speed had been less of an issue these last few years, with all those other metas in my body to give me attacks I could use at long range.

Now, though ... these old techniques were going to have to find new life, or else I'd be seeing the end of mine at the hands of someone faster and more prepared than me.

My forearm thudded against his wrist, turning aside his blow as I shifted my balance on my front leg. I don't know if the Terminator was expecting me to cower and retreat a little more—like I had in our last encounter—but he'd committed his full weight to his attack and my brain had recused itself from the immediacy of the threat. Adrenaline had kicked in, and now life was moving at both an alarmingly fast pace, and yet still a slow one.

Years of practice, years of training, had allowed me this detachment in the frenetic pace of a battle. The crazier things got, the cooler I got, because ...

Well, because I'd fought world-ending threats before, and this guy was just an aspiring Sienna-ending threat.

No big.

He twisted away from my block, trying to rechannel his force and hit me with his other hand. I acted from instinct and headbutted him, catching him forehead-to-cheek. Not exactly optimal, and it hurt, but I heard a satisfying crack that signified I'd broken his cheekbone.

The Terminator staggered back a step, his face slightly misshapen, that smoking effect melting behind him. It seemed to be some sort of by-product of his speed, something I'd never seen before, but I had the brief thought that something like that maybe had an illusory or distractive quality about it, as well. Meta powers didn't tend to fall into the realm of completely useless, not at this level, which told me he had some ability with it that I maybe hadn't seen yet. Because he probably hadn't felt like he was losing enough to employ it.

There was a nice cut on his cheek, a thin trickle of blood sliding down it just below his eyeball. He looked down for a second, then back up at me, and there was nothing in his eyes but vicious resolve of the sort I'd probably had whenever I was about to kick someone's ass. It was very intimidating for most of his subjects, I was sure.

"If it bleeds ... we can kill it," I said, staring him down. Then I blinked. "Wait. No. Sorry. Wrong Schwarzenegger movie."

"What?" His voice was deep and resonant. His genuine confusion shone through in his response.

"That was from *Predator*, but you're the Terminator," I said, readying for his next attack. "My bad."

He squinted at me, as though trying to determine whether I was crazy, bantering in the middle of a fight like this. He must have decided I was just stupid, because he came at me again. The fact that we were trapped between cars didn't give him a lot of room to maneuver, and he couldn't flank me without going wide around one of them or leaping over its top, both of which would leave him exposed to a counterattack. And also allow me to see him coming from a mile away.

The Terminator led with a short punch, a jab designed to knock me back, but I whipped an arm around it and captured his wrist under my armpit. I whirled, ready for him, because I'd seen which side he led with, and I shifted my stance as I came around. I stole his balance perfectly and whipped him face-first into my SUV.

He cracked against the passenger window glass, shattering it with the palm of his free hand, which he used to prevent his head from rattling against the car. I continued my motion, his left arm trapped under my right arm, and I pinned him against the car, hyperextending his elbow in the process.

I was almost back to back with him at this point, and even with him pinned against the car, this was not a good place to be against a metahuman. I hit him in the lower back with an elbow and then released him, whirling away and leaving him against the vehicle for a quarter second before he spun around on me, nursing that elbow I'd just jacked up.

"Human flesh over a metal endoskeleton?" I asked, rhetorically. "Not so much."

"What in the hell are you talking about?" he asked, low and gruff, cradling his arm against him. I'd given his tendons and cartilage a good bend in the wrong direction, and even a high level meta would feel that for a bit—unless they were Wolfe.

But nobody was Wolfe anymore.

I took a breath, trying to put the rampant stab of emotion I felt at that lonely thought behind me. "I'm making fun of you," I said. "It's this thing I do to annoy my opponents, get them off balance, even when they're faster than me. It's one of the few things I really remember about myself—"

He came at me without any blatantly obvious warning—except a subtle change in his balance as he set himself up for it. If I hadn't been paying attention, if I hadn't danced this dance with countless other people, if Mom hadn't taught me … I might have missed it and gotten blindsided, had to throw up a scattershot series of blocks and hope for the best.

But I saw it, and when he came at me …

I dodged, I blocked, I turned him aside and rammed him into the car door next to me. I had him pinned against the mass of the car, his arm barred this time, putting my knee into his back to keep him there. If he moved against me, he'd break his own bone, or at least dislocate his elbow.

Finally, I had the Terminator pinned between a rock and a hard case.

But he failed to acknowledge this fait accompli and gave the car a shove with his free hand. It squealed, tires moving against the pavement, and sending the family within into a frenzy. They scrambled to get the hell out of the vehicle, their faces pasty white within the confines of the car's cab. It was a mother and her three kids, and I could read the panic in her eyes, could hear her frantic screams as she climbed over the center console into the passenger seat and hurried to open the door and escape that way. She was screaming for her kids to follow her as the Terminator continued pushing against the car and moving it, tires skidding, across the pavement.

The kids were screaming now, too, trying to get out. One of them, presumably the oldest, had thrown open the passenger side door and was hurrying to unfasten a toddler in a forward-facing car seat. Their cries were drowned out by the squeal of the tires on the pavement, the Terminator was moving the vehicle, meta strength shoving two thousands of metal toward the van in the next lane over. I could see the eyes of the guy in the driver's seat of the van, and they were wide and panicked, because he saw what was coming.

The doors were open on the passenger side and the mom was standing there, screaming for the kids to get out. The car was creeping toward her like a slow-moving lava flow across the freeway. The open passenger door made contact with the side of the van and, caught too wide open to just close, it started to bend at the hinge joints. The metal squealed, protesting at this rough abuse, pressure being applied in a way it was not meant to be pushed.

A child's scream cut the night, echoing in my ear, and I realized that unless I did something quickly, they were all going to be crushed against the van in the next lane, unable to flee because of the bending doors that had them penned in. The driver of that vehicle was already pulled forward as far as he could, but he was butting up against the back of a semi-trailer, and if he inched forward anymore, the rear of the trailer was going to decapitate him.

I had this sorry bastard, the Terminator, pinned exactly where I wanted him, and then he'd had to go and put innocent people in danger. I panicked, some alarm going off in my head telling me that this was not acceptable, that this was wrong, that he was crossing a line into territory that I found absolutely detestable.

For a fraction of a second, I placed my bare hand on the base of his neck, touch the exposed skin. I imagined the burning pain, the searing as my powers started to work and his soul started to work free of his body, into mine—

And just as quickly I ripped him from the car as he shoved it, using my leverage to swiftly spin him away from it, placing myself between him and that vehicle, between him and the children and mother he'd been just about to mash into a paste.

I'd meant to crash him into my own SUV, parked only a few feet away, but as I yanked him around, he hooked his elbow and locked it in place, pinching two of my fingers so it took me an extra second to work them free.

A second is forever in a fistfight.

I hadn't quite gotten them loose when he whipped me into a punch I didn't see coming—hello, distraction, trying to free myself from his momentum and the whirl—and he leveled me into my own vehicle, neatly reversing the plan I'd set for him. I hit it with a lot more force than I would have been able to marshal against him, though, denting the door in solidly upon impact, the windows shattering above my head, bones cracking all up and down my back.

"So she shows her weakness," the Terminator said over the ringing of bells in my head and the screaming of every nerve in my back from my shoulders to the base of my spine. I was pretty sure I'd broken every rib, or at least it sounded that way to me in the chorus of howls as the neurons fired. "Do you consider yourself some kind of hero?" He loomed in my vision. "A funny thing from the most wanted criminal in America."

I tried to get to my feet, but without Wolfe to heal me ...

Wolfe ...

... I couldn't muster the strength. Muscles use bone to anchor them, to push off of, but with my ribs broken, my entire back in furious agony, I couldn't push up to my feet. The best I could do was lean against the car, trying not to topple over left or right, my legs bent, my body nearly in a sitting position.

It would have been handy to have some fire to throw ...

... *Gavrikov* ...

Or a light net ...

... *Eve* ...

Maybe a little fear to cast in the Terminator's mind?

... *Bjorn* ...

I'd settle for being able to turn into a dragon and bite his head off.

... *Bastian* ...

But there was no one here to save me now. No voice to encourage me to fight on ...

... *Zack* ...

Just me, alone.

On a freeway.

Broken bones scattered throughout my body.

Crippling pain running through me.

A question occurred as the Terminator took a step closer, and I couldn't raise so much a hand against him.

"Who are you?" I asked, my voice rasping. Every breath hurt.

"That's classified," he said with a tight smile, and raised his fist, one last time, to smite the hell out of me.

30.

"I bet the identity of your daddy ... is classified, too ... even from you," I said, holding my sides. Darkness was closing in around me, the man I had taken to calling the Terminator looming over me, fist raised high, ready to bring it down and crush me once and for all.

And this was my last gambit. A "yo daddy" joke. One step above the rhetorically classic "yo mama."

But the funny thing was ...

The Terminator actually hesitated. He kept his fist high, his face scrunched up in concentration, and he asked, somewhere between confusion and disgust, "What?"

I lifted my leg in a hard jerk and slammed my foot into his groin. It wasn't much; it still activated enough muscles in my core to completely wreck my ability to hold myself upright, triggering pain against all those broken ribs, and I slumped and fell over immediately afterward.

If I'd been a normal human, it'd have been a good, solid kick in the balls, one that would have sent my opponent to his knees, clutching his groin, wondering if my "yo daddy" joke distraction had just cost him the ability to be a daddy himself someday.

But I was freaking metahuman.

And I punted his ass across the damned road, his crotch riding at about the level of his shoulders as he Team Rocket'd over the car behind him and landed somewhere in the ditch beyond. "You shoulda made like a squirrel," I muttered as he flew, "and learned to protect your nuts."

I heard the landing over the screaming of my ribs. It sounded like it hurt.

Without a moment to spare, I heaved myself off my knees and fought against the pain surging through my body. I moved nearly bent double, clutching my chest as I navigated around my own SUV, now partially in the other lane, casting only a look behind me to see if the mother and her three kids had escaped the car behind me.

They had. Whew.

The mom was holding her baby tight as she ran for the exit ramp, the driver of the van next to her running alongside her, grabbing a couple of the kids to help them along. It was nice to see strangers helping each other, even if I had to watch it while bent double and hauling ass across lanes of parked traffic under the wide, watchful eyes of lots of drivers probably wondering what the hell they'd just witnessed.

I crossed the median, leaping over the barrier between lanes with a seething grunt as the landing made me almost scream. Pain ran through me with every movement, and I felt like I was blacking out on my feet. Near-instant healing was something I was sorely missing at the moment, as someone honked at me and I dodged a Cadillac Escalade by a matter of inches. The draft current almost knocked me down as it whizzed behind me at seventy miles an hour.

Lucky for me that whatever was causing this traffic jam had slowed things down in the eastbound lane, too. I managed to make it across the freeway with no major incidents.

I was looking around for Harry and the others, but I didn't see them anywhere. Sirens were going in the distance, and I knew that I had to make myself really scarce before they showed up, because the last thing I needed was legal entanglements right now.

There was a tall embankment and a ten foot fence dividing Interstate 94 from the world beyond. Darkness was still creeping in on the edges of my vision, and I was afraid I was going to pass out any second. I looked left, then right. Ahead, some few hundred yards, I could see the Radio Drive eastbound onramp. Flashing police lights told me that going that way was a terrible idea. Looking right, I saw nothing but empty freeway back to the Woodbury Drive exit, and that was a bad idea, too.

I looked at the fence, almost beseechingly. Couldn't it be shorter?

There was nothing for it, though, so I jumped it, damned near catching a foot on it because I was trying to leap with a shattered rib cage. My right foot brushed the top bar and then I descended in a steep dive.

I hit the ground and rolled, not intentionally or in an aikido way meant to diffuse the force of impact, but rather in a *my-freaking-lungs-just-collapsed-oh-my-merciful-heavens-arghhhhh* kind of way. I stayed on the ground for a minute, an hour, who knew at that point? All I had was pain, pain, and the world was probably ending around me. All I could hear was blood rushing in my ears, the coppery taste of it in my mouth, and the smell of wet, cold air seeping into my lungs.

Ah, home. If only I'd been in a reasonable condition to appreciate the fact I was kissing Minnesota soil again. Well, snow, anyway. But since it was Minnesota, and January, that was basically the same thing.

I was cursing under my breath when a car came to a coasting stop on the road in front of me. I hadn't even really noticed it was there, but it was, a frontage road that ran up to a well-lit shopping strip a hundred yards away that bore a tower with the words, "Woodbury Lakes," lit up on it.

There were no flashing red or blue or white lights to indicate that whoever had stopped next to me was a cop, but I wasn't holding out a lot of hope for escape by this point. My ribs were so wrecked I would have been lucky to fight off an aggressive caterpillar at this point—and fortunately there were none of those handy. Because Minnesota. In January.

A car door opened, and I heard solid heels clicking on pavement. Through the veil of blanketing pain, I realized I was being regarded by someone, very slowly, as they approached. But steadily; they weren't hesitating or hanging back. Strong hands gripped me beneath my underarms, and I was lifted, tearing a gasp from me as my entire rib cage realigned again.

"Don't fight it," came a female voice as smooth as an aged Lagavulin. It sounded familiar, but hell if I could have placed it, even with a gun right to my head. She dragged me, effortlessly, a few feet, until I heard the opening of a car door. I was lifted, bodily, into the passenger seat of a vehicle—I could tell because I could see the windshield right in front of me between seething gasps for air—and I settled into the least painful position as my savior walked back around and got in the driver's side, shutting the door behind her.

"W ... who ... are ... you?" I managed to squeeze out in agonized gasps as she slowly turned the car around and eased it back the way she'd come. I could only see her out of the corner of my eye, and blurry, because my vision was clouded by tears of pain.

She had brownish hair with traces of highlights, and it was in a kind of cool, wavy coif, something that looked like it had taken some time to make happen. I couldn't see her skin, but she didn't look old, just ... mature, I guess. She had the strength of a meta, maneuvering me around like that, but I couldn't really make out her eyes, or her face.

"You don't remember me, then?" she asked, turning to favor me with a look. "Remarkable."

"It's not that remarkable," I said, still struggling to find a less agonizing position. "I recently suffered ... tremendous memory loss."

"Is that so?" she murmured with a kind of disinterest that sounded funny at the time. Later, it occurred to me that she'd either known about it or else didn't care. Either/or.

"Yeah," I said. "Now my brain's like, all Swiss cheesey." I was mumbling, heading toward unconsciousness. "There are holes ... big enough to drive Harvey Weinstein's ego through."

"That's a big hole," she said.

I looked at her; for a moment I thought she was Ariadne, but no, I remembered clearly what Ariadne looked like. "Seriously ... I know you from somewhere."

"Of course you do." Such a smooth voice. Mm. Scotch.

"Where do I ... know you from?" I asked.

"The past." Crisp. Elegant. Totally evasive.

"Well, no shit. I didn't figure we'd met in the future. Though ... that actually did happen to me once."

"Akiyama?"

I blinked and a little tear dripped down my cheek from where I'd wept it a little earlier. From pain, purely. I turned to try and look at her again. "How do you know about Akiyama?"

"How many ribs do you think you've broken?" she asked, ignoring my question.

"How many ... are in the human body?" I gasped a little as it felt like a sharp piece of rib bone hung in my side. It felt like getting stabbed. "Because I would say that number ... plus a hundred more."

"You don't even stop when you're in agonizing pain," she said. "Same Sienna."

"You know me?" I asked.

"Well enough." Her voice melodic, and I stared at her through the wet veil that obscured my sight, blurring the world around me.

"Wait ..." I peered closer. That hair, the way it was styled, the color, the voice ... "Are you Sigourney Weaver?" I slumped a little more in my seat. "Wrong movie again. She was in *Aliens*, not *Terminator*."

"This is no movie," she said. "And since you don't remember me ... maybe I'm just a figment of your imagination."

"Figments of my imagination don't carry me away from the scene of my certain capture," I muttered, keeping my hands absolutely still. I'd found a position of pure equilibrium, where I didn't feel the need to pass out in pain, though the sensation of agony was lurking around the edges of my consciousness. "It takes an actual accomplice to do that."

"Accomplice after the fact, perhaps," she murmured, and I got the feeling she wasn't even necessarily talking to me anymore. She had such composure, though. She really did remind me of Ariadne in that way, but the voice was way smoother. Octaves lower, far more confidence.

Oh, and superpowered. Let us not forget that.

"Were you in Scotland with me?" I asked, feeling a wooziness set in.

"No," she said simply, and—I thought—with a tiny hint of regret. "But I'm pleased you made it through that ordeal."

"Ordeal?" I almost laughed, but it hurt too much. "Hell, that wasn't an ordeal, that was a freaking apocalypse."

"Yet still you stand."

"I'm really more slumping right now. Trying not to move."

"For now," she allowed. "But nothing keeps you down for long, Sienna."

"You know that about me, do you?" I asked, my head slumping against the seatback. It was comfortable, and I'd been sleeping in a car for the last day or more. Why not again now?

The darkness started to seep in, stealing my consciousness as she answered. "I know that about you," she said, and she sounded definite about it. "That ... and so much more ..."

31.

I woke in a motel room that was not half bad, my breath coming into my lungs with a thin reminder of pain that had mostly fled. Traces of it remained all up and down my ribcage as I moved, tensing the muscles in my abdomen and sitting up on a threadbare bedspread that had probably seen a better day or two.

"Ew," I said, rolling to the edge of it. I was still fully clothed, fortunately, though I hoped they boiled these bedspreads between hotel guests, and at a high temp, too, maybe five hundred degrees. I knew what happened in hotel rooms. I'd seen the news show investigations. And, uh, also been a hotel guest with a boyfriend or two.

The pain was mostly gone from my back as I looked around. It wasn't a very big place, a pretty typical two-bed hotel room. I ran fingers along my flanks, seeking places where the ribs felt disjointed through my shirt. No obvious points stood out, and there was no tenderness as I pressed harder.

I'd healed. However long I'd been out, it'd been long enough for my metahuman powers to bring my body back up to snuff. No small thing given how injured I'd been.

My head ached, probably the result of not having any Scotch for a while. I'd missed a good evening of drinking, and I wasn't sure how to feel about that other than annoyed. I stood, glancing at the dark curtains behind me. Light streamed through a small crack in them, giving the room a little illumination. Peeking between them I saw a grey Minnesota day.

At least, I assumed I was still in Minnesota. I could have been anywhere, though, really.

"Hello?" I called. There was a light on in the bathroom, which I couldn't really see into from where I stood in the room. I meandered over, shuffling, slow, just in case someone came jumping out at me.

There was nothing to worry about, though. My personal savior, Sigourney Weaver, was gone, not a trace of her left in the room. No purse, no keys, no suitcases, no personal effects at all.

She'd just dropped me off here to recuperate and … vanished?

"What the hell …?" I used the bathroom and washed my hands, then took a look at myself in the mirror. There was a little blood on my face, so I borrowed one of the wash cloths under the sink and fixed that problem, trying not to look at my too-thin face as I worked on making myself look—well, not presentable, but at least like I hadn't just been in a street fight. Which I kinda had. More like a freeway fight, I guess. Rumbling with the Sharks. Or the Terminator, in this case.

I went back into the room, which was quiet. The clock told me it was 11:32 in the morning. I looked closer at the phone and it had the name and address of the hotel, which was in St. Paul, pretty close to the Minneapolis city limits judging by the address on Snelling. Now that I listened, I could hear the sounds of the city outside the window, though when I'd looked outside earlier all I could see was a vacant lot next door and train tracks a little farther in the distance.

"Oh, man," I muttered and sat back down for a minute. I tried to take stock of my situation.

I'd damned near beaten the Terminator in a straight-up fight until he'd dragged innocent people into it. That was pretty dirty, and told me a lot about him. He seemed fully prepared to make a jelly paste out of those people if I hadn't put my life on the line to stop him. That made him a villain, full stop, and the next time I met him I was not going to hold back in my efforts to put a fist through his face and out

178

the back of his head. Not that I'd had much chance to be restrained thus far, but any thought that he might be some determined law enforcement operator hell bent on catching me had gone out the window when he'd tried to pulp that family. Decency and the benefit of the doubt definitely weren't going to hold me back anymore.

Now I found myself squarely in the middle of the Twin Cities. Someone had brought me here, and—who the hell was Sigourney Weaver, actually? Had I really met her before? Was she part of the memories Rose had sucked out of my brain, never to return? It was a shame my life didn't function like the movies, because if it had, I'd have had a happy ending when I'd blown Rose's own brains out. In a Hollywood ending, all my memories would have magically returned, and I probably would have gotten all those superpowers back that I lost, too.

But I didn't get the Hollywood ending. I didn't even get the happy ending, or the marginally happy ending, or even the kind of dirty, hollow happy ending that politicians pay for at a massage parlor. I got the drunken funk ending, where I retreated into my own shell again and stayed in a cloud of booze for months without resolving anything until shit in the world went so far sideways that even I couldn't ignore it anymore.

At about that moment, I was wishing the room had a minibar.

"What the hell am I supposed to do now?" I wondered, then remembered. The Terminator wasn't my only problem, and the mysterious Sigourney Weaver wasn't my only mystery. I had another one, one that had brought me here, and one that had left a trail of complications behind it.

Reed. Augustus. Scott. The team.

I scrambled for the TV remote on the nightstand between the beds. It clicked on easily, and the flatscreen on the wall lit up, going straight to a news station. I needed to know if my team was okay, if they'd had any fatalities, if Reed was conscious, was—

Trying to control my breathing, I waited the infinite seconds for the screen to brighten. It was already on a breaking news alert, fortunately, but …

I stared at the screen, which was a live feed of downtown Minneapolis. I could see the Nicollet Mall in the background where it crossed 6th Avenue. The sign for Murray's, Scott's favorite downtown steakhouse, was visible in the background shot. I could see Oceanaire, the awning for Ike's, and a Starbucks all in the foreground, and one of the skyway bridges that connected downtown buildings together like a webwork for easy traversal during Minnesota's bitter winters was in the foreground.

And there, in the center of the shot, occupying the middle of a downtown intersection—6th Avenue and Nicollet Mall—

Was our big bad guy.

He glowed, wreathed in fire like Gavrikov when I'd first encountered him, every inch of his skin engulfed in flames. There was another barrier shimmering around him, water vapor in the dry, cold air, and I had a guess what that was. There was also the sound of wind whipping, which was usually natural in Minneapolis streets, but in this case I had a worse feeling … that it was not natural, that it was totally related to the enemy hovering there.

A gunshot cracked through the downtown canyons, and there was a slight movement on the screen, the high-def image of the man on fire darkening around the shoulder for just a second, then a little drip of liquid running off like he'd been hit by a large, leaden raindrop.

He hadn't, of course. He hadn't been touched by it.

It only took me a second to figure it out; a police sniper had just taken a shot at him from down the street, and a couple things had happened that my meta eye caught. One, this barrier of water vapor and wind the bad guy had created had slowed the sniper bullet just slightly—or maybe more than slightly, it was tough to gauge that sort of thing even with meta eyesight at 2,500+ feet per second.

And when the bullet had gotten close enough to this man on fire, it had completely dissolved under the intensity of the heat, melting and running off like liquid slag channeled down a drain pipe.

I'd seen Gavrikov do something similar to bullets, at least relatively small caliber ones. Unless the police brought something bigger out there to challenge this guy, it looked like he was impervious to any threat they posed.

As if in response to being shot at, a rumble echoed through the ground, and the street beneath him started to shred as an ovoid wall rose to surround him to the waist. It paused there, crushed gravel and street sorted down to its base earthen components, this guy's Augustus powers clearly functioning at a reasonable enough level to allow him to rip up a street that was probably more synthetic components than actual dirt and sand and whatnot. I'd seen Augustus do this kind of thing before he'd had his power boosted and it tended to take a toll.

But this guy ... he was moving water, earth, air and fire, all while maintaining an easy hover. So he had flight, too, because if he'd been using wind to keep himself aloft, the strain would have to have been too much.

"Shit," I whispered. That number of powers narrowed things down for me. He had to be an incubus who'd jacked a bunch of people. There was no other way I knew of that he could get that many powers together.

I had a brief flash of memory, back to a village in Northern Scotland where I'd faced someone else with those seemingly unstoppable abilities. The thought of Rose's vicious grin made me shudder even now, set my heart to racing, and part of me wondered ...

Was this some sort of afterstroke for her? Some reaching-from-beyond-the-grave attempt to swipe at me, one last time?

If so, it had worked. She'd taken out my whole support team, had ripped them all away from me, cast their fates into doubt. If Rose's dead hand was still tormenting me from the other side, her aim remained unerring.

But no, I couldn't just jump to that conclusion. Maybe I was being egocentric. Maybe this had nothing to do with me. Maybe—

"Sienna Nealon," the man said, voice echoing through the TV speakers as I sat, alone, in that hotel room, and listened to him speak my name.

"Shit," I whispered.

"Where ... is Sienna Nealon?" he asked in a European accent, which leant a little credence to my 'It's Rose!' theory, at least in my mind. "Where is she?" His face, consumed by fire, spoke like some kind of horrifying deity of flame. "Where is the protector of this city?"

And he looked right into the camera.

Right at me.

"Come out," he said, no joy, no taunting, just a direct command. "Come out and face me. Once and for all. Our meeting is destined ... it is inevitable ..."

I blinked. I had gone beyond having a bad feeling about this; I was in the next county, where it looked like an impending passenger liner shipwreck combined with a three-plane crash and maybe a space station landing on the whole mess for emphasis was about to go down.

"Come out and face me, Sienna Nealon," he said, those black, shadowed eyes hiding beneath the glow of flames, "and we will meet our inevitable fate ... together."

32.

"Sonofabitch," I muttered as I walked out the front door of the hotel and was hit by the frigid Minnesota air. It was well below freezing and my thin windbreaker was somewhat shredded. Even if it hadn't been, it was completely inadequate to the task at hand. It was a Florida winter coat, not a Minnesota winter coat, and I felt the difference everywhere. My nostril hairs stood up and froze, goosebumps sprinted down my back and arms, my knees felt like they were going to knock together uncontrollably—all that within two seconds after I walked out the door.

I hurried across the parking lot, shoes crunching in the hard-packed and hard-frozen snow. It looked like it'd been a while since they'd had a fresh powder here, which sorta worked in my favor and sorta didn't. I didn't tend to drive much, and that went double for when there was snow on the ground. I probably hadn't driven in snow for almost two years, given that I'd been driven out of the state and gone on the run before winter had come last year.

Also, I could fly back then, a loss I was keenly feeling as I tried to nonchalantly stalk up to an older-model Ford Explorer. It looked like an early 2000's edition, which suited me.

I tried the doors, very casually, then looked into windows of the cars next to me, just to see if the doors were unlocked. No dice. I could scour the parking lot and hope to find someone who'd been sloppy about locking theirs, but this was about as good as I was going to get, I figured.

I busted the rear window on the driver's side and reached up, unlocking the driver's door and slipping into the Explorer. It was cold in the car, overnight temps having dropped, the chill long seeped in. There was a partially drunk diet cola in the cup holder in the center of the vehicle, and I lifted it, just to see. It was completely frozen through, the cola a hard chunk of ice at the bottom of the can.

"Yep," I said, leaning down to pull the wires out from under the dashboard, "welcome back to Minnesota."

It took me a couple minutes to strip the wires I needed and hotwire the car. It would have been easier with longer nails, but meta strength and my enhanced fine motor skills got the job done eventually. The engine purred to life, and I looked back as I shifted the Explorer into reverse and eased out of the parking space. Once out, I threw it in drive and engaged the four-wheel drive which had drawn me to this vehicle.

I pulled out of the parking lot and onto Snelling, gunning it down a side road a few seconds later. In order to get downtown, I'd have to cross the Mississippi River, and most of the easy routes would be jammed with people trying to get the hell away from the scary metahuman who was tearing up Nicollet Mall.

Such a shame. They'd just finished with what felt like a fifty-year reconstruction project down there.

My easiest route would be to approach from the north, Hennepin Avenue bridge. I'd sneak into downtown that way, and if the roads were too logjammed, I'd just ditch the Explorer and head north into the city on foot. I could cover the mile or less between the bridge and the intersection where my adversary was waiting in a matter of minutes.

I took the north route to circle around; Snelling started to turn into a freeway around just before the State Fair grounds; I could see the tower in the distance, and it gave me a little thrill, being this close to home.

The Explorer skidded on the slick roads as I hit the overpass at Larpenteur and slid through the intersection as I hung a left. Larpenteur became Hennepin under the bridge, and suddenly I was racing through a faded industrial area, passing old warehouses and shipping concerns as they slipped past at fifty miles per hour. Trees with no leaves hung over the street, their branches like skeletal bones trying to wave me off from doing what I was hell bent on doing.

Which was racing into a confrontation with a guy who had me so grossly outpowered as to make my fight with the Terminator look completely fair by comparison. But hey, I'd almost beaten the Terminator, so ... I had to at least stand a chance with this guy ... right?

I tried not to allow myself the luxury of negative thoughts, but reality is a mean mistress, and she came crashing in on me while I tried to accentuate the positive. This was madness, possibly suicide, which was a phase I thought I was past since I'd crawled my way out of Rose's clutches.

The Explorer shot under a rusted railroad bridge draped with ice stalactites and through an intersection where someone blared their horn at me for failing to acknowledge the rules of the road. Give way, idiots, I'm trying to save lives here! Or possibly kill myself in a blaze of glory and martyrdom.

How had my life gone so far off the rails? A year and a half ago I'd been living in this city, I'd been the most powerful meta in the world, I had a boyfriend, I had friends who were like family, I had half a billion dollars in the bank and was secretly working for myself, lived with my surrogate mom Ariadne, I was a hero who was instrumental in stopping the tide of metahuman attacks, was respected, and was just generally ...

Happy.

Shit. I was happy.

Now I was on the run from the law, and Ariadne didn't even remember me thanks to the machinations of the villain who'd borked my life from the highest office in the land. I had almost no powers. Who even knew what had happened to my boyfriend, my family and friends were beaten down, I'd lost most of my money and couldn't access the rest, and I was pretty much thought of as a villain throughout the world.

As the Minneapolis skyline appeared in the distance between

a couple of leafless trees, I had to ask myself ...

Was this really the consequence of some shitty decisions I'd made back when I was eighteen?

Did this really come down to the bad press I'd gotten from killing Clyde Clary, Eve Kappler, Roberto Bastian, and Glen Parks? From my intemperate actions as a metahuman superhero law enforcer, when I'd occasionally lost patience with people like Eric Simmons? From Cassidy's character assassination campaign against me a few years ago?

I was wanted. Hunted. In spite of my best efforts to save the world, I'd been framed for things I didn't do, and tarred because of the things I had done years ago.

Was this just the deal? Was I a villain, now and forever? Irredeemable?

I mean, it wasn't like the law was likely to just forget the Eden Prairie incident, since that was the pretext for my arrest. It was somewhat compounded by the LA nuclear incident (thanks, Greg Vansen) but astute eyes had at least blasted all over the internet the fact that "Sienna Nealon can't produce a nuclear blast!" which had apparently staved off any charges there, though I was still very much a person of interest in that investigation.

All the things I'd done, both good and bad, seemed totally weighted against me. The good counted for nothing, the bad weighed tons and was pressing down on me with the force of a dumpster filled with plutonium. And on fire, because my life was a nuclear dumpster fire.

I was passing the occasional house now, zipping past stores as I shot over Interstate 35W. I flew through more intersections, got more honks, flipped the occasional bird in response. Traffic was picking up in the opposite direction, and I was passing in the center lane, laying on the horn anytime I caught up with someone who was traveling the speed limit.

After blowing through a whole series of intersections, things started to build up. Condos and apartment buildings began to rise around me. Newer restaurants and stores had sprung up through this part of town. Disused industrial and light commercial sectors gave way to an aging and refurbed cityscape, the kind of neighborhoods where hipsters dwelled with their lumberjack beards and flannel shirts (no, seriously—a guy in a flannel shirt, in a perfect imitation of the Brawny Paper Towel man, was hauling ass down the street in the opposite direction).

I hit the split of Hennepin Avenue and 7th Street and raced on, joining up with 1st Avenue. A few blocks later, downtown Minneapolis was rising above me, just ahead.

Home.

Almost home.

A little farther ahead and I saw the bridge onto Nicollet Island.

And suddenly … I was there.

The bridge ended, and I was in downtown Minneapolis.

I turned left onto Washington Avenue and raced, ignoring the honks as I pushed my way through vehicles that were blocking the intersection, forming a line to escape the carnage on Nicollet Mall. I went straight ahead on Hennepin and hung a left on 6th, fighting through another string of stopped traffic. People were getting out of their cars and fleeing on foot, some wrapped up tight, some dressed completely inadequately for the occasion.

Here I abandoned my car on 6th, pulling it onto the sidewalk and honking to get people to get the hell out of the way. There was definitely not going to be any escaping from this by car, so … I just left it, hitting the cold air as I got out, letting it pour over me, infuse my bones as I stared down to the intersection with Nicollet Mall.

The little dome of rock waited, cracks in it that provided an opportunity to see the big bad guy's self-constructed oven. Flames were crawling slowly out of the sides, and that shimmering veil of water waited.

"Take my car," I said to a woman who was struggling under the weight of trying to drag along four kids, two of them very young and the others maybe six or seven, tops. I grabbed her by the arm and got her attention with a sharp shake as I pointed to the Explorer. "Go south. Hit 394." I pointed to the 394 signs just down the street. "Go the wrong way if you have to, just get out of downtown."

Her eyes were frightened and yet somehow dull as she stared

at me. She blinked, then squinted, almost in recognition. "Aren't you …?" she asked, like she was trying to put something together.

"Take the car, get out of town," I said. "Hardly anyone is coming this way, so take advantage of the empty lanes." I turned my back on her. "The Explorer's running, just get your kids in, buckle up and go."

"Thank you!" she called after me as she hurried them into my car. I didn't stick around to watch the operation. The crowds on the street were thinning already, the buildings around us probably near empty. The city of Minneapolis had seen enough metahuman incidents that no one wanted to be caught at ground zero when one was brewing right outside their door.

I took to the street at a run, passing the big Murray's sign, passing under the Ike's awning and then, once I'd gone past a couple garage entrances, past Oceanaire's windows.

Snow remained in the gutters, frozen in spite of the city's best efforts to clear it. Piles remained, draped on the edges of the sidewalks, waiting for some sucker to try and step over them.

I didn't try. I just jumped and landed on a spot on the road that was clear.

Approaching the little sphere of flaming, hovering stone was a daunting business. I kept my stride even and stooped, grabbing up a handful of snow and shaping it as I went. I made a snowball, of course, and walked right on up to the sphere, stopping about ten yards away.

Only one thing to do now.

I threw the snowball with unerring accuracy and it piffed right through one of the cracks, dissolving into steam and boiling water as it passed into the flames. I heard it sizzle, a little cloud bursting out of the crack where it had entered.

"Hey, Captain Planet!" I shouted, voice echoing over the street, "I'm calling you out. I've seen your earth, wind, water and fire, so why don't you shed your geodesic dome of a hidey-hole and show me the power of heart, huh?"

It was pretty classic Sienna Nealon to walk up to someone like this, sitting in an impenetrable (to me) fortress in the middle of the street, roasting flames cooking out the sides, and just toss out a challenge.

At least, it seemed like the sort of thing Sienna Nealon would do. Based on what I could remember. And I remembered ... most of it? Maybe.

That was the struggle, though, wasn't it? Not knowing what I didn't know, having no clue about what I couldn't remember. Were the parts Rose removed from my memory things that were critical, core to who I was? I'd been a flippant ass in response to what she'd done to me while it was happening, but with three months of separation since I'd killed her ...

That was a lot of time for doubt to sink in. And I had plenty of it, now.

"I don't have all day, sparky!" I shouted again. Black eyes appeared at the nearest split, Mr. Flames peering out at me. "That's right, dark-eyed boy. I answered your call, dick. You could have just used the phone, but no—you had to make a big scene. You know what that says to me? You're one of those dramatic guys whose mommy probably didn't love him enough. The kind who tried to trip girls to get their attention when you were in grade school, and never really progressed beyond that." I flipped my hair. "I get it, though, I'm totes smoking enough to get you jonesing, fire bug, but I'll be honest, I've been with hotter guys than you—"

The earthen armor around him shifted, cracking open like an egg as he floated out, staring at me like I was some unknown creature. "Sienna ... Nealon?" he asked, staring down at me.

"It's me," I said, spreading my arms wide. "You attacked my friends and family, you made an ass of yourself downtown in my city, you called me out—why are you surprised I'm here?"

He blinked a couple times, his eyes disappearing in flames, the black orbs simply vanishing as his fire-covered eyelids covered them. It was a trippy thing, like they just vanished for a quarter second or something, and he was left featureless save for a nose and a thin line where his mouth would be. Like an incomplete, flaming version of the old Dick Tracy villain, the

Blank. He leaned closer, staring at me. "You ... look so different ..."

"Well, if I looked the same, people'd be realizing it was me everywhere I tried to hide, dumbass," I fired back at him. I looked sideways and saw a local news truck parked a couple blocks down 6th, with one of those giant crane cameras extended up at the four-story level or so. The glint of a lens in the daylight told me that the world was watching. Probably wondering why I wasn't about the business of smiting this asshole yet.

Because they didn't know the truth.

That I was as powerless as a freaking kitten against a guy like this.

"You are ... too thin," he said.

"Way to skinny shame me, dickhead," I said. "You go to all this trouble to arrange a date, and you end up being the worst I've had since that Ricardo douche."

"I ... what?" Flamey looked taken aback. "I ... do not call you here to ... date you."

I rolled my eyes. Of course he didn't. Only the sickest and most twisted of admirers would try and approach lust and/or love from this angle. Like Sovereign, which this guy was starting to remind me of. I ignored the tight ball of fear in my stomach. "Fine. Why did you want me to come here? What do you want from me?"

Like I didn't know the answer to that.

His thin, flame-coated lips smiled wider, then wider still, curving up in a black line across the flames that covered his face. "A fight, of course." He spread his arms wide. "I come here to you ... for the fight."

33.

"Well, that's just effing great," I announced to the empty, echoing canyons of downtown Minneapolis. I didn't bother keeping my voice down because there was no one really around to hear me. No cop cars, no obvious police engaging this guy, just a news camera a few blocks away and probably some snipers providing impotent cover fire from minimum safe distance.

He blinked at me again, his fiery skin once more causing his black orbs of eyes to disappear as he did so. "Do you ... not enjoy the fight?" There was a curiosity in his tone.

"You think I enjoy fighting?" I gawked at him.

"Does it not ... remind you of who you are?" His Euro accent was strong, but the passion in his voice was undeniable. "Does it not remind you ... of your strength? Does it not bring you back ... to yourself when you feel lost?"

I cracked my knuckles and they made a loud noise as they popped. "I dunno. I feel like there might be other ways to get in touch with my inner awesome. Ones that result in less pain for others." I looked up at him. "So ..." Now came the moment of truth. "We can both flaming suit up and cancel each other out," I lied, "or you can come down here and fight me like a big boy without creating a rain of flaming wreckage all around. You know—recall your inner badass by going knuckle to knuckle with me instead of trying to prove your fire is stronger than my fire."

He cocked his head at me, but drifted closer to the ground.

"You ... would surrender an advantage?"

I shrugged, looking around. "We could burn this place to the ground in a flaming twister, and I don't know that it's going to get you in closer touch with yourself or whatever it is you're looking for. I've got fire, you've got fire—we use them against each other and it does nothing, you should know that."

He nodded. "That is true, I suppose."

"So are you out to cause utter devastation?" I asked. "Because there's a town west of here where that happened." I was playing a hunch; however much wreckage this guy had left behind—and shit, it was sizable—he hadn't out and out annihilated Reed or Jamie or Veronika. If he'd wanted to, he could have left them a pile of smoking ashes.

But he didn't.

"No," he said and drifted to the earth. "I will not snuff the flame shield, though; if I do, your police will shoot me."

Well, shit. How the hell was I supposed to beat him seven ways to Sunday with my bare fists when he was five thousand degrees?

"Fair enough," I said instead, my mind racing. "Shall we keep this to the ground?"

He frowned, another funny spectacle when wreathed in flames. "Why?"

"I thought you were looking for a test of strength," I said with a shrug. "Seems to me that if we're flying and I land one good accidental hit, out go your lights and you crash to your death. Fight over, all on the basis of a lucky punch."

He thought about it. "That ... is also true."

"You know my abilities," I said, the lying becoming easier as I went. "And I've seen yours—or at least some of them. Let's keep the destruction toned down and I will battle with you as hard as you want. You start ripping apart the whole city, I'm going to find a very unfair way to murder your ass as swiftly as possible. If you want a true contest of strength, fight me like a man, not a meta terrorist. Capische?"

"Your terms are fair," he said and set his feet. Flames smoked off of him. "Are you ready to begin?"

Not remotely, I realized, since I had exactly zero ways to cause him damage when covered with flames. At least, nothing at hand.

"Just a sec," I said, and strolled over to the corner of the street, where Oceanaire's outdoor furniture was sitting stacked on the sidewalk.

"What … are you doing?" he asked.

"Well, it's not going to do me any good to punch you when you're covered in fire like that," I said, looking over my shoulder at him, "and I can't get you with a light web. We're not flying. I mean, I could probably get in your head with Odin powers—"

"I have those myself," he said, still watching me walk toward the sidewalk patio space in front of Oceanaire.

"Which means those are useless for me," I raised my voice and he started to slowly follow behind me, warily, because we were about to fight and obviously I was going to bushwhack him somehow. "So what have I got left? I can't turn into a dragon here, we just agreed to limit collateral damage and that'd just make a mess of this building," I nodded at the tower that stretched out of Oceanaire's facade, "so … I'm kinda out of easy options." I stopped by the stack of furniture. "Advantage: you. We fight as is, fist to fist, and it's either a stalemate or you beat me with your superior quantity of powers, see?"

He stopped short of the sidewalk. "Well …" He shifted uncomfortably. "I do not like all this talking. I thought we would fight."

"And we will," I said, lifting a chair out of the stack. "But you can't expect me to walk into it with nothing to hurt you with. What's the point of that? How are you challenged by that? What's that do to—what was it you said? 'Remind you of who you are' or whatever?"

"That is a good p—" he started to say, but I winged the chair at him and he paused to try and stop it from taking his head off. He raised his hands and acted like he was going to catch it, but instead he tossed a little fire ahead of him, superheating the metal and turning it into a puddle of slag that hit him and steamed. His mouth pulled into a grimace, because he might have been able to absorb flame, but molten metal didn't just evaporate when it made contact with his fire shield. Not that much. A bullet, sure. But a whole metal chair? Nah.

It slid past his flame shield and onto his skin, sizzling as it burned him.

I'd already heaved a table at him to follow it up, and he tried to block that but it went low, like a frisbee, right to the gut. It melted as it struck, but not before it transferred some force to him. He made an "OOF!" noise as it bounced and got him in the gut, doubling him over on the wire surface. He melted through the surface instantly but stopped as he made contact with the sturdy steel beams that held the supports together. They boiled, turning molten, and he screamed as he recoiled away from them.

"Heads up!" I shouted, throwing another chair at him. He looked up, but I'd aimed low, throwing it like a shot put at his gut, chair-back first, and it caught him in the midsection, searing and sizzling as he melted that, and then caught the seat portion right in the chest and chin.

He wobbled, leaving another pile of slag on the street as I tossed another table at him, then another. They went frisbeeing at him as he wove on unsteady legs. One cleaned his clock and dropped him to the ground while the other took his legs out from beneath him. The fire started to fade as he hit the ground, elbows buried in the slushy mess in the gutter.

I bombed him with another chair, still about twenty feet away, then grabbed another two, one for each hand, clutching one by the wire back and gripping the other beneath the seat. I was going to tame this flaming lion, tame him or kill him, and I took off at a run to cross the distance between us before he regained his wits.

There wasn't going to be a lot of time to shellack this guy, and I was going to have to get him to drop the flame shield if I was going to even have a prayer of doing so. I rushed in on him and a little past, then whapped him squarely across the back with the chair in my right hand. It slagged, but not before the physical force sent him flying into the curb. I heard the rich crack of his collar bone as he impacted on the gutter, shoulder catching as he did a serious dive and ended up face up on the sidewalk, making little snow angels as the slush around him melted and ran off.

Brandishing my partially melted chair, I came at him like I was going to stake him with the melted remainder. I had a couple of points left of the tubing that secured the chair back in place before it had been turned to molten metal, and it came to a sharp end. Drive that through his heart and he'd be just about done, I figured, or at least he'd be in a bad enough way that I could turn his head into a pinata and shower the street with his brains before I called this thing a day.

I didn't telegraph my move before I came in on him, driving the point at his chest. I would have leapt high to drive it in, but that would be overly dramatic and also give away my intent. Instead I just came running up and—HOO-AH!—rammed it toward his chest.

I was about to make contact when something shredded its way into my mind like a physical punch inside my brain. I'd been hit by Bjorn's Odin power before, when he and I had fought, lo those many years ago before Old Man Winter had forced me to absorb him and he'd become a complaining part of the cadre of powers I kept in my head. His powers tended to manifest in the form of a raven—your dark thoughts given mental form—blasting their way into your mind.

That ... was not what happened here.

If Bjorn's power could be called a psychic assault, akin to someone jumping into your mind and pummeling you with your fears, this could only be described as a psychic blitzkrieg, the entire Nazi army plowing through my brain and leaving nothing but trammelled dirt and wrecked villages behind. I screamed and dropped the chairs, heard one make a satisfying sizzling as it ran over him, and I staggered back and fell off the curb.

This was worse than any hangover I'd ever felt, worse than taking a direct hit from a Thor type when they were standing in a field during a lightning storm. Scenes from my past flashed in front of my eyes, and they were like a montage of

Sienna Nealon's absolute worst hits—the murders I'd committed, the people I'd screwed over, the accusing faces of those whose lives I'd upended by my action or inaction.

I saw Ariadne, and somehow she remembered me, and all the crap I'd brought down on her.

Then there was Reed, looking pathetic in a hospital bed, tubes threading out of him, the guilt-inducing sound of a life support machine beeping in the background.

And finally ... there were my souls, surrounding me in silent judgment.

Wolfe. Gavrikov. Bjorn. Zack. Kappler. Bastian. Harmon.

Their forces were distorted, but their expressions were unmistakable.

I'd failed them.

And they were letting me know.

"No!" I shouted, coming back to myself as I landed in the slush in the middle of the street. Cold water soaked through my clothing, and it was like a shock that brought me back to myself. I wanted a drink of scotch more than I'd wanted anything in my life to this point. I wanted it now, I wanted it quick, I wanted to cut my wrist wide and shove the bottle right into my veins so this sick, uneasy feeling I'd been running from for months, this sense that I'd—I'd lost something, that I sucked, that I was the worst person in the entirety of the world, that I was weak and pathetic and horrible—I wanted it gone, I wanted to be in blissful stupor, and—

My face lay against the rough pavement of 6th Avenue, my fingers cold in the melted ice that this bastard, this ... this fight seeking, this danger hunting ... this Predator had left behind. The chill was seeping in, Minnesota winter come back to get me. I'd been warmed by his flames, distracted by the horror of what he'd done in my mind.

I remembered Veronika, when we'd first met, saying that she'd conditioned herself with an ex to resist the power of the Odin mental attack. How I wished I'd been able to do that now.

"Why do you just lie there?" the Predator slurred. I turned and saw him floating, his shoulder at a funny angle. "Why do you not shrug off my Odin attack?"

"Because no one's ever hit me with it like that before," I said, rising to my feet. "Either that power has been enhanced or you've been living a thousand years and working with it."

He looked frozen in place, caught in headlights, me about to run him down. Unlikely, since the mind assault had frozen my entire body, and I was just shaking out of the paralysis. "I have not lived a thousand years," he said stiffly, answering that question.

"Then why are you so good with fire?" I asked. I was starting to get a feeling this guy was no incubus.

He flared for a second, and then rushed at me, streaming flame. I was forced to dodge back, to go low, and he shot inches over my head. His black eyes passed me, and even covered in the fire, I could see the curiosity.

My bluff was about to be called. If I'd still had my Gavrikov powers, I would have taken his charge head on, and we would have gone flame to flame.

Instead … I'd dodged out of his way. And I'd already faltered under a mental assault that an Odin type should have theoretically been prepared for, at least in general if maybe not in scope.

I rolled back to my feet, a little slowly because of the stiffness, and he paused as he came around. He threw a burst of flame at me, one I should have been able to absorb, then another, then another.

I dodged them. Because there was nothing else I could do.

The shiny lens of the news camera caught it all, blocks away, over his shoulder, and I knew that now … the world was drawing its own conclusions.

Now … the whole world knew.

They knew I was powerless.

Weak.

"What are you doing?" Predator leaned toward me, throwing more fire. I dodged, rolled, sidestepped, and he upped the tempo. I moved, ducked, flipped, and spun out of the way of successive shots, no time to grab something and hurl it toward him for a counterattack. "What is wrong with you?"

"I could ask the same of you, really," I said, my breaths

becoming ragged from all the rapid movement. "I mean, really, who goes looking for fights? What are you, Tyler Durden? Are you a figment of my imagination?"

"This cannot be." He stopped throwing flames. "You … are not her?"

I paused, ready. "Oh, I'm her. Or as her as you're going to get these days."

He just stared at me, almost crestfallen, like he was another person I'd hit with crushing disappointment. "You have none of her powers."

"You think so?" I stared him down. "Drop the flames, come over here and hold my hand for a bit. See if I'm missing that power."

"You are … weak." It was a sick sounding declaration, like a gunshot in the street.

"Fuck you," I said and turned, reaching the corner in a second. I grabbed hold of the light pole in front of Oceanaire and ripped it out of the ground as he stood there, stunned. I tugged it carefully, working to not tear the electrical wiring as I pulled it free of the street. Then I put it on my shoulder, holding the pole like a massive baseball bat. "Come here and say that to my face, you son of a bitch."

He raised a hand to shoot flame, but I brought my improvised bat down on him like he was a Whack-a-mole. It hit, hammering him, melting as it did so. He let out a little cry of pain as the molten metal dripped through the fire shield, and I dragged it forward, taking care to keep the structural integrity of the wires that had powered it connected—at least for now.

I smashed him over the head with the melting pole a few more times before he got irate enough to do something about it. And the something he did about it was a billowing cloud of fire that forced me to go sideways and ripped my electrical wires out, severing the power pole from the ground.

There went one plan, unfortunately. And it was a good one, too. Zap zap.

"You are not what I thought you were," he said, steely and pissed now that he'd managed to blunt my constant bonking and burning attack. He was still holding his shoulder at a funny angle, though, and his head looked like it bore a wound, judging by the way the flames danced over his forehead, casting a consistent shadow over his brow like a scar. I'd hurt him and he couldn't heal it, at least not immediately.

"Hey, man, I'm sorry I haven't updated my dating profile yet," I said, taking advantage of the newfound freedom of the pole in my hand and bringing it overhead like a log, hurling it at his midsection. He started to go up and then changed his mind at the last second and went sideways, a nearly terminal hesitation and a pretty rookie mistake. He caught a glancing blow on the side as he tried to get out of range and the crack of his ribs echoed down the street. "But honestly, you lose a little weight, you ditch a few psychological demons, stop hearing voices—most guys would consider that an improvement."

He fell to the ground, clutching his side, fire starting to subside from his feet and hands. He was wearing clothes beneath, a trick I'd never managed to master with my flame shield, but one that Aleksandr Gavrikov had at his disposal. It suggested a high level of control of his fire, something I'd already suspected just from watching this guy work. Still, the ability to control it millimeters at a time? Enough to run a shield just over the surface of your skin and not consume your clothing? Way beyond anything I'd ever been able to do.

I darted in and kicked him in the knee, wrenching it by making it go in a direction it was not supposed to go. He let out a little cry, and I did not let up, especially as the fire receded from him. I kicked him in those already-wounded ribs, sending him flying through the air and into the facade of the building across the street. He crashed into it, leaving a cracking impression in the concrete, and I was all over him as he flapjacked down onto the sidewalk, not giving him an inch of space to recover.

"I didn't ask for this fight," I said, stooping and punching the shit out of him. His face was bleeding after one hit, nose shattered after two, cheekbones out of place after three. "I didn't ask for any of this." Blood spattered my clothing as I gave him the business, the Sienna Nealon special, which was face punching with no a la mode. His skull made a cracking noise—or my knuckle did, hard to tell with the adrenaline pumping—and I worked him like a punching bag as he lay there.

"I didn't ask for any of this!" I shouted, raining blows down on him. Fury pulsed through my hands, ravaging him as he tried to raise his hands to shield his face.

I didn't ask to be made a fugitive for shit I didn't do.

I didn't ask for every meta asshole on the planet to see me as their number one rival.

I didn't ask for some crazy Scottish bitch who lost her family in the war to latch onto me as the avatar of every wrong that had ever been done to her.

I didn't ask for the president of the United States to decide I was a threat to everything he was trying to accomplish, I didn't ask for Cassidy and the Clary family to come after me for revenge, I didn't ask for freaking Sovereign to decide that I was his one and only chosen bride, or my mother to die, or for her to imprison me, or—

My adversary exploded in a burst of fire that flashed over me so quickly I barely had time to react. I moved on instinct, hurling myself away from him, seeking cold, seeking ice, and I landed in the nearby snowbank at the edge of the road and rolled, rolled furiously and without thought, even as the ice melted and steamed and sizzled around me.

When I stopped, I was face up and looking into a cloudy sky. I raised a hand and saw scorched skin, blisters already appearing between the angry red. "You … ass," I said, to no one in particular. Or at least no one I could see.

He floated through the air toward me, head at a funny angle, creases in his flame shield in a few places where I'd worked his frigging smug, fight-seeking face. His nose was out of joint—literally—and his jaw hung a little to the side.

"You … are not what I was looking for," he said, muffled through the broken jaw. It was probably causing him a lot of pain.

"You weren't looking for an ass kicking?" I asked, unable to get my body to move. I was, after all, flash-fried, and that wasn't a condition that leant itself well to anything but rolling around on the ground wishing for the burning pain to stop. I was feeling the first traces of it, but I suspected his earlier mind assault might have been occluding some of the pain because my nervous system was still not fully back to operational. "Because if you called me out, you should have known I wasn't just going to send you away with a little chiding."

"Look at you," he said, almost sneering down at me. "You talked your way through my advantages, lied your way through part of the fight, counting on me to be too dumb to realize you were ... weak." Here he sneered and spat a little, still talking like he had a mouth full of cotton. Which, he probably would, later, because I was pretty sure I'd knocked out some of that son of a bitch's teeth.

"Yeah, well ... it didn't seem likely you'd fight me fair, fist to fist, you loser," I threw back. I was trying to move, to do something—hell, grab another snowball and throw it at him in defiance, maybe turn it yellow first if I had any pee left—but my body was just ... not working. I glanced around, seeking some sort of impromptu weapon, anything would do.

All I saw was empty sidewalk and snow. Nothing to my advantage at all. Quite the opposite, in fact, if he melted the snow that enshrouded me. He could drown me right here and there wasn't a damned thing I could do about it.

I twitched, my fingers moving slightly, and I gathered a small amount of snow in my palm. With jerky movements, I lifted my hand, and tossed it at him.

The small snowball hit his chest, sizzled, and evaporated.

"You are pathetic," he said, disgust just dripping from him. "What happened to you?"

"I ran across someone badder than me," I said, looking him right in the eye. "But I still killed her ass. And I'll do the same for you."

"You are like an old dog that still barks even though he can barely move." He just loomed, sneering down at me.

"This old dog bit you harder than anyone who's bitten you yet, dickweed."

"No," he said, and his voice went hushed. "No ... you are not even close. This?" He motioned to himself. "This is a pleasant sleep compared to what I have been through."

"That so?" I stared up at him. "Well, next time I'll make sure to turn it into a nightmare you'll never wake from."

"There will be no next time," he said, shaking his head at me as he raised his hand. I could feel distant thunder, like the earth was moving beneath me. It was a strange, faint hammering sound that seemed to grow louder the longer I lay there.

I stared at him as he raised his hand to strike—

And the ground beneath me gave way, the sidewalk crashing in as I fell beneath the street.

Something snatched me out of midair, and I was moving, moving like someone had me on their back. I didn't even feel like I'd lost consciousness, just that somehow the sidewalk and snow had dropped from beneath me, and then I was being hoofed through tunnels. An explosion went off where the light had been streaming through into the darkness of this sewer, and the pressure felt like a hard shove.

The person who carried me did not even stumble, sure-footed as he rounded a corner and kept moving at a hard run. "So," came the voice of Harry Graves in the darkness, "that could have gone better, but not much. You did well."

"Harry? I ... just got my ass kicked," I said to him, feeling oddly reassured that he had kept his word.

He'd found me, like he said. Just when I needed him most he'd ... uh ... jackhammered through the concrete beneath me, pulled me out as it fell, and then dynamited the tunnel entrance behind us to cut off my adversary's ability to follow us.

Damn.

"Damn," I said, because it just came out.

"I know, I know, I'm amazing," Harry said, huffing lightly as he rounded another corner. "I'll have you out of here in five."

That was exactly what I'd been thinking. Safe on the back of Harry Graves, I felt myself lulled by his movement, my body traumatized beyond the ability to function. I let my neck loll, swayed as he ran, and just gave myself over to the darkness I'd been fighting since the man on fire had burned me, and off I went, into waiting sleep, my fight now finished.

34.

I sprang awake in a dark room, cognizant, dimly, of the fact that this was the second time I'd been beaten into near unconsciousness in the last day or so. The thought crept in as I found myself wondering, once more, where the hell I was.

"Hey," a soft voice said, and a lamp snapped on. I stared into the face of Harry Graves, and my frenzied breathing, loud and gasping, started to subside.

"Harry," I said, my near-panic at the memory of how I'd most recently gotten my ass beat starting to fade. I looked around; we seemed to be in a fully-furnished house, though one with extremely faded décor. "Where ... are we?"

"Oh, I just looked around for an uninhabited house and checked ahead to make sure we wouldn't get caught," he said. "So long as we're out of here by next week, we won't run afoul of the owners."

"You're into burglary now?" I asked, looking around. There was a collage photo of a married couple on the wall in black and white, and the grandma-style throw pillows arrayed on the bed next to me and on the floor next to Harry's chair, plainly discarded, told me a lot about this house's occupants.

"I've always been into burglary," he said, smiling. "It's like an Airbnb that they didn't sign up for. And I always try and leave the place better than I left it."

I shook my head. "Between your breaking and entering, Eilish's unrepentant shoplifting, and Cassidy's cyberterrorism

... I've fallen pretty far." I plopped back into the plush pillow. It even smelled like I'd imagined a grandma pillow would smell.

"You want to talk about it?" he asked as I buried my face in the pillow.

"I got my ass kicked, Harry," I said, opening an eye and staring into the white cloth, made yellow by the lamp glow. "What else is there to say besides the obvious?"

"What's the obvious?"

I sat up and looked at him. "It's so patronizing when you do that."

He started to say something—I was pretty sure it was going to be another question that he already knew the answer to, but he stopped. "I told you ... it's kinda rude if I just finish your conversation for you. Then you don't learn anything."

"I don't need to learn anything else right now," I said, swinging my legs over the side of the bed. My clothing was scorched, blackened, really, but still nominally functional, like rags held together by frayed knots. Cover myself up in a blanket and I'd be more or less fine. "I think I've learned enough today, attending the school of hard knocks."

"You almost beat him, you know." He was looking at me ... beseechingly? A hint of pleading present in his eyes and tone.

I reached behind me, trying to figure out what the lump at my back was that was annoying the crap out of me. I pulled out a carbon-scored Walther PPK and stared at it before putting it back in my waistband. It wasn't damaged, at least not badly enough to have set off the ammo or melted the barrel, and given how crappy I was doing these days for defending myself, I might just need it before long.

It was the weapon I'd killed the most powerful person in the world with, after all. Albeit with an assist from Greg Vansen.

"Everybody knows, don't they?" I asked, staring down at my empty hand. Yeah. I'd need the PPK, sooner or later, since I couldn't throw flame, shoot light webs, fly away, assault minds, read thoughts, or turn into a dragon anymore.

"Yes," Harry said, thankfully not bothering to play dumb

and ask for clarification like, "Knows what?" Instead, he said, "The news caught the whole fight. Commentators assumed, of course ... Everyone's wondering how it happened. Cable airwaves are filled with the speculation, but to my knowledge, no one's even close on the how."

"How could they?" I asked, staring at my empty palm, pale white and powerless. "I'm still a villain to them. I'm sure they're wondering how I got my comeuppance. Whoever breaks that story is going to get beaucoup ratings."

Harry sat there in silence for a moment before answering. "There's nothing I can say here that's going to make an ounce of difference to you right now."

"You got that right."

"There's a bar down the street," he said instead, rising a little stiffly. "There's a few, actually—we're in St. Paul—but if you go to any of them but the one named Pete's, you're going to get recognized, and the cops will show up before you even get down one glass."

"We wouldn't want that, would we," I said sardonically. "Because I doubt I could fight them off, and I damned sure can't flight them off anymore." I stood and started to brush past him.

He caught my arm, and I almost fought him, but he only held me for a second. "It's not over," he said, looking me right in the eye.

"It's over," I said. "I can't beat him. I can't beat the Terminator. I'm not what I once was." He let my arm go. "I used to be the most powerful metahuman in the world, Harry. And look at me now." My voice was hoarse, a whisper. "You said it just now, without me even asking—"

"Because I knew what you were going to ask before you even—"

"All I want to do is get a drink," I said, looking up at him and feeling the burning self-pity. "I don't care about the Terminator. I don't care about the Predator anymore—"

"Nice names."

"—I don't even care who Sigourney Weaver is. I just ... want a drink." I smacked my lips. "That's all I want. All I want to do now." I looked him in the eyes. "Whatever else I might have been before … it's gone now. Okay?" I patted him on the shoulder, almost sarcastically, like I was giving him reassurance in the locker room after a hard defeat.

"Okay," Harry said as I went for the door. He didn't say anything else.

The guy who could predict anything I was going to say, could counter any argument I might make …

He didn't say a damned thing.

He just let me walk out so I could go get stinking drunk.

And that was when I knew I was right.

It really was over.

I was done.

35.

"Hey," Cassidy said, looking from her computer monitor as I came into the grandma's living room. "I was just reviewing tape, and I think—"

I held up a hand to shut her up, and pinpointed the door most likely to be the front door. There was a quilt on the back of the couch, and I grabbed it, wrapping myself up as I went. It looked dark beyond the cracks of the curtains, no natural light shining in, which meant it was almost certainly well below freezing out there, and my clothing was pretty frigging useless against the weather by now.

"Where are you going?" Eilish asked, emerging from a bathroom as I stalked past toward the door.

"Sienna's going to get a drink," Harry answered from behind me. I did not look back as I opened the front door, which was helpfully unlocked.

The subzero air hit me full in the face as I stepped out onto a quiet street. Squarish, boxy houses stood all up one side of the street and down the other, but we were situated on a corner; the street came to an intersection to my right, and it looked like a main road. US Highway 61, if I was not mistaken, which snaked through St. Paul heading north.

I picked my direction and headed out onto the main drag of 61. The area was a little run down, but not terrible, and as I reached the corner I could see a half dozen bars just from where I stood.

There was one with a neon sign that said "Pete's," and

although the T was burned out, I got the idea. I thought, briefly, of being a defiant ass and just ignoring Harry's guidance, but I wanted a drink a lot more than I wanted to get into a tangle with the cops, so I made myself a makeshift cowl with the purloined quilt and headed toward Pete's— Pee's, without the T, actually—crossing 61 at a jog, my blanket trailing behind me like a cape.

Stepping into Pete's was like dragging myself into a junkyard. There was no pretense about this place; the bare concrete were floors unrepentantly cracked, and the old plaster on the walls suggested to me that St. Paul's building inspection team was either falling down on their jobs or their code was at third-world standards. A motley collection of old signs and beer memorabilia was the primary decoration, but none of it looked like it had come from this century.

I bellied up to the bar, encouraged by the many, many bottles on the shelves behind the bartender, and tried to ignore the collection of older, biker-looking dudes at one end of the bar, a couple of leather-clad gals with them giving me the eye, like I was going to steal their men or something. Draped in a freaking quilt and wearing clothes that looked like they'd been barbecued. Ladies, if I could steal your man dressed looking like this, you have bigger problems.

The bartender was a gruff old guy with a squint. "What'll you have?"

"Got any scotch?" I asked. He nodded. "Whatever's good, then." As he walked away to fetch me a drink, I fumbled for my wallet and found it gone. That was going to be a problem at some point.

A jukebox played a classic rock tune, maybe Roy Orbison, though it was hard for me to tell. I put my elbow on the bar and then my face on my hand. There were no TVs in here, which was good, because I needed the outside world to intrude on my serious drinking like I needed to get into a brawl with all those old biker guys. Sure, I'd kick their asses, but what the hell good would that do? The Terminator and the Predator would still be out there. All I'd have done would be adversely de-stimulate the St. Paul bar economy and inject a few Medicare dollars into the local hospital. And

Pee's (I sniffed; the name almost fit) seemed like it could use all the help it could get staying open.

The bartender dropped off a drink for me and asked, "Get you anything else?"

"A refill, once I go through this," I said, and he nodded, then meandered off, probably planning to return once I'd done some damage to my scotch. I hoisted it, preparing to drink; it wasn't going to take long.

"You're her," a cracked voice said, and I almost slopped scotch down the front of me. I turned my head to look, and found myself staring at one of the biker gals. She was all done up in boots and with a leather jacket all her own, faded straw hair and looks that had probably really been something once, before now. Now she was a biker grandma who was trying real hard to just look like an aging, cool, biker mom. No amount of hair dye could hide the wrinkles and hard lines, though, and her sandpapery voice suggested cigarettes had been a constant fixture in her life.

"I'm a her," I said, holding my scotch just inches from my lips. The heavy smell of alcohol rose into my nostrils, begging me to complete the circle, to dump it back down my throat, to let the healing begin. Or at least the numbing effect.

She sat down next to me, unasked, and I started to favor her with a vicious look that would send her skittering away. She didn't skitter, though, instead looking around, left and right, surreptitiously, like she was about to confess something that she'd rather no one hear. "I know I don't look it, but I'm a grandmother."

I stared at her, trying to contain my shock. "You don't say."

"I had a baby at seventeen," she said, keeping her eyes forward. "A little girl. Her daddy and I used to sit down by the river in Minneapolis ... so I called her Mississippi ... Missi for short."

"Original," I said, scotch still perched in front of my lips, wondering what the hell this had to do with me.

"She got married to a man who works for Lifetime Fitness out in Chanhassen," she went on, treating me to the worst dinner theater I'd ever seen—because the dinner theater out in Chanhassen (actually a real thing) was quite good. Also, my scotch was my dinner, so that didn't add any points to the current experience. "And they had a little baby of their own. Called her Clara."

"That's nice," I said, my scotch still in a holding pattern. I was going to down it soon if she didn't get to the damned point. I don't know why I was holding back; taking it down might have made me more apt to listen. Except ... I was listening, without fail and only the occasional sarcastic interruption. Maybe I was curious about where this old biker chick was taking this story.

"One night when Clara was real young," she said, "her momma kinda hit her limit. Cooped up all day with the baby, she needed to get out. So she decided to take her out shopping. And Chanhassen has a few places, but she wanted to go, to really get out for a while—so she took her to Eden Prairie Center."

I started to feel a little tingle across the back of my neck, working its way down my spine.

"And you'd think, you know ... peaceful night of shopping. Nothing bad ever happens when you're shopping ... except something did." She was still staring straight ahead, at the bar, but she was starting to get choked up. "Some man ... some ... superpowered man ... he came charging through the store wearing this ... this black armor." She sniffed a little. "He was running from someone, see?"

Now I really started to tingle. Mainly because I remembered this. Remembered the man in black armor. His name was David Henderschott.

"He tosses a clothing rack across the damned store," she said, and now she turned to look at me. "And Missi is right there, inches away—but she'd stepped back from the stroller where Clara was sitting to look at something—and that rack is just whizzing at Clara, and Missi told me—'Momma, all I could think was our little girl was going to die.'" She shuddered. "Makes me sick every time I think about it—how close she came."

I just sat there. My hand shook a little, and a cold drip of scotch hit me on the leg.

She pulled out a phone and tripped the touch screen so it lit up. A picture of a ten year old girl was right there, long pigtails and ... a Grateful Dead t-shirt?

"You saved my little granddaughter," she said, sniffing a little. "You threw yourself in front of that clothing rack and yanked her out of the way so fast her momma barely even saw it. She told me—told me later after—after the world found out who you were, she said—'That's her. That's the girl that saved our baby.'"

Scotch was spilling all over the place now, and I sat my drink down in front of me, hand shaking. I remembered that night, now that she'd reminded me. It wasn't a memory I'd lost; it was one I'd buried, an afterthought, jumping in to save that little girl—Clara. Some offhand action by me, pure instinct.

And here was the consequence. A little girl who'd grown up because I'd acted.

"I know," Biker Grandma went on, "you find yourself in some trouble lately. And I don't believe a bit of what they've said about you. Because I *know* who you are. You showed us when you saved my Clara, when you risked your life when you didn't have to, when there was nobody who knew who you were. That told me everything I need to know about you."

She reached over and brushed my hand. "The cops and the government and the press can say whatever they want. Call you a criminal. But I know who you really are—"

"Who am I?" I asked, a little afraid to find out.

"You're a damned hero," she said. "And you don't let anyone tell you any differently." She stood up, turned to the bartender and said, "Her drink's on me. As many as she wants." And with one look back, and a smile, she started back to her friends.

"Thank you," I said, and stared at the spilled scotch in front of me. "But ... I hope you're not offended if I ..." I smelled the scotch on my hand where it had dripped, strong and pungent, and ...

... I didn't want it anymore. Not a single sip. "... If I don't, because ..." I stood, composing myself. "... I've got somewhere

I've got to be. An ... ass ... I've got to kick."

"You go get 'em, girl," she said, with that same, encouraging smile.

"I will," I said, as I turned to leave. "I just gotta figure out how."

36.

Eilish met me at the door, peering in just as I was heading out. She sniffed the air once and declared, "Not exactly JD Wetherspoon's, is it?" as I passed her.

The cold air hit me, bracing and powerful, frosting my cheeks where—frigging again—I'd been crying. I mopped my eyes and resolved that this was the end of the waterworks for a while.

No more tears. From me, at least. There were going to be lots of tears from the Terminator and the Predator. I was resolved to make those little bitches cry, then cry uncle.

"Harry sent you?" I asked as Eilish tried to follow beside me but failed to keep up with my quickstep.

"Uh, yeah," she said as a car honked at me when I went to cross 61. I flipped him the bird and kept walking. "Seemed to think you were about done."

"I am about frigging done, that's right," I said, clutching the quilt tight around me. "But why did he send you? I was heading back."

"Hey!" the driver shouted out the open window from where he'd screeched his car to a stop. "You're Sienna—"

"Would you kindly get back in your car and drive on?" Eilish asked, waving a hand at him. "You're not going to call the cops or do anything else except drive home and go to sleep, right?"

The man just sat there, head stuck out his window. "I'm just going to drive home and go to sleep."

"Good boy," Eilish said. "Also, obey all traffic laws and make sure you yield to pedestrians, even when they're not in the crosswalk, all right?"

"Yes," he said. "Of course." And stuck his head back in the window and patiently waited for us to clear the lane before slowly accelerating away.

"Guess that explains why Harry sent you," I mused as I stepped up on the sidewalk and headed back toward the house. "He doesn't move in very mysterious ways."

"I don't exactly consider him an open book, though, do you?" Eilish asked. "I mean, you still don't know why he's here."

"Said he needed my help with something," I said, turning the corner back onto the residential street. Even though the sidewalks were icy, I stuck to them because snow was piled on the lawns. "I assume I'll find out what that something is when the moment comes, since he's not exactly Mr. Forthcoming, and he's been overly solicitous thus far in terms of giving help and asking for none in return."

"Aye, he's probably got a big favor to ask," she said, nodding along.

"What about you?" I asked as she pulled her hands out of her pockets and blew on them ineffectually. This cold was miserable, probably way beyond what Ireland got in winter.

"What about me?" Eilish asked, stopping alongside me.

"Don't give me that crap, Eilish," I said, pulling the quilt tight. "You came to me in Scotland because you wanted to know the truth about Breandan. You got drawn into a fight you didn't ask for, it's true, but you could have left and gone back to London afterward. Instead, you got on the plane with me, came to America, and you've been hanging out ever since."

"I appreciate free food and unlimited drinks, which, by the by, is a considerable incentive for most human beings," she said with a totally fake twinkle of amusement. "Why, that's the very incentive most casinos use to snare people in. Take it from someone who used to spend all her time in the company of a top-notch gambler."

"Why are you here?" I asked, trying to cut through the BS,

looking her right in the eyes.

She shuffled her feet slightly and looked at them. "Well, it's a funny thing, y'see ... I don't really have anywhere else to go. My family ... they went with the cloister outside Connaught, and Breandan ..." she shrugged. "Well, ye know. So, you're right ... I could have gone back to London, where I still have an outstanding arrest warrant, and my days of dodging the female cops are probably waning. So damned many of them now, y'see; female empowerment—good for the soul, not so good for the Siren on the run who relies on men she can bend to her will."

"What do you want to do, then?" I asked.

"I don't know," she said, shoving those hands deep in her pockets. Her jacket was wholly inadequate to the task of keeping her protected from Minnesota's vicious cold. She stamped her feet, but I was guessing that was unlikely to do much. "That's why I've been hanging about with you. Doesn't exactly require soul searching, what you've been up to of late."

"Reed could use your help, you know," I said softly.

She frowned. "How'd you know he was all right?"

Now it was my turn to hem and haw a little, though only because I hated to have to explain my chain of reasoning. "Because Harry didn't say anything when I woke up, and it was the first question on my mind. I watched him as I was storming out; he didn't have any bad news to deliver."

"Yeah," she said with a nod. "They're all still in the hospital, but no fatalities. We don't have much of an update on them, though—they're just ... in stable condition, as these things go."

"I figured," I said, drawing a frosty breath that made my lungs ache. "That means they'll all recover, probably. Metahuman healing and whatnot. But this guy ... the Predator ..." I shook my head. "He's looking for a fight. For a real fight, someone that can ... I dunno, make him feel alive or something. He's dangerous."

"Harry said he was actually going to kill you," she said, "if he hadn't pulled you out."

"I did piss him off," I said. "And he's causing no shortage

of property damage." I started back toward the house. "I have to find him. Have to wrap this thing up."

"Uhm ... forgive me for being all gloomy now that you're ... full speed ahead, because I don't mean to be an anchor on your, uh, cheerfulness, but ..." She paused. "How are you planning to kick his arse seeing as last time you bluffed him into taking it easy on you? And he still dusted the city streets with you?"

"I don't know yet," I said, "but that's the least of my worries."

"The least ...?" Eilish asked as I moved on and she followed in my wake. "Hell, girl, what's the greatest of them, then?"

"The Terminator is still after me, somewhere," I said. "And he's got a habit of showing up where I show up."

"Yeah, how's he doing that, by the way?" she asked as we walked up the path to the house. Someone had shoveled it; probably some kind neighbor or maybe a plow service. Either way, it was done, and the remaining snow so hard packed that it wasn't too slippery.

Harry opened the door for us a second before I reached for it myself, so I just cruised on in, Eilish in my wake. "How's the Terminator finding us, Harry?" I asked as he closed the front door behind the Irish girl.

"Every time you make a scene or an anonymous tip—a credible one—is received about you, he uses it to triangulate your current position," Harry said, folding his arms as he walked forward.

"His accent is American," I said, "his bearing is military. And this isn't the first time they've employed soldiers against me."

"You are leaving faint traces," Cassidy said, piping up from her spot in the corner, lit by the glow of her monitor. "You were stealth in Florida. No tips, no nothing. But when you started moving, you started exposing yourself to more random people, casual encounters."

"Before, I was hanging out on the beach, I'd go to the occasional restaurant," I said. "You're telling me that no one noticed me then, but the moment I started moving—"

"You were acting like a vacationer among people on vacation," Cassidy said, blinking. "The minute you started moving, you were back to old habits, whether you realized it or not. And so you looked like—"

"A dangerous fugitive," I said.

"I was going to say a real bitch, but whatever," Cassidy said.

"Yeah, your natural RBF ... it's the stuff of legends," Eilish said, gesturing to my face. "It makes me want to surrender to the authorities. And you weren't really like that in Florida, see. Too drunk, I guess." She shrugged.

"Sobriety ... why is this worth it?" I muttered. "So ... people are going to recognize me now, even with the weight loss and different hair color."

"As long as you've got that working scowl on your face ... yeah," Harry said.

"So help me if you tell me to 'smile more,' I will dedicate my life to making sure that when next you smile, you do it with less teeth," I said. He shrugged, and he was smiling, the bastard. "Whatever. This is not a problem of the moment. I need to deal with these assholes that are out there causing me problems." I shed the quilt, dropping it back on the couch where I'd found it. "How do I beat these guys? How do I level the playing field?" I looked at Eilish.

She looked back, and her eyes widened. "Oh. Uhm. Me, then?"

"There's only one of us in this room that can wrap men around their finger like they're talking seductively to a sailor on leave," I said.

"It's me, isn't it?" Harry asked, smiling faintly. "I've got a way with words." His smile disappeared. "A word of warning about what you're thinking here ..." He explained.

"Uh, let's not do that," Eilish said once he'd gotten it all out.

"Fine," I said. "We'll work within the frame ... work."

"How?" Cassidy asked. "I'm sorry, I'm supposed to be the smartest person in the room, and while I'm very encouraged by the beating you were able to deal out to this ... Predator, I guess you have chosen for him, namewise—"

"It's a good name," Harry said. "Fits the 80's theme of our slate of villains. Plus, the Predator really did go looking for a challenge."

"Whatever," Cassidy said, totally brushing off Harry's keen observations. "I like what you did to rearrange his face and skull, but I am slightly skeptical of your ability to repeat."

"Let me tell you a little trick about humanity, Cassidy," I said. "This guy? He thinks he's the apex predator of the planet. That's why he was seeking me out. He wanted to be the best, and ... now he thinks he is." I smiled. "But the problem with being the champion ..."

"Is that you have to defend the title every now and again," Harry said with a smile. "Otherwise, you're not the best anymore. We learned that in *Rocky III*." He shrugged when I gave him the eye. "Sticking with the theme."

"That kind of thinking on his part is dumb," Cassidy said. "He beat you. He should take his well-earned victory and be happy with it."

"Logically, yes," I said. "But this drive of his—whatever demons are fueling his fire? Logic ain't in the picture at this point. He's running on fear and ego, and if he gets challenged, he's going to fight. Which is why he's dangerous. If this goes on much longer, his little over-the-top aggressions are going to stop finding hard targets like metas and he's just going to run roughshod over everyone." I walked over to Cassidy. "I need a place where I can fight him ... and beat him."

Her eyelids fluttered, but she answered almost immediately. "Try in your dreams."

I started to fire off an angry retort, then stopped myself. "That's ... not bad."

She smiled. "It's a start, anyway. I expect that'll get him ... nice and ready for your next meeting." She started tapping again at her keyboard. "And while you're doing that, I'll see if I can find a place where you can even the odds."

"A maths class, then," Eilish said, very straight-faced. "What? Even the odds, get it?"

"I got it," I said, "it was just terrible, that's all. All right, people," and I headed back for the bedroom, "I'm going to go take the most productive nap I've ever taken. Hold down the fort while I'm gone, will you?"

"You'll be safe until you come back out," Harry said, giving me a fake salute. "Kick his ass, Sienna. Kick it hard enough he'll carry a grudge from here to eternity. And—never mind," he said, shaking his head. "You've got this."

"Damned right I do," I said, disappearing into the bedroom, dark and inviting, waiting for me—a battlefield fit for a succubus.

Because if there was anything I was good at, it was pissing people off.

37.

"So it is you," the Predator said as he entered the darkness of the dreamwalk with me, looking around at the hints of broken street, of the shadow of buildings beyond the lines of dark that hung in the distance like night closed in.

I'd chosen the scene of our fight because it seemed likely to put him at ease, to remind him that yeah, he'd beaten me hard. I needed him lulled for a few minutes, anyway, before I got back to the business of throwing down the gauntlet. Right on his junk. "Yeah, it's me," I said, "the girl who dealt the hardest ass kicking you've yet experienced in your brief supervillain career."

He was dark of hair and fair of skin, absent the flame that had consumed him when I'd met him in the almost-flesh. His face in the dream lacked the creative alterations I'd made to it through my punching. That was interesting; I doubted he'd healed yet, but maybe. At the very least, he hadn't taken the beaten I'd given him onboard psychologically.

So, in his mind ... flawless victory. It was time to turn that feeling around.

He shook his head at my jibe, made a noise of disdain, and then a shoving motion as if to ward me off. "I beat you, and you ran."

Overconfidence. I like that in someone I'm about to pummel.

"Well, you kinda overpowered me like, ten to one," I said, flippant. I had dreamwalked myself into a new wardrobe, something that felt more classically Sienna—leather coat, jeans, stylish t-shirt, and some steel-toed boots. Yes, steel-toed even in my dreams. Because they're my dreams, duh. "I suppose I could have hung around and taken the killing punch, but it seemed stupid to do so since my intention is to whip your ever-loving, superpowered ass, and to date you haven't killed but maybe one of your challengers." I cocked my head. "So … was it because you felt threatened? Or was it because you realized that you're really a chickenshit at heart, and that me being a threat to you scared you enough to want to kill me?"

A dark cloud ran over his face, a shadow not unlike the ones hiding the scenery around us. "You don't frighten me."

"Au contraire, mon frère," I said, going to that chipper tone of voice I only used when I was really trying to piss someone off. So … often, I guess? "You tried to blast my face into oblivion." I touched my cheeks gently, probing. "My pretty, pretty face. Why would you want to destroy something so beautiful if not from fear? I mean, I guess I could understand spite as a motive, since you are not so pretty, but …"

"You are trying to goad me," he said with a patronizing smile. "It will not work."

"What are you afraid of?" I asked. "Losing your temper? You already lost that, Bubsy. Or was spiking my head into a sidewalk like a normal Thursday for you?"

He frowned. "It is Monday."

"So sue me, I can't keep track of the days anymore." I shrugged. "Your superpowers … they're lab grown, aren't they? You didn't manifest them naturally. Not at your age." I had him pegged as in his thirties by looks, and he didn't have that air about him that screamed old meta.

He hesitated, then surveyed his surroundings as if trying to assuage his worries. Which was good, because the fact that he was talking and answering the question meant I'd riled him enough to talk, but not enough to break off all contact—yet. It was coming, though. "I have been a metahuman for two years, yes. Very good guess." He smiled tightly. "Long enough to learn that I am stronger than you, or any of your friends, the supposed light of mankind."

"If you're calling me the light of mankind, you must be from somewhere super dark," I said. "Another guess ... Revelen?"

He stiffened visibly, almost flinching. "I am not from Revelen." He seemed to draw back, wary eyes on me. "But it is where I was ... made. Or made powerful, perhaps."

Huh. An interesting little item of note, I thought. "So ... did you meet Vlad?"

He frowned. "... Vlad?"

"The man in charge," I said. "The one everyone is terrified of when they meet him."

He nodded once, slowly. "I have met him."

I stared back at him. "And you're terrified of him?"

He stared back at me, and there was a hint of uncertainty, then he nodded, just once. "Only a fool would not be."

"Are you running from him?" I asked, bypassing the other pressing question I had.

He nodded again. "Only a fool would not be." And this time he smiled again, but his eyes were hollow and his look utterly without joy.

"What's your name?" I asked more softly, guiding us away from being confrontational. I had a couple more weapons in my arsenal that I could use, but I didn't want to use them unless he proved ... difficult.

"Stepane," he said. "Stepane Abraam."

"You had two powers when you manifested?" I asked, and he nodded. Suddenly it made sense.

Every so often, a meta would be born with two abilities, one each from their mother and father. Aleksandr Gavrikov had gotten flight and fire, for instance.

Stepane here had probably had latent powers; a metahuman way up the family tree somewhere, so far back that the abilities would never have shown up on their own.

But with the serums developed in Revelen, they'd unlocked his basic powers. "Fire," I said, "and ... the Odin ability? The Warmind?"

Stepane nodded again. He seemed withdrawn now that I'd confronted him directly. "They were what I started with."

"And they gave you other serums," I said. "The one that boosts those base powers. Which is why your fire and your Warmind are so damned epic in strength." I thought about how he'd blasted the fear through my head in a way I'd never felt before, and how his control over the flames was second to ... well, maybe Gavrikov, and that was it. "And the one that unlocks tangential abilities—which is why you can use wind, water, earth ..."

"I have illusion powers," he said, "flight ... some others of small note."

"They gave you serious juice," I said. "You took me on, took on my team ... and you won. Congrats on that, by the way, it's not an easy thing to do."

"When I left Revelen ... when I escaped ..." He stared into the darkness, as though it were going to leap out at him, "I did not wish to be afraid again." Now he looked at me, and there was darkness in his eyes. "Do you know what it is like ... to fear someone? Someone ... unstoppable? To know they are out there, that they can rip you apart at any time? That they are just waiting to do so until it is convenient? Until they *want* to?"

I had a flash of a girl with flaming red hair and mad eyes, anger flowing through her like her countless powers. I thought about her, dead on the Scottish soil in her own village, and suppressed the shudder. "Yes," I said. "I know what that's like."

"I came here ... to become the best," Stepane said, voice echoing hollow. "To find my strength. Because ... *he* ... is out there. And he will come for me ... sooner or later. I must try and be ready. Be the best. To find the strength to beat the best."

"What did he call himself with you?" I asked.

Stepane looked at me, puzzled. "What need did he have for a name? He was simply *him*. Anyone who met him knew to whom you would refer."

Hm. That didn't answer anything for me.

"He was the most evolved among us, you see," Stepane went on, and I let him monologue. "The most powerful."

"You make it sound like that's all that matters," I said.

Stepane let out a cackle. "It *is* all that matters. This is what we humans do—prey upon each other. The weak die or capitulate and serve, the strong ascend and rule over them. One of your presidents said, 'The only thing we have to fear is fear itself.'" He shook his head. "Those are the thoughts of a privileged man coddled by civilization, softened by the rule of law."

"Well, he suffered a debilitating illness that left him in a wheelchair, so I don't know that he lived an adversity-free life ..." I said.

Stepane shook his head. "Adversity is not the issue. By the law of the jungle, he would be eaten."

"I'm glad we don't do that anymore. Pretty sure I'd be forever trying to get the flavor of certain people out of my teeth."

"You joke, but you don't see it," Stepane said. "The laws of civilized society are a ruse. A mask that hides what truly happens. The strong still rule, just more gently now."

"Why wasn't I ruling when I was strong, then?" I asked.

"You were a threat to those with a different type of power," Stepane said, eyes glimmering in triumph. "That is why you were cast out and chased. The balance had to move, all society had to be put against you, because you were too powerful then for just one person or two people to simply take you out."

"Well, this has been a fascinating discussion on strength and Darwinism with a nice little detour into cannibal land," I said, "but here's the thing ..." I heard a faint whisper, somewhere outside the dreamwalk.

Deltan Data Systems. South Minneapolis. It was Cassidy's voice. An address followed.

"Yes?" Stepane asked, looking around. I couldn't tell if he'd heard it, or if he was just responding to my eyes darting around, like Cassidy's face was going to appear out of the darkness.

"You got strong, I congratulate you on this," I said, staring him down. "Why, you may even be the most powerful meta in the Western Hemisphere, since it seems like you think old Vlad in Revelen is still a little too much man for you to take on."

He looked at me evenly, seeking out signs of deception. "Thank you."

"But ..." I said, dropping the other shoe, "you're really only powerful in the waking world." I smiled. "In here ... I'm way stronger than you."

"How—"

He didn't even get the question out before I was all over him, applying my succubus pain-generating powers with complete abandon. I'd never assaulted anyone in a dreamwalk the way I assaulted him now, dredging up every sort of nightmare I could, pouring on the agony while I bound him tight and immobile, unable to so much as twitch here in his dream.

Stepane was paralyzed, his mouth open wide, screams trying to come out, but I'd blocked them. I could hear them echoing in my head, resonating throughout the darkness of the dreamwalk as though they were transmitted by sound wave across my skin. He screamed and screamed and screamed—

And after about fifteen seconds that made him feel like it was an eternity, I let him loose and turned down the agony.

"That's a fraction of what I can do," I said as he huffed, breathing hard, into the black emptiness that was the ground in here. "And I'm going to come visit you every night, until you get to a point where you don't dare sleep for fear of knowing that this moment is coming—

"That *I'm* coming for you." I leaned in and breathed the last words in his ear, and where with lovers past I'd infused my whispers with sweetness, here I went the opposite direction, and he shuddered in revulsion and fear. "How's that compare to ol' Vlad? Who do you fear now?"

"What ... do you want?" He looked up at me, gritting his teeth. Now I'd pushed him over the edge into fury.

"I want a rematch, bucko," I said. "Away from police snipers, away from prying eyes—at least until the cops show up—and far, far away from interference by anyone who might want to stop our little battle to see who the strongest really is."

"You are weak," he said, oozing a little drool down his chin. "You stand no chance against me."

"I almost kicked your ass before, sparky," I said, brushing his cheek and making him scream in agony once more as I sauntered off, casting one look back before leaving him with a taunt I knew would have its desired effect. "And this time? I'm not going to go nearly so easy on you."

38.

I woke from the dreamwalk with a gasp, sitting up to find Harry next to me, and Cassidy tapping away in the corner of the room, still lit by her screen. She glanced at me for just a second, then went back to typing.

"You heard?" Cassidy asked.

"Deltan Data Systems in South Minneapolis," I said, shivering a little, either from the torture I'd just performed or the realization I was about to go into another fight that would probably end up in an incredibly brutal fashion. "You sure about that one?"

"It'll work," she said, not looking up.

"Harry—" I started to say.

"I'll go get us a vehicle," he said, already on his feet. He brushed my hand as he stood, and I realized he'd been kneeling at the side of the bed when I'd awoken. He tossed me a smile, then vanished through the bedroom door. A few seconds later, I heard the front door open and close.

"I think he might have a crush on me," I muttered under my breath.

"Duh," Cassidy said. "Even I can see that." Then she paused, looking at her computer screen, eyes unfocused.

"You're thinking about Simmons ... about Eric, aren't you?" I asked, putting my legs over the side of the bed.

She looked down, almost trying to hide behind the screen of her laptop, but it was so small it afforded no protection from my prying gaze. "Yes," she whispered.

"Is he dead?" I asked.

She didn't answer for a moment, staring straight ahead. "I don't know."

"You don't?" I asked. "No body found, I assume?"

She shook her head. "No body. No confirmation."

I let her baste in silence for a beat. "What was he doing in Virginia? Why was he attacking that aircraft carrier?"

"I don't know," she whispered. "I ... when I got out of the Cube, it was before everyone else. Harmon let me loose ... to come work with him on destroying you and completing the serum. When Eric got out ..." She turned so I could see her profile. "I don't know what happened, but when I finally got free of Harmon a few months later ... he had already disappeared."

"I suppose a guy like Simmons wouldn't want to be found by the cops again."

"No," she said, turning to look right at me, eyes burning. "He didn't disappear from the cops. I could have found him if he'd gone underground. He disappeared, Sienna. Vanished. Not just off the grid, off the continent. No record of travel under any alias. No one matching his description. He was gone, like he'd never even existed." She turned away again. "Not many people have that kind of power to ... make things disappear and reappear—like he did in Virginia. No customs record. No passport. The FBI investigation?" She touched her laptop screen. "It's like he dropped out of thin air. Eric wouldn't have gone after a target like an aircraft carrier just for the fun of it. He'd need a reason. Someone *made* him do this." Her face hardened. "They pushed him in the path of this maniac." She looked away. "They got him killed."

I felt a little chill, like a familiar boogeyman had come strolling behind me and stroked my spine. "There's only one group I know of that seems to have the ability to make things appear and disappear out of the United States these days without any trace."

Her gaze hardened. "Revelen."

I nodded. "It's hardly conclusive, but ... yeah."

"I don't know much more about what's going on over

there than you do," she said, focusing back on her screen. "They've got someone who's pure dynamite working Infosec for them."

"ArcheGrey1819," I said, taking a breath as I slid off the bed and stood.

"Probably," Cassidy said. "But her architecture is so good it's tough to tell without seeing inside the walls for hints of her ... signature code."

"Are you going to be okay?" I asked, thinking again of her use of pep pills during our road trip. She had the dark circles under her eyes now, and I wondered how long it had been since she'd slept.

"Your false concern is unnecessary," Cassidy said, focusing her attention back on her screen and typing again. "You don't really care if I'm processing these amphetamines properly."

"I care a little bit," I said, trying to be gentle. "From a purely utilitarian standpoint ... Cassidy, you're watching my back on this. I need you in the best possible working condition."

"I'll be fine," she said, not looking up from whatever she was typing. "I can work for seven and a half days without sleep, and I'm on day four, hour six. As you know from your recent experiments with alcohol consumption, narcotic effects are lessened among metahumans due to superior liver and kidney function—"

"I was expressing concern for you as a person," I said. "You don't have to explain yourself to me."

She paused her typing. "Oh," she said, not looking up from the screen. Her pale skin glowed in the screen light and she glanced up at me. "I know you're not doing this for me anymore. Because of our debt."

I sighed. "And here I was hoping this would square things between us. Kinda annoying that you finally learned enough about detecting human motives to figure out mine had changed in the course of this thing."

"I'll make you a new deal," she said, thinking for only a millisecond before speaking, leading me to believe this was something she'd scripted out ahead of time. "When the day comes that you go to Revelen ..." She kept talking, even though I opened my mouth to protest, "... and we all know it's coming ..." Her gaze got hard, furious, and I saw hints of the depths of anger within Cassidy, and it was ... boundless. "I want to go, too."

"You could just buy a ticket tomorrow," I said, shrugging. "It's not like the country is under embargo. Airfare is like a thousand bucks, no obstacle for you."

She shook her head. "Going in that way? They'd see me coming a mile off." She shut the laptop and leaned forward. "No. I just want you to tell me when you go—so I can come at them my own way."

My brow puckered as I frowned. "Why?"

She smiled thinly. "Because when you go in everyone will be paying attention to you and the mess you're making. They won't have time to spare a thought for me." She leaned back and opened her laptop once more.

I tried to decide how to take that, and finally settled on pretending it was some kind of compliment. "You've got a deal," I said and met her gaze over the gulf between us. Once upon a time, I would have said the distance between Cassidy and I was light-years. But now, looking at her as she typed, planning her revenge ...

It didn't seem nearly so far.

39.

Deltan Data Systems was an old building, constructed in the seventies but carefully maintained. It sat just off Highway 55 in the southern part of Minneapolis north of Richfield and the airport. It was a section of the city that was caught between degeneration and renewal, old houses being refurbished in some pockets and decaying in others.

Here on the commercial strip, things followed the same path. Next door was a decaying strip mall that bordered Highway 55, and it had definitely seen some better days.

Snow dotted the Deltan Data Systems' parking lot, most of it pushed to one corner as plow trucks tended to do in the middle of winter, and I stood outside the running van, absorbing a little of the heat as Harry stared out at me, Eilish in the passenger seat next to him.

"Are you sure about this?" Eilish asked. Harry looked like he might have wanted to ask but knew better.

"I am sure of very little lately except that scotch is a foul yet tempting mistress who held the key to my heart," I said, staring at the forbidding two-story across the parking lot. I felt a little bad about what I was about to do to Deltan Data Systems, but hopefully they'd backed up the hard drive elsewhere. And were, uhm … insured, I was going to say, except insurance didn't tend to pay out for metahuman incidents.

Alas. Maybe they had a stockpile of cash. Or could get FEMA assistance once this was over. Something to mitigate the prickle of my conscience, because it was unlikely the federal government would be totes cool with me transferring cash out of my bank account in the Caymans to cover the damage. Pretty sure they'd consider that money laundering or something.

A flicker of light streaked across the sky, and I drew a breath. "Cassidy ... drop the dime."

"Dime dropped," she said. "I reported you as two blocks away in an email to the FBI from an anonymous account. They won't catch it until tomorrow, but the NSA should already have it. Based on previous experience, your Terminator should be along in less than thirty minutes."

"All right, well, get clear," I said, and slammed the van door as I started across the parking lot toward the building. "And Eilish—"

"I know what I'm doing," Eilish said, nodding at me like she was a rebellious teenager and I was her hopelessly square parent. "Go on. Try not to get your arse kicked too hard."

"That's like my mantra," I muttered as the van pulled out.

Harry hadn't said anything, and I hadn't looked back at him.

"No time to think about that now," I said under my breath as I broke into a jog, avoiding slippage on icy portions of the blacktop and running up to the front doors.

The building had a Plexiglas entryway, a vestibule to keep some of the winter cold out of the actual lobby, and I kicked in one wall as a streak of burning fire came in for a landing behind me. I stepped inside before he could follow, opening the interior door and leaving the Plexiglas lobby behind for the real one, a squarish affair with old white tile that looked like it would never be clean again.

Deltan Data Systems looked about like I expected it would from Cassidy's schematic drawings. She'd pulled the architectural blueprints, which told me exactly where I needed to go, fortunately—

Because Stepane came flying in through the hole I'd made in the door outside and then proceeded to make one of his own through the interior doors. Plexiglas melted under his heat as he cruised through in hover mode. I sprinted around a corner out of the lobby.

I found myself in a long hall and tried to recall the layout. I needed an alternate route; I was headed to a room at the end of the hallway, but if I ran straight, Stepane would catch me in the open with nowhere to run. I didn't want to battle him in a long, empty hallway, without anything close at hand to batter his skull in with, and no way to stop him from burning me up.

On the other hand, I had to put up a little fight before I ran, otherwise he might suspect he was walking into a massive trap. Which he totes was.

I threw open a door and ran inside, leaping over a desk in a small cubicle farm within. I was two rooms away from my destination, and Stepane blasted the door off its hinges with a gust of wind so fierce that the damned thing would have decapitated me if I'd been right in front of it.

"Nice try," I said, like I was in control, and kicked loose a piece of cubicle wall at Stepane as I dodged up and over into the cube behind me and kicked loose the wall on that one, too. I could smell him burning his way through my distractions midair.

He'd started a fire already. Damn. I'd been hoping to hold off on that until we were a little closer to my destination, but hey … when you play with fire, you better be prepared to suffer a third-degree or two.

I vaulted and rolled over two more cubicles and then ran low down an aisle between two rows as Stepane blazed overhead. I snatched a stapler off a desk and hurled it at him over the walls with perfect accuracy. I heard him mutter a curse in some unfamiliar language as it melted and drizzled stainless steel through his fire shield.

"This is how you prove your strength?" he asked, a little taunting. "By hiding like a mouse?"

"More like a fox," I muttered meta-low, so that he could hear me as if I were whispering, and in such a manner as to not give my position away.

"You are a fool," he said, "to challenge me in this way. My power is obvious, and we are outside your domain of dreams. If you could have killed me in there, you should have."

"But then I'd fear you physically like you fear Vlad, and I'm not a little punkass like you, so ..." I whispered again, sneaking between the cubicle rows. I was headed for the back wall, and as I turned a corner, I got a glimpse of it—forbidding concrete block, and my next challenge.

Because there was no door in this wall.

I'd known that when I'd gone into this room, but I hadn't realized it would be a concrete block wall dividing me from the next room. I'd figured drywall, which was a pretty easy thing to bust through. Smash on in, take out a few studs, boom, onward.

A thump on the other side of the room, near the entrance, drew my attention for just a second. I didn't dare stick my head up to look for fear of having it burned off by a blazing fireball.

"What are you doing?" Stepane called to me from across the room. I frowned; he wasn't anywhere near where that noise had come from. He seemed to be drifting that way, though.

"Oh, man," I muttered before I could stifle myself. I did say it very quietly, which was about all the brains I could claim in this situation. Also, I didn't say, "Oh, shit," which was kinda what I was thinking.

I needed a way through that wall, and fast, because things were about to heat up in here. The smell of smoke was already wafting through the room, but I had a suspicion that Stepane had stifled his fires after burning through those cubicle pieces, probably in an effort to keep the fire suppression systems in here from drowning him. Or not, since he could control water.

Making a beeline for the back wall, I started trying to think of things I could use to bust through concrete. My fist seemed the ever-present option, but that'd do some damage to me in the process, and would make my later face-punching endeavors more difficult. I marked that as a last resort. The rolling chairs in this place seemed too flimsy, and I passed a rolling metal cart that held a printer, plugged into its very own power supply. Sadly, this was the best of my options so far.

I didn't really have an abundance of time to seek out better, because I could feel the heat from Stepane looming overhead and getting warmer. So I grabbed the cart, printer and all, and hurled it into the wall about fifteen feet away. Then, without waiting to see where it landed, I made a full-on, bent-over sprint across the nearest aisle and dove into a cubicle as far from impact as I could.

The printer cart shattered against the block wall, sending a spray of chips through and leaving about a six-inch hole where one of the corners of the cart had hit. In terms of damage, it wasn't enough to do much more than bury a hand through, and I was a little disappointed because I'd hoped for more.

A glowing figure shot overhead, stopping at the wall. "Where are you?" Stepane asked, and I corked in a laugh because I didn't want to answer his stupid question with an even stupider response that would instantly give away my position. He sounded pretty pissed, not that I cared. He was going to kill me if he caught me anyway, so why worry about offending him further?

I debated throwing a whole cubicle at the wall, but with him hovering between me and the weakness I'd created in it—and thus the best target—I had a little time to search out an alternative. And also to hope he moved.

Creeping out of the cubicle and away from him, I kept nice and low. With my head turned so I could look back over my shoulder, I moved parallel to the wall I wanted to go through, keeping in cover behind cubicles as I headed toward the aisle that moved from the door where I'd entered (across the room) toward the wall where I wanted to smash through, and behind which—through just one more wall after that—lay my destination.

The server room.

I glanced at the corner ahead, then looked behind me as I tiptoed, still bent double, out into the intersection of the aisles. Watching the glow of Stepane as he hovered, waiting for me to show myself, I chuckled a little inside. He should have been sweeping the aisle, watching for me everywhere—

Something tickled in my brain, and I stiffened. A little

warning stabbed into my subconscious, and I turned because I felt movement ahead, like something jerking out of the corner of my eye—

And I got a momentary glance—enough to see the Terminator, leering at me, bent double just behind the corner of the intersection—before his punch caught me squarely in the chest and hurled me backward.

The blow hurt, force spreading itself through my chest and launching me off the ground. I had enough presence of mind to tuck my knees against my chest and make like a cannonball as I flew through the air—

I crashed through the wall, most of my momentum dispelled by the impact, and hit the one opposite—also concrete block—coming to a hard landing on my elbows and knees and sending a shock through my whole nervous system.

"Yay," I croaked, lying on my freaking face in the darkness as I heard movement in the room I'd left behind, "Made it through one wall."

And then I collapsed on the floor.

40.

I dipped into unconsciousness for a few seconds, and when I came to, I heard an argument out in the cubicle farm, echoing through the Sienna-sized hole the Terminator had made by shooting me through six inches of concrete block.

"She's mine," the Terminator said in that low rasp of his. Ominous. Foreboding. Totally a voice-over actor gone wrong.

"I must kill her," Stepane, the Predator, said, sounding pretty firm in his conviction.

"Okay," I said a little woozily, "you boys fight it out while I take a nap. I'll battle the winner for the lifetime supply of dog food … or whatever crappy prize goes to the champion in this contest of fools." I didn't even have a dog anymore.

"You are not my mission," the Terminator said, and I heard him crack his knuckles, kinda I like I did sometimes to intimidate people. "But you were involved in the *Enterprise* incident … some of my brothers in arms died there … which means I will have no compunction about getting knee deep in your ass. Stay out of my way, or I'll *make* you my mission."

"Yeah … you tell him, Terminator," I muttered, still woozy, but still awake enough to trash talk. "You … stomp him a new ass. Superspeed style."

"You seem strong," Stepane said. "Perhaps I will simply fight you both tonight."

"Oh, good," I said, and fell down on my face once again,

promptly passing out.

When I woke, the concrete wall in front of me was coming down, pieces of block shaking loose. I pushed myself to all fours, my body aching in places I didn't even remember it could ache. I pushed to my feet and blinked as a fist shattered the wall in front of me. I gasped, jumping back in time to avoid a two-inch square piece of concrete that smashed into something behind me with resounding ring.

I moved laterally in the narrow room, which was probably only ten feet wide but ran a good forty or so feet long, with a door that led out into that hallway where I'd entered, and which was sandwiched between the cubicle farm and the server room. The Predator and the Terminator were having their 80's movie dream face-off among the cubicles, and judging by the fact that I'd seen the Terminator's hand come smashing through the wall a moment ago, it looked like there was no clear winner yet.

If somehow the Terminator came up aces in this little conflict, I was going to need to suss out a way to beat his ass to unconsciousness ASAP, which was well within my capabilities and kinda played to my strengths, given that my specialty was face-punching.

On the other, if Stepane the Predator came out ahead … well, I still had the marginally more difficult Plan B, which my heart was set on, and all I needed to do was access the server room behind me with as little damage to the wall as possible and then … do one other thing.

I looked around the room, recalling what it was for. It was the room with all the transformers and serious electrical wiring to support the server farm next door, as well as the rest of the building. One of the main power boxes lay just a few feet ahead of me, and I regarded it curiously for a moment—

That ended when Stepane and the Terminator came crashing through the wall. The Terminator had three big pieces of cubicle wall in his hands as a shield between him and Stepane's flames, and as he came through he shoved Stepane forward, sending him into the back wall of the power room with sheer brute force and speed. Stepane impacted and bounced, flames sputtering a little as the Terminator roared and flexed his mighty frame.

Stepane burned through the cubicle pieces like they were nothing, and they stood just a few feet from each other, facing off like two bulls about to charge.

I sidled over to the electrical panel and casually ripped the conduit wire I'd been eyeing before, tearing it loose of the power box. I carefully gripped it by the insulated part, then I tossed it like a spear at the Terminator as he started to raise his fist to go after Stepane again.

The exposed wiring hit the Terminator just under the armpit and the reaction was immediate. He jerked and flailed, legs twitching as he did a dance that wouldn't have looked much out of place on a headless chicken. Then the wire must have grounded out, because he stopped jerking after a few seconds and pitched over, landing in the rubble of the hole he'd made through the wall.

"Don't think this will spare you from—" Stepane started to say, rising up again.

I hit him with a lightning-fast kick that sent him into the wall, and he crashed through the blocks just a little. A second hit—swift enough that his flickering fire didn't burn me— sent him tumbling through, and I leapt after him, trying to keep light on my feet as I moved past him and into the server room.

Stepane rose again, hovering as I fished in my pockets and pulled out a handkerchief I'd borrowed from Harry (such a classic gentleman) and a lighter I'd picked up at a gas station on the way here. I casually lit the cloth on fire as he watched, probably wondering what the hell I was doing. "You know I control fire, yes?" I nodded, and he indicated the flaming handkerchief with one outstretched hand. "You think to battle me with ... this?"

"Oh, this isn't for you," I said, waving it in front of him, then raising it up and wafting the black smoke pouring off of it into the dark ceiling of the server room.

A klaxon sounded, loud and furious, like a fire engine had been parked behind the dark servers behind us and now decided to turn its lights on and blare its horn.

Stepane's black eyes blinked from beneath the flame shield. Dawning realization that he'd been had trickled in, but he didn't quite see how. "You know I can control water, too—" he started to say.

Then the fire suppression system kicked in.

"And that'd be totally advantage: you ... if this room used water to suppress fire." And I grinned.

Halon 1301 flooded the server room, breaking the chain reaction that allowed combustion and fire. Tricky, interesting stuff, Halon—pretty much safe for humans to breathe, it still managed to defeat flames with ease. And preserve electronic equipment, which was why Deltan Data Systems had probably installed this kind of system. Sure, there were environmental concerns, which was why Halon 1301 systems were devilishly uncommon these days, but ...

Hey. It put out fires as easily as breathing.

I smiled as the Halon descended, snuffing out Stepane's flame shield and causing him to waver as he blinked, exposed at last.

Rushing in while he was still getting used to his shield being gone, I pummeled Stepane's exposed flesh, beating him as hard as I had in my dreamwalk. The rage I'd been sitting on after Scotland, and now after watching my friends hounded and hunted by this clown, after being shellacked by both him and the Terminator, from being chased by the damned law for something I hadn't even done ... all that came out, channeled through the techniques learned in a thousand training sessions with my mother.

It all came rushing out through my fists, and I remembered as I shattered his orbital bone, as I broke his jaw, as I smashed his nose—

I remembered who Sienna Nealon was.

I brought up a knee and drove Stepane into a server, denting the metal. Then I hit him with a frenzy of punches, driving him into it over and over, watching his head rock back. He was woozy, bleeding, bones broken all over his face and body.

Ripping a server out of the ground next to me, I lifted it above my head and brought it down on him, mid-chest. It shattered ribs, rent open flesh, and buried itself halfway through him. I raised it again, brought it down as hard as I could—

And Stepane Abraam was split cleanly (well … not *that* cleanly …) in two just beneath his armpits.

Then, for good measure, I drove the server down again, splitting his arms off and raised it once more. This time, I was prepared to strike off his head.

I paused, the server raised high above me. I stared down at his eyes as he struggled for air with lungs that, uh … weren't entirely there anymore.

For some reason, I cast my impromptu bludgeon aside and knelt next to the man I'd dubbed the Predator. There was panic in his eyes as he gasped to take a breath that would never come, as he tried to writhe and control a body that I'd completely shattered.

He couldn't speak, so I brought my hand down to his face and touched his cheek, pressing my palm to him. I held my breath, staring down at this utterly destroyed human being …

Yeah. This was who Sienna Nealon was. Face-puncher was sugarcoating it. Sienna Nealon was a destroyer. An annihilator.

Death.

My fingers touched him, and my power started to work. I'd almost forgotten how this felt in the last months, burning through my skin like a pleasant flush, like I'd had a little too much to drink …

And then it went straight to my head.

I plunged into the darkness akin to the dreamwalk, and I found myself in Stepane's mind. It was dark here, just as it had been before, but there he was, standing before me, pale as death, and clutching at himself.

He looked down, seeing his body whole once more, and breathed. "I am … dying?"

A vision of all the damage I'd done to his body flashed before my eyes. "Yes," I said. Because what else was there to say?

He stood in silence a long moment, and then a resigned smile graced his lips. "Good."

241

I cocked an eyebrow at him. "Good?"

"He can't reach me now," Stepane said, smile turning to a grin. "Now … it doesn't matter how strong I am, or how I weak I am … I move beyond his grasp." He staggered, turning a whiter shade as death seemed to take hold of him. "But you …" he looked up at me, and his eyes were …

Haunted.

"I'm heading for a collision with ol' Vlad, I know," I said. I paused, trying to decide how best to say what was on my mind. "I could really use some help."

"Your friends will be fine," he said. "I did not hurt them badly enough that they will not recover. None of them angered me … as you did." He seemed relaxed, almost as if this were a victory rather than a defeat that had led to his death.

"I could use some powers of my own," I said, looking at him, keenly aware that out in the real world, my hands were firmly on his cheeks, and though time had more or less paused, within his mind … my powers were still working out there, establishing the connection between our souls that would harmonize, allowing me to draw him out completely.

He got it in that instant, and a change came over his face as he seemed to light up, though no flame appeared on him. "No." His vehemence made me take a step back. "You cannot do this to me."

I took a step forward. "I'm stronger. You're weaker. Isn't that how this goes? Didn't you tell me that?"

"Please … do not do this to me," he said, and his mouth fell open, desperation shaping his lips into a hideous, fearful look. "I … I was to be free. Free of him—and you—you would have me be your puppet into death as you throw yourself into his open jaws?"

I stared at him. "No. No, I wouldn't do that to you." He relaxed, just slightly. "Because I'll tell you something, Stepane … strength is a nice thing if you want to live by the law of the jungle—and heaven knows more than a few people I deal with in the world want to. It's a job and a calling for me, to greet them with force and make them realize the error of their ways, but …" I shook my head.

"That's not how we do things in this civilized society you seem to eschew. We're supposed to persuade to get what we want. To win someone over to our way of thinking."

"You will never win me over," he said, shaking his head. "Not to face him. Not again."

"I know," I said, and the darkness started to swell around us as I began to withdraw my hand from his face, breaking the connection before my powers could drain his soul dry. "And I won't make you."

I stood, pulling my hand from his face, and taking up the server again as he lay there, looking up at me with glazed eyes. He knew what was going to come next, but there was no fear in them now.

Bringing the server high, I raised it above his head—

Then brought it down with lethal force, snuffing out his fire—his life—once and for all.

41.

I walked out of the server room through the hallway door, letting it groan and shut behind me with the mechanical whine of a hinge. Now I was back to nearly where I'd started from, the lobby ahead. I saw the door to the power room just a few yards down the hall, and was on my way toward it when it groaned open, the Terminator staggering out, murder in his eyes.

Then he looked at me.

"Hey, military guy," I said, pausing as he dragged himself into my path, "I don't want to fight you. And I damned sure don't want to have to kill you."

The shadow effect smoked off his shoulders, and I had a bad feeling he was about to go blurry with speed. "You don't have to worry about killing me. But fighting ..." And he put up his dukes.

"You're awfully arrogant for a guy who got his ass launched back on Interstate 94," I said, settling into a defensive stance of my own. "If you hadn't put lives at risk, or if I was the kind of cold psycho the press seems to think I am, you'd be a dead man already."

He twitched, just slightly. "Enough talk. Now—"

"I don't think there's been enough talk yet." A female voice came echoing down the hall, and Eilish stepped out of the lobby, Harry a couple steps behind her. "Let's keep talking, darling. Let's just talk and talk and talk until we can't chatter any more."

The Terminator stood there, stiff, for just a moment, and then he seemed to relax an iota. "Yes, ma'am," he said, like she was an officer he had to obey.

"You all right?" Harry asked, hustling over to me. He tugged on my sleeve, which was a little tattered from fighting and getting hit and beatings and whatnot. Also, bloody from lots of punching, and maybe a little from being punched.

"I'm fine-ish," I said, feeling the sting of a thousand aches. Going through a wall didn't come without some costs to your bone structure, but nothing major was broken, and hopefully if we could get out of here I'd have a chance to heal. "Cops on the way?"

Harry shook his head. "Cassidy's got them chasing about ten different leads right now. We've got ten minutes or so to get clear." He looked at me a second longer than he needed to, then switched his attention to the Terminator. "Still … might want to ask your questions so we can get going."

"Not a bad point," I said, and walked over to the Terminator, who strained a little, looking like he wanted to hit me.

"Uh uh," Eilish said when his fist twitched. "No hitting, now, my dear."

"Yes, ma'am," the Terminator said, his voiced clipped in that stiff, military way.

"Who are you?" I asked, looking the Terminator right in the eyes.

He stiffened to attention. "Lt. Colonel Warren Quincy, formerly United States Marine Corps."

"And now?" I asked.

"Would you kindly answer all her questions?" Eilish asked.

He looked at me, then dropped to at ease, hands behind his back. "I work for a special operations group within the Department of Defense, reporting directly to the Joint Chiefs of Staff." He twitched slightly. "Until recently."

I exchanged a look with Harry, and he nodded. This sounded important. "What do you mean 'until recently'?"

"I am currently on detached duty to the Federal Bureau of Investigation," Warren Quincy said, "to aid in their apprehension … of you." And he looked right at me.

ROBERT J. CRANE

"No surprises so far," I said. "Who ordered you to come after me?"

"The Director of the FBI," Quincy said.

I raised an eyebrow at that. But then, I'd watched the last FBI Director get murdered in front of me, so I supposed it was no huge surprise that this one might be antsy, thinking it was a vendetta against the office. It wasn't; I hadn't even killed the last guy (much as I might have wanted to when I was working for him). "That's ... interesting," I said. "Maybe this one thinks he's pursuing justice."

"She," Quincy corrected.

"What do ye think of her?" Eilish asked, probably detecting the same reserve in Quincy's reply as I did.

"I think she's a stuffed shirt pencil-pushing lawyer who's probably never been in the field a day in her life," Quincy said, staring straight ahead, stiff as a board. "If she heard the sound of gunfire she'd think it was fireworks in the distance."

"So you're just after me?" I asked, trying to wrap this up. "And you work alone?"

"I work alone," he said, staring right at me, like a caged tiger, "and you are my sole mission."

"Lovely," Eilish said, "well ... feels like we should be getting along, now." She clapped Quincy on the shoulder. "You stay here, darling. Wait for the cops. Go ahead and forget I was ever here, or that she was—actually, just forget everything that happened since you took this mission. It was all a distant dream; you don't have any idea at all how this happened, how you ended up here. It's a big mystery. All right?" And she smiled at him.

"All right," he said.

"Go ahead and sit down right here and wait for the police," she said, and he did just that as I started past him.

"They're not going to stop until they catch you," he said, calling after me as I went by. "They know you killed Harmon. They want this settled." He turned his head. "My orders said dead or alive, but I just wanted to beat you. You're a fellow warrior to me; I've seen what you've done over the years and it's beautiful work. But these are soft people, the ones who sent me, people who don't understand fighting, don't understand war. You're a murderer to them. They won't be as merciful next time."

I looked down at him. "Thank you, Warren."

He looked right back, and beneath Eilish's control, I almost felt like he was saluting me … and warning me. "Ma'am."

I walked on by, and Harry fell into step behind me, Eilish a few behind us. "Did Cassidy erase the surveillance footage here?"

"Yep," Harry said. "And without any affirmative witnesses—"

"This won't be provable as a metahuman incident," I said, smiling that Harry got what I was driving at immediately. That'd be an insurance payout for Deltan Data Systems, and it meant my conscience could rest easy about all the property damage I'd done here. Hell, with one of their people caught at the scene, maybe the government would get involved and throw in some hush money.

The van was waiting in the parking lot, and Harry slid open the door for me as I stepped up, cringing at a couple of my lesser-realized pains that adrenaline had wallpapered over during the fight. Cassidy was waiting inside, face in a tight moue, watching me.

"You got him?" she asked. "I couldn't see on the feed. Which is erased now, by the way."

"I got him," I said, and she slumped back in her seat as I slid in next to her and fastened my seatbelt. Eilish and Harry loaded up in the front, and then we were on our way, before the first siren even reached my ears.

42.

We pulled up in front of the wrecked house in Richfield, Minnesota, the street deathly quiet and a light snow starting to fall around us. Cassidy had already gathered her things, and I was left staring out at the destroyed house as I opened the door on the silent street and let the frigid air rush in, chilling me. "Are you sure about this?" I asked, nodding at the house. My brother had wrecked it while dragooning Cassidy into his service to rescue me from Scotland; it didn't look like she'd done much to repair it yet.

Cassidy frowned at me. "I own the one next door, too." She shrugged. "I liked the neighborhood, and it felt right to expand, so …"

"Oh," I said, glancing at the wrecked house again. "I just … thought you were sleeping in the ruins of the basement or something."

"I need an active power supply for the sensory tank," she said, shaking her head as she crossed over in front of my chair and I squeezed my legs to the side to let her pass. "And the computers. And—well, everything, really." She stepped out onto the curb. "Though I think I've missed the sensory deprivation tank the most these last few days." She glanced at each of us, then lowered her face. "Good times, people. Let's never do this again." Then she looked at me. "Except us. We have a future date."

"Way to make it weird, Cassidy," I said, then added, "So … we're not square, huh?"

248

She hesitated, yellow light from a nearby streetlamp casting her pale face in shadow. Snowflakes came down around her, giving her a case of artificial, frosty dandruff around the shoulders. "No. But ..." She looked me right in the eye. "This ... thank you." Then she glanced away. "Your friends ... they're all in stable condition. Some are waking up now, others will be within hours." Now she looked right at me. "They'll all be fine, every one."

"I know," I said, feeling my breath catch in my lungs, and not just from the rush of col. "But ... thank you, anyway, Cassidy. And ... I'm sorry about Simmons."

"I know you are," she said, looking down again. "Which ... is strange, because were I in your shoes ... I wouldn't feel the same." She shook her head, like she was trying to rid herself of troubling thoughts. "Let me know when you go to Revelen," she said, looking me straight in the eye once more. "And we'll call it square."

"I like how you're the only one that believes that I'll be able to square things if I go to Revelen," I said, taking a deep breath. "Because everyone else is all like, 'You're going to die if you go to Revelen.'"

She blinked a couple times. "Who told you that?"

"The voices in my head before they died," I said, "Stepane—the Predator—that's where he came from. Where he got his powers. Their serum."

She took this in, processing. "That affects the calculus in my equation."

"Unfavorably, I assume."

She nodded, just slightly, as she stepped up onto the driveway, which had been plowed, despite the house being wrecked. "Yes, unfavorably." And then she started to walk away.

"Do I even want to know the odds?" I asked, wondering how she could even render such an equation without any freaking idea of what we'd be facing in Revelen.

"No," she called back, not turning around. She picked her way around the snowy lawn, walking down the cleared sidewalk, bag on her back comically large for her thin frame.

"Maybe we should go right now?" I asked as Harry eased

the van forward.

"No," Cassidy and Harry chorused as one. I looked back at him, he shook his head.

"Bad odds," Cassidy said and gave me a little wave.

"Very bad odds," Harry agreed. "The worst, in fact."

I frowned, and slid the van's back door shut as we passed Cassidy, now making her way up her driveway. Any other time, even when I had her locked up in prison, I would have dreaded seeing her again.

This time ... and for some reason, related to this growing fear and awareness that the nation of Revelen was a growing menace I was going to have to deal with at some point ... this time ... I almost looked forward to seeing her again.

Almost.

I mean ... I wasn't totally crazy.

43.

"Oh ... it's you," Reed said, sounding a little dazed, like he was suffering from cotton-brain, that medicated feeling where your head feels like it's stuffed with ... well, cotton. He was blinking at me furiously against the darkened backdrop of our dreamwalk, and smacking his lips together like the cotton feeling had spread to his mouth.

"You sound surprised," I said, slipping out of the darkness toward him.

"I guess I am," he said, peering around, that dazed look in his eyes. "I didn't really expect to see you again for a while after our last talk." He frowned. "Wait ... what happened after our last talk?"

I hemmed for a second before I composed a straight answer. "You got on a plane to Minneapolis and as soon as you got off, you got your ass kicked by the bad guy."

"Oh, man," he said, closing his eyes, putting fingers on the bridge of his nose to knead it. "The team." His eyes snapped open and he looked straight at me. "What about—"

"They're all fine," I said. "Our bad guy ... wasn't quite so bad, at least to you guys. No fatalities, and everyone seems to be recovering. You'll walk away from this one with nothing scarred but maybe your pride."

It was his turn to hem. "Did you, uh ... kick his ass? In your own, inimitable way?"

"He's dead, yeah," I said, looking away. "I tried to spare him, but ..." I shrugged. "He wouldn't have any of it."

251

He stared right at me. "Did you try and absorb him?"

Why did this dreamwalk suddenly feel so desperately uncomfortable? "Yeah," I admitted after an awkward pause. "He wasn't interested, so I let it pass."

Reed just stared at the dark ground for a few seconds before replying. "Damn."

I stared at him, a little surprised. "Why 'damn'?"

He shrugged. "I mean ... obviously you beat him without any additional powers, and ... you're totally a badass and all, it's just ..." He did another shrug, like he was trying to squirm his way out of having to answer an awkward question. Finally he broke through with a sigh. "I just want you to be safe, and having all the powers you can ... makes you safe ... er. Because there's no way you'll ever be totally safe, at least not the way you live."

I gave him a jaded eye. "The way *I* live? Which one of us is presently paid to deal with metahuman criminal menaces?"

"Yeah, with an agency *you* set up."

"But you're doing the dirty work—well, most of it, anyway. I mean, sure, you gotta call in little sis every now and again when things get really hairy—"

"I did not 'call you in'—I left you day-drinking on the Gulf of Mexico—"

"But you knew I wouldn't just sit this out when it got personal—"

He sighed again. "Yeah. I had a feeling that if anything would pull you out of your funk and back into the game ... it'd be a serious meta threat."

"I'm, uh ... done with the drinking," I said, looking away. "I mean, I've probably still got some mild withdrawals to go through—thanks, metahuman powers, for blunting the impact of that—but, uh ..." I looked up and found his eyes. They were, thankfully, kind, and filled with concern for me. "... I'm done."

"Good," he said, and he sounded a little hoarse. "I'm glad you're ... done. I wish I could have helped more, but ..."

"You did it right," I said. "One mental crisis at a time. Honestly, I was ... such a mess. I'm surprised you actually thought I'd leave my stupor to get in on this."

"It's who you are," he said softly.

"A crazy person?" I said, half-joking.

"A hero," he said, not.

"She took everything from me, Reed," I said, looking at the infinite blackness below. "My powers, my memories ... pieces of who I am. She even broke my confidence, though apparently my ego is so massive she couldn't take all of it. But ... strip that all away ... and I have to ask, what's left?"

"A hero, still. Duh," Reed said, answering instantly. "Also ..." His voice softened. "My sister. Who'd be kinda super even without a single power."

My throat got very tight, and my eyes misted up. "Thanks ... bro. I love you, too."

He brought it in, and we hugged, his arms around me and mine around him, for what felt like forever—in the best way. Finally, he said, "So ... this is goodbye for a while, I guess?" And he pushed back slightly, so he could look me in the eye. "Since you can't call me anymore, and I presume you're ... headed on your separate way."

I held his gaze, and smiled. "Maybe we should make this a weekly thing? Like, 'Sienna Nealon, phone home'? But with dreams?"

He smiled. "I'd like that. A lot." And he hugged me tight again, and didn't let go for a long, long time. I liked that, too.

44.

The van rolled to a stop outside a hotel in Burnsville, Minnesota, just south of the cities, off Interstate 35. Harry was at the wheel, and I sprang out the side door as Eilish stepped out of the passenger side, her little bag slung over her shoulder.

We both peered inside; there was a man at the front desk, and Eilish sighed in relief. "Excellent prospects." She was tense all the way through, looked like she was about to spring a leak from contracting her muscles so tight. "You sure about this?"

"Reed said he'd be happy to have you on the team." I looked her right in the eyes. "You'll be fine, Eilish. It'll give you a chance to see if doing this ... heroing thing ... is something you want to do. It'll pay ... well, I might add, and ..." I shrugged. "He's got connections. You'll be able to stay here for a while if you're of a mind to. It'll give you a chance to work things out without worrying that you're going to be ... y'know, implicated in assisting a fugitive in her flight from justice, decency, and railroading." I shrugged. "They probably wouldn't write up the indictment quite like that, but ..."

"I appreciate it," she said, staring back at me with a curious intensity in her eyes. "I've been ... lost ... without Breandan. It's been years since I felt ... steady, I guess? And ... I hope you don't take this wrong, but these last few months, after Scotland, coming over here with you, watching you dive into the bottle? It's really woken me up to the fact that I need to work on a life for myself. So ... maybe I will find it here."

I looked back at her. "I'm guess I'm glad that somebody got some benefit out of me hitting rock bottom."

"That's thinking positive," Eilish said, and thrust out her hand. I shook it quickly, and she headed for the door.

"They're good people," I said, calling after her. "My friends. Take care of them."

She looked over her shoulder at me. "I'll do what I can." And then she went into the hotel, already speaking to the man behind the counter as the doors whooshed shut behind her. "Would you kindly …?"

"She'll be just fine," Harry said as I climbed up into the passenger seat next to him.

"I know she will," I said, settling in and staring at the glove box and the dashboard. Now Reed was gone, at least for a while, and I was separated once more from my team. With Eilish saying her farewell, and even Cassidy being gone, I was left alone with Harry Graves.

I looked at him, and he looked at me. He smiled and shifted the van back into gear as he took us out of the parking lot. I was left to wonder how long it would be until I was on my own again—

"A good long while," Harry said, smiling over at me.

"Oh," I said. Question answered, I guess.

We headed south as he turned onto Interstate 35, and I held the rest of my questions in, just basking in the quiet glow of having another person with me—at least for 'a good long while.'

However long that might last.

45.

South Dakota
Daybreak

We'd followed Interstate 35 to Albert Lea, Minnesota, and then headed west on I-90 over the flat plains. We made great time, zooming through the night with Harry at the wheel, not a word spoken between us. My mind was on spin cycle, trying to digest everything that had happened; the fights with Stepane and his fear of Revelen, of the info that Warren Quincy had given me about the threats that still remained with the law on my ass ...

Oh, and there was a nagging doubt or twelve about exactly how long 'a good long while' meant to Harry.

Plus ... this one other question that had yet to be answered.

"You didn't actually need my help at all, did you?" I asked as the sun started to rise in our rearview mirror. It was glinting outside my window, the reflection bright orange and beautiful over a cloudless winter morning. I could feel the chill seeping through the van's window and into my arm, against the glass as I stared at Harry.

He was smiling. Damn him. It was handsome, too, as per usual. "Not this time, sweetheart," he said, in a way that might have seemed patronizing from anyone else.

Harry Graves, though? He pulled it off and actually made it sound ...

Nice.

"You were here for me?" I asked. He nodded. "Why not just say so, then?"

"Well, I don't know if you remember how you were feeling a few days ago," he said, ambling along in his explanation, "but if I'd said, 'Sienna—I'm predicting a ninety-nine point nine nine percent certainty you're going to die in the next few days,' how do you think you would have responded?"

"Reasonably, I would hope—"

"You'd be hoping wrong," he said with a shake of the head. "Where you were, mentally … you were going to tell me to take a walk. Or try to ditch me at the first opportunity. But bring a girl a bottle of scotch to warm her up, and present this—this selfless lady with a chance to once again save a soul in need—"

"Oh, screw you," I said, surly. Then, after a brief pause. "But thanks, I guess." That came a little more abashed. "How'd you know it was you who could help me?"

He furrowed his brow at me. "Oh, you mean because I can't see my own future. Well, funny story about that … I can't, obviously. But what I can see is that Sienna Nealon has a 99.9% probability of death impending, and there's no visible factor that can save her. But there's still some … rogue, random element of chance, unrelated to you or anyone around you …" He grew quiet for a second. "And I looked again, and it was still there, gleaming in the possibilities … but I couldn't see anything related to it. I tried to look closer, to dive into it, did everything I could to figure out what the hell it was …" He shrugged. "I'm ashamed to say how long it took me to recall that I can't see myself or the probabilities related to my future."

"So by elimination, the only factor that could save me was you," I said. "Sounds dicey, Harry. What if you have other blind spots, other people you can't see?"

He smiled, and it was dazzling. "Then you got the benefit of my company for absolutely free. What a deal, huh?"

"So … how did you save me?" I asked. "You know, to get past that probability of 99.9%?"

"Well," he said, "first you have to understand … that

probability, the 99.9%? It was that this 'Terminator' as you call him ... was going to kill you back there at Deltan. If you'd fought him again, alone ..." He shook his head. "There was no way out for you."

"Damn," I whispered. "But I kicked his ass on 94."

"You still had to limp away from that one, as you'll recall," he said. "No ... he had a trick up his sleeve, something he'd been saving. You were going to put him in an impossible position ... and that was going to be the end of you." He said it with quiet certainty. "Just the same, if Eilish had intervened in your fight the way you suggested before the battle—"

"You said she'd die." I looked at him and he nodded, once. "That Stepane would kill her before she got control of him."

"Without doubt," he said. "One hundred percent. But the moment he was out of the picture—"

"You told Eilish to come in," I said, working through it. "You came with her, directed her right to me."

"And I knew I was doing the right thing, because the probability of your death started to drop as we headed in that direction," he said. "See, that's how I know to guide myself. I don't know how *my* fate will unfold ... but I figure if your odds improve ..." He smiled again. "... Well, I'm heading in the right direction. I take care of you, you take care of me."

"'For a good long while'?" I asked.

His smiled faded a bit. "If you don't mind some company on the road. I could help, after all. Keep you a few steps ahead of trouble. Maybe ... provide a little company." He didn't arch his eyebrows enough to be lascivious, but the suggestion was there, if subtle.

I stared at Harry Graves, who'd somehow come back to me after a year of just ... being gone, and now ... he'd saved my life. Again.

And he was handsome.

And he was decent.

And oh, it had been forever. I could tell by the way my heart was beating, my pulse quickening and my breath catching in my chest.

"It might be nice to ... have some company for a while," I

said, trying to play it cool even though I knew he knew. The smile gave it away. I figured he'd seen a certain sexy probability in my future grow exponentially in the last thirty seconds, and that was just fine with me. I reached over, and brushed his arm, my bare fingers running over his sleeve.

"Oh, I brought you these," he said, and reached down into the pocket in his door. He tossed something at me, and I caught them.

Gloves.

"All the way from Florida?" I asked, staring at them.

He actually blushed. "Well … I held onto them until I, uhm … knew you might need them for … something."

"Hm," I said, favoring him with a crooked smile, then slipping them on one by one. They were leather, smooth, comfortable. "What do you get for the succubus who has it all?"

His smile matched mine. "You're on the run from the law. Do you really think you 'have it all'?"

I smiled again, this time more mischievous. "No, but … considering where I am and what I've been through … I think I'm doing okay. Now …" I touched his face. "Take your eyes off the road for a second, Harry. Because I see something in your future that you don't." And I kissed him for just a couple seconds.

We broke, and he said, "Whew," and then swerved slightly before getting the van back under control and back on the road. "Yeah. I did not see that coming."

I settled back in my seat, but reached out with my left hand and took his right, interlacing our fingers. "Wait 'til you see what happens next," I said, and smiled at him as he smiled at me, the infinite possibility of the future ahead of us on the horizon. I couldn't see it, but …

I had a feeling it was going to be good.

46.

Secretary of Defense Bruno Passerini, Admiral, USN (Ret.) still walked with the cadence of a Navy man. It was something he'd picked up in Basic and never let go of, the precise movement style that came from drill. He couldn't have shed it if he'd tried—not that he had—but it was bound to him like a second skin, and almost as tightly as the anger he felt pulsing through his veins right now.

"Director Chalke," he said, trying to catch up to the woman in the grey suit as she strode through the West Wing lobby toward the exit. She probably had a car waiting for her, and he didn't want to miss this opportunity to catch her. Otherwise he might have to make an appointment and drop by FBI Headquarters, and that didn't suit his disposition nor his mood.

Someone had misappropriated his department's vital resources without even consulting him, and that was the sort of thing that Bruno Passerini found ... aggravating.

FBI Director Heather Chalke spun, giving him no more than a look over her shoulder before she paused and let him catch up. "Secretary Passerini," she said, a hint of levity running through her words—the Director always seemed to be speaking with great irony, like she was telling a joke that only she was in on, regardless of who she spoke to. It was irritating, because it bore the marks of a mind so impressed with itself that she didn't allow for the possibility that anyone was smart enough to realize she was speaking down to them.

Thank God she's not under my command, Passerini thought as he caught up to her. But to her he only said, "The Orion Protocol."

She made a face, squinched up her small features, like this was funny. "Is that your name for your little hunter guy? Cute."

Passerini held in the cold irritation he felt, but only just. Passerini's patience was not legendary in the Navy, and for good reason. Because when he lost it, you could only wish you were sitting under an F/A-18E Super Hornet as it dropped its payload. And that was the reason he'd been assigned the callsign Hammer. "I wasn't informed that we were offering one of our top programs to the Justice Department."

"Homeland Security, technically," Chalke said with that same veiled amusement. "But I know it's all very confusing, way more complicated than Army, Navy, Air Force, Marines, and—whoever else. There's a fifth one, right?" She tapped her chin, eyes looking up like she was trying to remember.

"This was my project," Passerini said. "Quincy was my operative. And now he's sitting in the Cube."

"We'll get him released," Chalke said with a light shrug. "I mean, I should have known better than to throw a blunt instrument like a soldier into this given how badly the last few attempts to use them have gone—"

Passerini bristled; Chalke was smiling. She knew she'd gotten his goat with the crack about the military.

"Well, since you haven't been able to get the job done with anyone else," Passerini said, not above a little passive-aggressive shot or two of his own—this was DC, after all. No one here spoke openly about their intentions; they just catted like teenagers at one another, and it drove him nuts. "It probably made sense to you to seek out the best trained fighters on the planet. But my people are not police," Passerini said, adding an edge to his voice that his junior officers when he'd commanded the *Enterprise* task force had called "Hammerfall," "and we were never meant to be used in the way that you and the previous administration have. There's a reason for the Posse Comitatus Act—"

"I guess you guys don't take the 'domestic' part of 'enemies foreign and domestic' seriously, huh?" Chalke snarked. If she was under his command he'd have broken her down to private for insubordination.

"I take my duty very seriously," Passerini fumed. "I take the safety of my people very seriously. And when one of them gets assigned to cannon fodder duty, thrown at Sienna Nealon by another department, one that doesn't give a damn for their well-being—"

"Soldiers are expendable," Chalke said with an uncaring shrug. "You should know this, you're the Secretary of Defense."

Passerini drew himself up to his full height, eyes blazing. "Listen, lady—"

"Sexist. Why are you military guys so sexist? Wait. 'Military guys.' Think I found the answer."

"We've got plenty of female brass," Passerini said, neatly avoiding adding, *And every single one of them is less of a horse's ass than you,* bypassing it to say, "And they all know the value of human life—especially that of the people that we're responsible for. You don't borrow my soldiers, sailors, Marines, Airmen or Coasties—that's the last branch, by the way—without asking me. Period." And he started to leave it at that.

"Oh, I wouldn't dream of it," Chalke called after him, "but that order came from the president."

Passerini paused. It probably had, but there was no doubt in his mind who'd convinced Gondry to issue it—and she was standing behind him in heels, the devil in Chanel.

"By the way," Chalke said, "I heard about your near miss with the *Enterprise.* You and the president, both very fortunate. Fifteen more minutes and you would have gone down with the ship. Lucky thing your helicopter was delayed, huh?" She had a gleam in her eyes as she said it, and Passerini couldn't tell if it was some kind of threat or just the words of a gloating, snide pain-in-the-ass.

Passerini just seethed, staring at her. He was wondering if he'd missed something. There was definitely a glow in her eyes, one that he'd always attributed to smugness in the past, but ... maybe ...

No. Passerini shrugged that thought off. Plenty of people were difficult, or assholes. That didn't make them traitors or part of some conspiracy to false flag their own countrymen. It just meant they were assholes.

And FBI Director Heather Chalke had to be one of the biggest assholes he'd ever met in his life.

"I wouldn't worry about your people getting roped into future operations with us," Chalke said, taking a couple steps back. "It didn't go so well for us, trying to use your ... jarheads or whatever you call them. We'll look elsewhere for help in the future."

"Good," Passerini said tightly. "Good luck in your hunt."

"Oh, we won't need luck," Chalke said, still smug, and walking away. "Didn't you hear? Sienna Nealon is powerless now." Chalke let out a hearty chuckle. "Her days are numbered." Then she muttered something else as she turned.

Passerini froze, watching Chalke as she walked out the lobby doors. She looked back at him and smiled infuriatingly, and he just stood there, fighting back his warrior's instincts.

Because he could never have proven it, not in a million years, but he could have sworn what she said was ...

"Her days are numbered. Just like yours."

Epilogue

Breddocia, Revelen

"She called me Sigourney Weaver," the woman said, strolling placidly through the lushly appointed office in the old castle.

The man who'd perhaps been most famously known as Vlad watched her, his fingers on his chin as he contemplated this small bit of information. He frowned, studying her. "You do look a little like her, now that you mention it. With your hair like that. You resemble her in *Ghostbusters*."

"And you look like hell itself shat you out," she replied, only a little ire coloring her response.

Vlad smiled. "You have such a way with words."

She slowly paced toward the window, looking over the city of Bredoccia below. Vlad still remembered when it had been a simple village and not the bustling metropolis it now was, a hub of growing trade for Eastern Europe.

And all that ... was because of him.

"She didn't remember you, then?" he asked, finding his way back to the point.

"It was as you suspected," she said, staring out the window. "All those memories are gone."

He coughed, a hoarse one. "Suspected? No. As I commanded when I struck my bargain with Rose."

She turned slowly to look at him, intense concentration writ upon her face. "You couldn't know she'd triumph over Rose."

He coughed again, that lingering ailment troubling him, just as it had lo, these many years. "I didn't. But you did." He pointed at her, trying to give her credit for her foresight. "You knew she would win in the end, and that ... was enough for me to believe it."

"She knows about us now."

"Surely." He coughed again. "We've certainly placed enough difficulties in her path. If she didn't see it by now, she'd be a fool."

"She'll turn her eye in this direction." She turned back to the window. "And I assure you ... she is no fool. Nor is she to be trifled with."

"I have no trifles in mind for Sienna Nealon," he said, turning his attention to the open file on his desk. Files. Bureaucracy. If there was a common thread linking the days of old to these new ones, it must surely be the growth of bureaucracy and paperwork. He picked up one of the pictures from the file with interest, staring into the face, intent, furious. It was a still frame capture from Sienna Nealon's recent battle in Minneapolis, taken from the news coverage. She looked ...

Determined.

Dangerous.

Like ...

He shook off the thought. "I trust your judgment enough to know that she remains a threat so long as she is out there. But the wheels are in motion, and they cannot be stopped." He smiled, a dark, malignant expression that had induced fear in so many souls. "She is fated to come to us now, and when she does ..." He snapped his fingers. "She will be dealt with." He coughed. "Sigourney."

At the window, he could almost hear her rolling her eyes at him. "You ass."

Sienna Nealon Will Return in

TIME

Out of the Box
Book 19

Coming April 3, 2018!

Author's Note

Thanks for reading! If you want to know immediately when future books become available, take sixty seconds and sign up for my NEW RELEASE EMAIL ALERTS by visiting my website. I don't sell your information and I only send out emails when I have a new book out. The reason you should sign up for this is because I don't always set release dates, and even if you're following me on Facebook (robertJcrane (Author)) or Twitter (@robertJcrane), it's easy to miss my book announcements because...well, because social media is an imprecise thing.

Come join the discussion on my website:
http://www.robertjcrane.com!

Cheers,
Robert J. Crane

ACKNOWLEDGMENTS

Editorial/Literary Janitorial duties performed by Sarah Barbour and Jeffrey Bryan. Final proofing was once more handled by the illustrious Jo Evans. Any errors you see in the text, however, are the result of me rejecting changes.

The cover was once more designed with exceeding skill by Karri Klawiter of Artbykarri.com.

The formatting was provided by nickbowman-editing.com.

Thanks to John Clifford and Jennifer Ellison (J Ells) for reading ahead.

Once more, thanks to my parents, my in-laws, my kids and my wife, for helping me keep things together.

Other Works by Robert J. Crane

The Girl in the Box
and
Out of the Box
Contemporary Urban Fantasy

Alone: The Girl in the Box, Book 1
Untouched: The Girl in the Box, Book 2
Soulless: The Girl in the Box, Book 3
Family: The Girl in the Box, Book 4
Omega: The Girl in the Box, Book 5
Broken: The Girl in the Box, Book 6
Enemies: The Girl in the Box, Book 7
Legacy: The Girl in the Box, Book 8
Destiny: The Girl in the Box, Book 9
Power: The Girl in the Box, Book 10

Limitless: Out of the Box, Book 1
In the Wind: Out of the Box, Book 2
Ruthless: Out of the Box, Book 3
Grounded: Out of the Box, Book 4
Tormented: Out of the Box, Book 5
Vengeful: Out of the Box, Book 6
Sea Change: Out of the Box, Book 7
Painkiller: Out of the Box, Book 8
Masks: Out of the Box, Book 9
Prisoners: Out of the Box, Book 10
Unyielding: Out of the Box, Book 11
Hollow: Out of the Box, Book 12
Toxicity: Out of the Box, Book 13
Small Things: Out of the Box, Book 14
Hunters: Out of the Box, Book 15
Badder: Out of the Box, Book 16
Apex: Out of the Box, Book 18
Time: Out of the Box, Book 19* *(Coming April 3, 2018!)*
Driven: Out of the Box, Book 20* *(Coming June 2018!)*
Remember: Out of the Box, Book 21* *(Coming August 2018!)*
Hero: Out of the Box, Book 22* *(Coming October 2018!)*

World of Sanctuary
Epic Fantasy

Southern Watch
Contemporary Urban Fantasy

The Shattered Dome Series
(with Nicholas J. Ambrose)
Sci-Fi

Voiceless: The Shattered Dome, Book 1
Unspeakable: The Shattered Dome, Book 2* *(Coming 2018!)*

The Mira Brand Adventures
Contemporary Urban Fantasy

The World Beneath: The Mira Brand Adventures, Book 1
The Tide of Ages: The Mira Brand Adventures, Book 2
The City of Lies: The Mira Brand Adventures, Book 3
The King of the Skies: The Mira Brand Adventures, Book 4*
(Coming January 2018!)

Liars and Vampires
(with Lauren Harper)
Contemporary Urban Fantasy

No One Will Believe You: Liars and Vampires, Book 1* *(Coming Early 2018!)*
Someone Should Save Her: Liars and Vampires, Book 2* *(Coming Early 2018!)*
You Can't Go Home Again: Liars and Vampires, Book 3* *(Coming Early 2018!)*

* Forthcoming, Subject to Change

Printed in Great Britain
by Amazon